RACHEL NEUBURGER REYNOLDS

THE WIPEOUT AFFAIR

RED FROG BEACH MYSTERY SERIES #2

COPYRIGHT

This book is dedicated to the memory of
Theresa Pisanelli,

Fearless wonder, lover of life, and perpetual enigma...

DAY ONE

SUCH AN EASY SLIDE

*L*ife in paradise. Like the past four months of Sunday mornings, I stood submerged in the Caribbean Sea as far down as my shoulders, hanging onto the ladder off the back of a large catamaran. It was eight in the morning, and we were moored over Coral Garden, a reef commonly referred to as Grandma's Garden. Was that to make it sound more comforting? No one seemed to know.

And, just like every Sunday, I stared intently at my silver-and-black snorkel fins, which reflected the perfect light four feet into the calm bay. It's not that I couldn't see how beautiful and clear the water was over one of the healthiest reefs in Panama's Bocas del Toro region. It was as placid as a pleasantly warm bathtub, but I was still reluctant. It might have been true that a dozen dive instructors and marine biologists were moments away to save me if needed, but that didn't mean it was one hundred-percent safe.

I took one foot off the ladder and wiggled it in the water. I considered it good progress for the week. I'd been reading lately that sometimes it's all about small victories. I'd made the uncharacteristically brave jump to move from New York City to Bocas del Toro in July. Now bettering my life was one step at a time.

"It's such an easy slide," said Jazz. She was in the water about five feet away from me, swimming around like a mermaid in her stunning blue one-piece bathing suit.

Every so often she would free dive down for what felt like hours. I'd be petrified that she needed immediate saving, and then she'd emerge from the water, smiling. It was seductive in a non-sexual way. "You've been sitting with a snorkel mask on for almost four months. How about just putting your face in the water, like we practiced. Once you see a trumpet fish, you'll never want to come out of the water."

Her real name was Jasmina Belmonte, but I'd never met a person who addressed her by her first or her last name. She was Jazz to everyone. She had quickly embraced me as a friend, and I saw something about myself that I hadn't seen before: that I needed a good female friend. I hadn't had one for a long time.

She was patient and always promised to stay next to me if I went in the water, if I'd agree to make that jump. She'd taught me breathing for those scared of the water a dozen times.

"The world is so beautiful down there. Parrotfish, four-eyed butterfly fish. And the reef. So beyond above the sea. See it now before it disappears." She clapped her hands as if she was performing a magic trick. "Lexie, it's at max 12 meters deep. It doesn't get deeper than that. You're safe."

"I know you must be sick of having this conversation with me every week, like talking to a broken record player, but..." I calculated. "12 meters? That's 36 feet." I climbed up the ladder, pulled my fins off and tossed them back on deck. "Correction. That's 39 ½ feet. That's almost three apartment stories." I followed my fins to the safety of the deck. "It's not that I'm not going to learn how to snorkel. It's just not going to be today."

She followed me out of the water. "If you just put your face in the water for 30 seconds, I will buy you all the food and drink you want tomorrow night. I'll even find a way to deliver you a Maine lobster roll."

It was tempting. Over the last months of our developing friendship, she'd guided me through the good and bad of the islands, while I fascinated her with the strange world of New England. She'd shake her head in amazement. "Why would anybody suffer through winters like that? But tell me more about snowshoeing."

"We've got four seasons, beautiful summers, which may be hotter and more humid than here. And everyone loves the Empire State Building. I can walk through the worst areas of town and it scares me less than taking that slide into the Caribbean."

"You've had a lot to deal with. Don't ever forget that. You're great considering what you've been through." That would be almost drowning at a destination wedding here in April.

I'd keep my life vest on until we returned to the marina in an hour. My motto was "better safe than sorry." Truth be told, it would probably be the phrase inscribed on my gravestone one day in the hopefully distant future. "Sorry for wasting your time again, Jazz."

"You, my dear, are never wasting my time. It's an honor that you trust me to help you fight your demons," Jazz said, taking off her gear. She touched her heart while staring in my direction. "You know when I offered to get you in the water, I knew it wasn't going to be a quick thing. I'm in it for the long haul, Lexie."

She stood and grabbed us each a bottle of ice cold water out of a cooler. The beginning of October in Panama was still hot. It wasn't too much cooler during the rest of the year, being closer to the equator than the rest of the Caribbean islands.

Jazz was what you would call cool as cucumbers. She looked slick as anyone's business, hardly ever taking off her sunglasses even when it rained for the twenty minutes a day that it usually did. She was ten years older than me but had a timeless look, classic, even if she was in cut-off shorts and a ratty old t-shirt. Blacker hair than mine, and lighter brown eyes. A stunner.

She was born in Bocas and married an American ex-pat ten years her senior named Cam. They owned the biggest fleet of snorkeling, diving, and deep sea fishing boats in the area. They were doing well, with a staff of almost thirty dive maniacs working out of the Aqua Point marina on Isla Solarte, a smaller and less populated island than Isla Colon, where I lived.

Jazz always took out a Sunday morning trip for her friends and some choice employees. Most tourists were scrambling towards their 12 p.m. checkouts and heading to the airport, so scuba and snorkeling instructors were essentially off the clock.

The airport only had two flights out: one morning and one afternoon. In a region where the economy was dominated by tourism, the 24 hours between check-out on Sunday and check-in on Monday was the unofficial day off to chill and recharge. Without a doubt, the Sunday morning outings were one of the highlights of my week.

She comforted me. "You fit in down here. You don't know it yet, but this is your home. I see how you love it more every day."

She was 100 percent right. I'd moved down a few months after my first visit in April, when I was the maid of honor at a wedding gone disastrous, which included a few murders and a nearly drowned narrator. My trip was the impetus to remove myself from a group of very toxic New York City friends and to start over. Case closed, moving on.

She threw me a towel. "You make sense here, Lexie. I hope that you are beginning to feel like you belong."

I had never felt I belonged anywhere. "I'm getting there."

"Six months from now you'll practically be a dolphin yourself. When you decide to let yourself slide… Ok, I'll be back." She gracefully dove off the boat to join some of her friends, having a conversation in the middle of the ocean as easily as if they were gathered around a table at one of the islands many crab shacks.

Due to my rather traumatic experiences in April, any rational person would have assumed I'd move to someplace like the Joshua Tree desert in California, devoid of any water for a hundred miles. However, these islands had me by the heart and pulled me back into their arms. True love.

And sometimes, after living in New York for a long time, you leave it for a while. When you come back, you realize that either it's the only place that you could ever be. Or, as in my case, that it never had you in its grasp at all.

Jazz's trip in the water was a quick one. She was out and laying on a towel as quickly as she jumped in. She didn't even bother toweling off, knowing the sun would take back the water in minutes.

Her pleasantry had morphed into deep thought and she put her hands over her eyes. She'd changed a little over the last month. She was still loving, generous, and understanding, but there had been a bit of a black cloud hanging over her that shouldn't be hanging around in the Caribbean.

"Are you okay, Jazz?" I put my hand on her shoulder.

I asked her all the time. She never confided, but I'd ask none the less.

She shook her head, and said, "Yes. I'm fine. I just have a lot on my mind. Just a stupid problem I've been having, but I think I finally took care of it. Better days are coming. My mind is just a little elsewhere." She closed her eyes meditatively then shifted as her pack started to return. "Hey! Look! They're coming back. How was it?"

Maybe a dozen undersea lovers were climbing back on board, positively over-the-moon with the things they had seen. With their voices overlapping, I wasn't sure who said what:

"Did you see that damselfish that was all over my *culo*? Crazy!"

"I'm all about the batfish."

"Ah, well those hatchet fish. Those vertical bottom feeders own my dark heart."

It all sounded nice, except for the damselfish attack. Granted, they were tiny. I had googled it. I had googled everything.

I'll admit that I had a tiny crush on one of the divers who'd just got out of the water. His name was Renaldo Silva, but everyone called him Renny. Everyone had a nickname in Bocas. Even I had one that I was determined to lose: Avanti.

At first, I'd thought it was kind of sweet and pretty when people started calling me that. I soon found out that the inspiration for the name came from the fact that I still wore life vests every time I got on any boat at any time. The most popular safety vest this year was a Maris Avanti Quattro, hence Avanti. How I longed to go back to my previous Bocas nickname of simply "Tall Girl."

Renny towel-dried his hair before grabbing a glass of

tamarind juice. He eyed my dry hair piled in a bun on top of my head and gently pulled on it. "Didn't make it in today?"

I didn't want to be the scared person I'd always been, but I wasn't going to pretend either. "Not this time."

"Don't worry. You'll make it in when you're ready. I've got faith in you, *chica bonita.*"

I could go with that nickname. A Spanish phrase I'd already committed to memory.

Pretty girl.

Renny had seemed nice and kind and regular looking when I'd met him. It took a few months in the tropics for his appeal to come to the fore. After talking to him for an hour one day while looking into his big brown eyes, it had dawned on me that he was attractive. He was handsome in a way that crept up on you. He had short dark hair, a quirky sense of humor, and charm like you wouldn't believe. A bonus for me was that he was taller than me when I was barefoot. With three inch heels? Maybe not.

He was single, but I was nowhere ready to date. I was coming out of a five-year relationship, which was followed with a disastrous rebound with a guy I had met at the wedding.

Renny was funny and charming. We liked the same music, movies and books. We shared a wickedly dark sense of humor. Every so often we'd go out for an afternoon on his boat for a couple hours, sing along terribly to The Cure or some other old band, and go our separate ways. That's where it ended. In the friend zone. We'd be great karaoke friends. Trust me, I was happy crushing on him from a distance.

The lady doth protest too much.

He was one of the many reasons to look forward to Sunday mornings like clockwork, and to gussy myself up a little (as much as you can in a wetsuit).

Renny and Jazz had gone to Cal State Long Beach, where they both majored in marine biology. They migrated back south to make some quick cash during the summers on luxury fishing and diving charters on the Pacific side of Panama. Jazz soon met Cam who had chartered one of the trips, and that became that.

I loved when Renny and Jazz would nerd out, talking the newest developments in the marine biology world they were no longer a part of. They debated things like marine population dynamics, molecular data on mangrove oysters, and the anti-inflammatory properties of coral reefs. Needless to say I was in the dark, but I enjoyed it much like I enjoyed living in a Spanish country while hardly knowing the language.

Besides, their enthusiasm was contagious. I was excited to learn that there were somewhere between 700,000 to a million species making their way through the oceans, two thirds of which had never even been named.

But lately, they weren't nerding out nearly as often. They bickered. Like fighting parents, they'd move just out of earshot so the rest of the crew couldn't hear their yelling, but we all had eyes.

The disagreements were something new. They'd been best of friends until the last month. Both of them blew off the subject if anyone asked. Each of them would rattle off some excuse about the dangers, saying the fights were about fire corals or if casiopias actually existed. True fodder for disagreements between marine biologists. No one believed them. No wonder Jazz felt a little sad.

We motored back to Aqua Point. Jazz and Cam had eight charter boats out of the marina, and another two over in Pinas Bay on the Pacific. They made a good but unlikely couple.

She was an ex-academic marine biologist with an edge

and an adventurous nature, but with a subtle darkness that made you wonder just a little. When you'd tell a story, she was watching from the outside. She absorbed everything.

Cam liked fun and he liked luxury. He had done very well in the not so exciting world of what he humorously referred to as widget making: knobs, switches, and lock catches. He also always got a laugh out of saying, "I was the doohickey King of Greater Houston." Great to be around, but lacking that certain *je ne sais quoi* his counterpart rocked. They were on the surface a very unlikely couple, but they really seemed to work.

The happy group of divers disembarked the catamaran and walked towards solid land. Renny held his hand out to me to help me off the ship. He looked at me with a smile that extended to his honey brown eyes and asked, "Are you still coming out with me on Wednesday?"

Jazz heard his offer and turned in our direction.

Renny hadn't yet let go of my hand as I replied, "Maybe. Yes. Yes, I'll be there." I collected my cool. "We can talk about it when I see you tomorrow."

"I've been studying up on your Red Sox for tomorrow night. I'm counting on you to explain all the finer points of baseball to me."

My heart skipped a beat, while the wise angel on my shoulder whispered, "Stay away from the charming ones. You know better."

There was a group of American ex-pats who met every Monday at one of the restaurants at the Red Frog Beach resort on Isla Bastimentos. To say I had a bad experience at the hotel was the understatement of the century, but I was determined to replace traumatic memories of the place with great new ones. The group had embraced me as soon as I'd walked off the plane, Jazz inviting me to socialize with them as soon as I was introduced to her during her surf lesson on Bluff Beach.

The Doohickey King had worked with the resort to install service to broadcast American baseball games, and we were all set up to watch the Red Sox beat the Yankees the next day. I was looking forward to donning my Red Sox t-shirt (too hot for my baseball hat) without having to endure the wrath of my former clique of New Yorkers.

"Good," he said. "I'll see you then."

This area should be renamed Flirtsville Island.

He yelled over to Jazz, "I'll bet you fifty bucks and my signed picture of Jacques Cousteau that I can get her snorkeling before you can."

"Oh, leave her alone, Renny," she called over her shoulder. I still had my life vest on as Jazz walked me the short distance to the water taxi rank. She didn't look at him to allow an opening for a reply. "Lexie, seriously. He's not the kind of guy you want to get involved with." Months ago she'd said that one day he might be a good match.

"Well, no one is the kind of person that I want to get involved with right now." I was serious about that.

"Just remember... just remember. He's no good for you." She put on her sunglasses and pulled her hair back. She grabbed me for a moment. "You're working at Hywel's camp this afternoon, right?"

She was referring to one of my two part-time jobs, a jack-of-all-administrative-trades at a surf camp.

"Yup. *Sayōnara*, surfers."

"That's Japanese, so you know."

Argh. What a doofus I am.

"Can you pass a message on to Hywel?" She was coy. "It's a surfing thing."

Flirtsville Island indeed.

"Tell him, *Cuidado con las curvas peligrosas.*"

That struck me as curious.

I got in the rickety water taxi, which would take me to Bocas town on the more populated Isla Colon and my semi-professional occupation. I'd been taking Spanish lessons twice a week for months, but languages and I were not a match made anywhere near heaven. I pursed my lips before saying, "You're going to have to write that one down." I reached into my waterproof purse and handed her my note-book, watching her write. "What does it mean anyway?"

"Watch out for dangerous curves." She didn't give the pad back right away, choosing to write something else on the note. She carefully ripped the page out of the book, folding it in fours, not wanting to share the rest.

As we took off, Jazz waved. "*Sayōnara, Lexie.*"

2

HYWEL AT THE MOON

𝓛ady Luck, my 1980 red Toyota Land Cruiser, was parked on the street not far from the launch in Bocas Town. Cars weren't really much of a thing on the islands. Besides the small grid of the town itself, which wasn't even a square mile, there were precisely one and one-half roads on the island of Isla Colon. Okay, maybe one and five-sixths, as there was another tiny road on the north side of the island that went from my favorite restaurant, Yarisnori, to nowhere in particular. The restaurant was in Bocas del Drago, Mouth of the Dragon, and not too far from my current living situation. If anyone knew the name of that particular road, they weren't sharing it.

The one paved road (called Paved Road) went inland, north to south, from Bocas del Drago to Bocas Town: eleven miles and forty minutes to make the trip. Then there was Dirt Road, a six and a half mile drive up the east coast terminating at the end of crumbling concrete, Bluff Beach, where Hywel's surf camp was.

The roof of my jeep didn't come off and there was no

air conditioning, but more than half the drive from my house was through the deep, dark, inland rainforest so it was cool enough. Capuchin monkeys, sloths, and hummingbirds were a welcome view when you could spot them. Howler monkeys still scared the pants off of me. I'd never actually seen one, but sometimes in the mornings their cacophonous wails could be heard up to three miles away.

The road from Bocas Town up to Bluff Beach started as bumpy-at-best and quickly went from bad to worse. I'd drive until the road disintegrated, which still entailed a ten-minute walk up the beach to *Grito Mono* Lodge. Ironically, that means howler monkey when translated.

Upon meeting Hywel in April, he'd explain the pronunciation of his Welsh name, saying, "Hywel, like howl at the moon," and then he'd bay into the sun. His guests seemed to like it, and that's all that mattered.

I'd met him in passing on my first trip when we did an event at his camp. He was one of the few locals I'd stayed in touch with after my return to the big city. When still on the fence about moving (though teetering towards the tropics), I'd emailed him, and he'd immediately offered me a part-time job. He'd also known of a very cheap rental that an old surf buddy from California had semi-abandoned - jalopy of car included. He'd gone out of his way to introduce me to great people when I'd arrived, including Jazz, who I'd met on one of her lessons with him.

Sunday mornings at eleven, I punched my timecard. Generally by this time most of Hywel's students were tired and had skipped out on the last morning of shooting the curl. They'd kick back on the deck of the nine-room hotel, eating Mother's Lollypops, also known as Mamón Chino, also known as Chinese suckers. Picture a fuzzy red version of a lychee with a grape texture. I will only say that it is an acquired taste.

Hywel was outside the board shed, cleaning the decks, getting ready for tomorrow's new onslaught of eager novices. All six feet and four inches of the lanky blond worked quickly, the task being pure muscle memory at this point. He owned seven pairs of board shorts, and he was wearing his usual Sunday flamingo number with an old punk rock t-shirt and his omnipresent aviator sunglasses.

He smiled as he always did when I showed up, which was more than welcoming. "Hey there, what's up, Avanti?"

That's the thing about nicknames. They stick.

"If you keep calling me that I'm going to quit soon." I'd at the very least learned how to stick up for myself.

Have you really, Lexie?

"I think it's cool," he said. "It's very Italian. Like you. It actually means 'forward, the direction' in which you are definitely going."

"Can't you just call me Tall Girl?" It was hardly better, but I didn't want to be known as the safety-first nerd, even if I was.

He looked down at me from his very high perch. "I think we can agree that five feet and ten inches is not very tall to me."

Fair enough.

"Hold on, that guy is going to kill himself." Hywel wiped his hands on his shorts and walked quickly towards the water. "There's always one!" He screamed to the heavens.

Hywel was now off to save the day, as he did on all Sundays. Usually, the victim was the worst surfer of the group yet nonetheless determined to conquer a junior wave before getting back on the 2 p.m. plane to Panama City. Instead of playing it safe, this person would go farther out into dangerous territory, as if a nasty wave would, by nature, lift him up and sail him across the top of the universe. Hywel headed out to the edge of the beach to try to reel in this week's victim.

I'd seen a lot of surf injury in my time working for Hywel, and none was drowning related, to both my delight and chagrin. Cuts on faces from the fins, concussions from your own board or someone else's. Then just the general falling over one another; whether in the surf or just trying to run around on the beach carrying seven feet of polyurethane. Surfing injuries were like the boo-boos of kids – they only hurt when you were done playing. And nobody ever wants to stop surfing.

I made my way back to the bar on the porch and stepped behind it, standing alongside Jules, the bartender, another blond California transplant. She handed me the paperwork on the guests so I could start tallying up the bar tabs and checking everyone out.

"Any drama this week?" I asked while tallying up the major bar bills that had been tracked merely with check-marks and initials.

"I'm going to call it the stilt incident and leave it for another day." Jules looked at the group of tourists with just a little bit of disdain.

I was calculating one of the guest's bills, and he was going to be down about $230 for the week for booze alone. "How is that possible?" I said. "Was he picking up the tab for everyone?" It was a very cheap island, known for $2 beers.

"Bottles and tips." She pulled her blond hair back and looked at my sheet. "The title of my memoir…"

I didn't doubt it.

She cracked open a beer, offering it to me. When I thanks-but-no-thanksed the offer, she took a big long sip of it herself. "You have no idea how much I need to just kick back and...oh no," she said, staring down the beach. "It's Daisy coming again."

Daisy had a nickname, but I'm not one to recall that kind of language.

I'd only met Daisy since she and Hywel had split up. They'd been going out, and having it out, for years. I'd been privy to only some of the seriously intense drama on her part. She'd become legendary in her wacky ways, especially in her ongoing obsession with her ex. She had been a commuter from the Costa Rican mainland, as many who worked on Bocas were. She had a nice little business of running huge parties at her open-air club, The End of the World, which attracted the hostel and backpacker crowd.

She was five foot even, but you could never miss her; her pixie haircut always some shocking shade of color framing her delicate face. She wasn't covered with tattoos, but had one very distinctive piece on her shoulder of a little angel looking wicked with vampire's teeth. Ever since they'd split up two or three months ago, she'd kept the short hair a shade of sapphire.

Picturing the laid back Hywel with the spitfire Daisy never made sense in my mind. He was luxuriating in the silence that was life without Daisy, but she wasn't going quietly. I'd seen her on at least a couple occasions on the outskirts of the Grito Mono Lodge surfing with some random guy; never the same one. On a number of special occasions, she'd mosey over to the hotel. Now the little piece of dynamite was angrily walking down the beach, sporting a white cover-up and huge red sunglasses.

Hywel had caught sight of his approaching scorned woman and grabbed the surfboard from the gentleman he'd just recently coaxed to shore. He quickly paddled out, dealing with her in the most mature of ways.

"Can you please go talk to her, Lexie?" Jules looked at me with fear in her face. "Four times now she's accused me of having a thing with him. Daisy told me..." Jules pouted her lips, put one hand on her hip and another in my face, in a perfect impression of the ex. "'I know Hywel got something going on with some new *zunga*. I know you're the one, Jules. Fess up.' She's mean. And I don't even know what a *zunga* is! I mean, she almost made me cry, and I didn't even do anything wrong. And she's some kind of karate master or something. She hasn't turned on you yet. Lexie, I've heard you're good with difficult people. Please?"

"He's not seeing someone new, is he?" I asked. He had seemed very happy to howl at the moon on his own lately. "He told me how relaxed and at peace he is flying solo."

"No, I'd know. I mean, how could I not? She's mean, and she calculating, and I really don't think I can deal with her right now." She grabbed a pitcher of beer and another of rum punch and did the final round for the Grito Mono graduates. "Seriously, if you could just try to get her to turn around, it would be a great help. Please. Pretty please. Pretty please with a cherry on top? Talk her off the cliff?"

I'm bad at saying no.

I reluctantly shuffled down the beach to try to have a civil talk with Daisy. She was yelling out into the harsh waves, "Very adult way of dealing with me, Hywel. Why don't you be a man and talk to me to my face?"

Hywel was miming that he couldn't make out what she was screaming at him. I don't think you needed the audio on to get the gist of the scenario. We'd all seen this play. He'd sit out there and pickle before coming back in, with the lady waiting for him.

"Men can be…" I started to speak. She turned around and sized me up. I'd met her a few times before the breakup, but she had mostly ignored my existence. I thought speaking to her woman to woman about the challenges of a breakup might be an excellent way to calm her down. And I currently knew all too well about the emotional turmoil of a split.

"Men can be what?" she commanded, looking like a pretty little general.

I looked out at Hywel who was choosing to let wave after wave go by, looking anywhere but our direction.

"They don't always act like adults in situations like these. Maybe it's not the best time to talk." I was cautious about trying not to blame her in any way.

She looked me up and down again and took off her big red sunglasses, signaling a potential moment of peace. "You were part of that wedding terrorist group, right?"

I did not comment.

"That was some crazy, crazy business."

"That it was. I'll tell you about it one day."

"And why are you back, lady hero? Do you think that because you saved the day you belong here?"

Do I?

That really was the question, wasn't it?

The short answer was that I loved the place and that I needed to figure out what I was doing with my life. The long answer was one that I didn't have an answer for myself.

She listened to me intently while I explained why it might not be the best time for them to have any kind of showdown. Though she'd been making scenes all over town, I convinced her that the most elegant thing to do was to walk away right now. You could see that she enjoyed seeing herself as the sane one. She flipped him off from the beach, though I don't think he saw or would have cared.

She leaned in as if she was telling me a secret. "He's seeing someone. Did you know that? I'm not a stupid person. I don't like looking like a stupid person. If there is one stupid person in this couple it's not me. No one can keep things from me on this island. No matter what he thinks." She was gathering herself together, ready to retreat.

"I don't know everything that goes on, Daisy, but from what I've seen and heard, he's alone."

She surprised me by giving me a big hug and a peck on the kiss, saying, "You're nice. I like you. But if I find out that you knew anything... let's just say it's better you tell me."

I'd have been foolish to think that I made any lasting impact in our brief conversation. She confirmed this with her final words, "Just tell him... he's won the battle, but not the war."

I LIKED my job at Hywel's. Sunday, I'd check out a satisfied group of novice surfers. Half of Monday, I'd check in a new group of wannabe wave riders. Tuesday I was responsible for social media, which was a fun day of taking pictures and making every day look like a party. Finally, Thursday morning was a half-day of whatever additional admin was needed for the week. I'd held my breath waiting for a response when I had originally replied to Hywel's offer, clearly stating, "I don't clean bathrooms, change sheets, or deal with brides of any kind."

The contract was binding.

When I first started working for Hywel, I always thought that hanging around with him or Jules on Sundays after the campers were on their way back to Bocas del Toro

International Airport would be what we did on our night off. But it didn't work out that way.

Just so you know, International Airport is a kind exaggeration. The single runway airport couldn't accommodate anything bigger than a Fokker 50, a sixty-two-seat plane that flew between Bocas Town and Panama City. 'International' was simply for the one weekly Miami flight. There was a dingy bar at the airport, and you could also get your nails done, so people seemed to like it. I'd spent a number of rainy afternoons waiting for late planes, and I'd left with various shades of sparkly colors that cheered me through the week.

But back to the story.

Jules? Sunday night was the night that she liked to drink too much by herself at home and go on eBay. She'd find last-minute auctions on high fashions from Panamanian sellers that she'd buy for dollars and then sell for fifty times as much to vintage collectors in the States.

So buddy-buddy bonding night with Hywel? No such luck either. "Avanti," he'd tease while I cringed, "Let's do a Tuesday thing. I get-twenty four hours off every week, and without the blue *loco* ding-a-ling of an ex in tow, I get to decompress for the first time in years. Surfing alone and naked by torchlight only. Kidding! Or am I?"

I wasn't going to take my chances with that one.

It's okay. Making my own way is a process.

Jules had everyone rounded up to take them back to the airport in our terrible excuse for a bus. Hywel now saw it safe to come in from the sea.

Getting ready to leave and searching for my keys in my waterproof purse, I came across Jazz's note to Hywel. Her surf lessons were on Wednesdays and Fridays, so I hadn't run into her at Grito Mono very often since that first time. "I have something for you." I handed him the note.

He took the note and laughed, but not lightly. "Jazz is really something, isn't she?"

"She said it to me, but I still can't speak ten words of Spanish, so I asked her to write it down. What does it say?"

He looked at it for way too long and I thought he wasn't going to share it with me. Finally he read, "*Cuidado con las curvas peligrosas.* Beware of dangerous curves. Obviously talking about La Curba Beach. It's a crazy break," he sighed. I noted that there was a second sentence she hadn't said out loud when she'd passed me the message.

Adios, a Santo Amaro.

I pointed at the note. "What's that? *Santo Amaro?*"

"Inside joke." He folded the note and put it in his pocket. He looked off into space for a while before coming back to Earth. "Oh, and by the way, thank you for getting Daisy to chill. She'll get over it someday. Hopefully sooner than later. But until then, just a little peace."

He mussed my hair and walked back to the surfboard shack. That was my cue to hit the road.

3

WELCOME TO MY INTERNAL MONOLOGUE

*D*espite being rejected by my surfing co-workers, Sundays were turning out to be a good day on my social calendar. I'd been petrified I'd be completely isolated and lonely, and it had been going better than I thought. I was excited to drive back home after work.

Still, there was too much solitary activity in my week. My work life provided me with some friends and things to do. My Fridays and Saturdays, however, were just me, myself, and I sitting on the dock trying to spot dolphins and waving at the dozens of snorkeling boats that drove by my house.

With Lady Luck, I took a right turn on to Paved Road. The light was good, and the jeep wasn't showing any sign of strain, so it was a good day. I counted the capuchin monkeys I spotted, which was a very cool thing to do.

A good lesson I'd immediately learned was to keep your mouth closed as your first line of defense in the fight against insects. You never knew if a swarm of invisible chitras were on their way down your vocal tract. Citronella candles at home, lots of Off, double that on DEET, and coconut oil seemed to work a charm. I'm just saying that life in Paradise has some ups and downs.

New York had become more down than up, especially since coming back after that wedding I've been talking about. Besides the obvious tragedy of murder, it had ripped my social circle apart. By my choice. At the ripe old age of 35, I was finally able to see the bride, my childhood best friend Olivia, for what she was: not my friend.

It was clear when I returned to New York City that I'd be starting a new chapter in my life, but I didn't want to start that chapter in the Big Apple. Bocas del Toro was the best place I'd ever been. And as Frank Sinatra sang, "If I can make it there, I can make it anywhere…"

Had I made it in New York?

Moving down to Bocas took hardly more planning than calling the few people down here I knew and depleting my American Airlines frequent flyer account. The person who I'd become friendliest with when moving down here was one of the police detectives I'd worked with during the wedding incident. Alajandro LaGuardia had been over-the-moon happy when he found out I'd be moving down. He'd tried to find a way for me to work as an adjunct of sorts for Bocas P.D. Thankfully it didn't work out. Murder investigations? Been there, done that, got the t-shirt, and threw it out.

I was immediately welcomed by LaGuardia's friends and family. Every Sunday night they'd prepare a huge feast at someone's place. Finally I felt comfortable enough to ask everyone over to my bayside cabin. I had good outdoor space, and enough repellant and traps that you didn't need to worry about flying critters when the sun started to set. I'd beat the chitras (only on my deck, but like I said…small victories). I was up to try cooking up a local feast, but they were looking for a real American style barbecue. This took a whole lot of wrangling, but I was ready. And excited.

I needed to find myself.

But that could wait until after the dinner party.

I took a left off of Paved Road just south of Bocas del Drago. There was a hint of a road that made its way down to my little blue bungalow. It was only a road in that Hywel's friend who owned the place had made a path purely out of disrespect for the half-mile of land he'd been driving over repeatedly.

When I'd moved in, I had spent the entire weekend cleaning the place. Not that it was super dirty, but when you are on the hunt for a social life, you've got to make a space worth visiting.

I raised a giant flag at the end of the private, deep-water dock so they'd be able to find the place. It had room for a few sailboats, small motorboats, and the random kayaks that came with the house.

My little blue cabin… The bungalow was pretty standard for the multitudes of hidden small places around the island. Solar panels everywhere, rain catchments, and the requisite hammock or two. I had the extra luck of having new appliances, a nice wrap around terrace, and a big deck for entertaining. Ceiling fans in every room.

If you are looking for air conditioning, you're on the wrong island.

My pad was remote and I had my reservations when I arrived, chaperoned by Hywel in a small motorboat. I'd seen a few pics. The long dock, a cracked path leading to the cabin on the outskirts of the rainforest. Solar powered lights were dim, cellular service and wi-fi were bad at best, and I was a stone's throw from dark woods filled with creepy critters and crawlers that I'd never seen before.

Had I made the biggest mistake in moving to a Caribbean island I knew nothing about?

Though my bed was under mosquito netting and locks on the doors were more of a suggestion than anything else, I acclimated quickly.

I'd lived in New York City for fifteen years and was almost killed on this very island. You take things into your own hands. I'd also taken self-defense on my brief return to the city. I had a baseball bat near the door and various things around the house that didn't look like weapons but could protect you if you knew where they were: scissors, pencils, brass candlesticks. Jules had given me a present soon after I arrived: lipstick pepper spray and a round brush that had a concealed stiletto dagger in the handle.

Truth be told, how much can anything really protect you?

And trust me, I now know what every insect in the rain-forest is.

Don't google Giant Rhinoceros Beetle.

I told you that you'd be sorry...

After a month of being petrified of the silence in my new digs, I started heading towards peace. I parked my car in an area of my pseudo-driveway that I knew was mainly *chitra* free. Living on the edge, you see...

Hours later, I was still unprepared for my visitors when a couple of boats pulled up to the dock. I'd spent an hour making way too much guacamole using my mom's recipe (secret: leave out the cilantro), and the rest of the food had been put in a holding pattern.

It's just burgers and hot dogs, Lexie. Get it together.

But what about the slaw and the...

Shhhhhhhh....

While everyone made themselves comfortable on the deck, I checked myself in the mirror to make sure I hadn't smeared avocado across my forehead. I had. Though I was starting to have a nice, natural tan that suited me, I still wore 50 SPF every day and was not convinced that was indeed enough. The Italian in me was starting to show, instead of a vampirically white New Yorker.

I'd started to smile again.

LaGuardia's twin five-year-old boys, called Tikki and Tavi, were the first ones to run in the house. Since I'd brought them a Spanish edition of Rudyard Kipling's Rikki Tikki Tavi, they'd demanded to be referred to as such. Twins were hard enough, and I'm sure that the detective was happy that there wasn't a Rikki to complete the namesake.

"Candy," Tikki forcefully asked.

I think it was Tikki. They were identical.

I'd bribed the kids to like me when I arrived with American candy, so perhaps not off to the best start. I passed them some mini Reese's Peanut Butter Cups.

"Oops. Is that okay?" I asked Gabby, LaGuardia's wife, nervously as she walked in with a bowl full of tropical fruit. She was a curly-haired, freckled, and adorable woman who everyone loved. She'd been a teacher before having kids, and she was the one giving me Spanish lessons. She wouldn't accept money for her lessons, but I'd think of some reciprocal offering one day.

LaGuardia followed with a case of the local Soberana beer, always looking like he'd been surfing rather than fighting crime. Often that was the case.

Gabby nodded, walking as comfortably around the kitchen as if it were her own. I'd moved down to the tropics with my clothes, one crate of books, and six boxes of the American food and toiletries I thought I might miss. I wrongly guessed that they'd last me for a year at least, but just heading into October and the USA cupboard was looking a little bare.

Gabby looked around the kitchen at the mountain of guacamole, and nothing else. "Can we help you?" I didn't have a moment to answer when the couple started pulling meat out of the fridge and spices out of the cabinet. They looked strangely at the two crates of coconuts on the floor.

"What are you going to do with those at a barbecue?" LaGuardia asked.

"Chop off the tops and pour cocktails in them?" I had tried to open one earlier to disastrous results. But now what was I going to do with 24 coconuts?

"It's a beer crowd," Gabby said, before grabbing a few of the Soberanas and heading towards the door. "I'll start passing these around." Before she left, she kissed my cheek and said, "Lexie, you don't have to try so hard. These people are your friends. You don't have to impress them."

She headed out with her Reese's-filled twins at her feet. One of them grabbed the baseball bat and dragged it behind him.

LaGuardia washed his hands and started unwrapping the ground beef, preparing an enormous amount of herbs and spices to mix into the burgers.

"LG, no," I almost screamed. "These are American burgers. We just make 'em plain." He was the first person I'd ever given a nickname to. Not that it was genius or original or anything like that.

He spiced the air in my direction with *achiote*, a local spice made of annatto seeds. He was an amazing detective, but on an island with a population of just over 10,000, he didn't often get the chance to show it. Bar fights and stolen property were the mainstay of unlawful acts on the island. However the few murders over the last five years showed what a fantastic investigator he was. So if he surfed on duty on occasion (or a lot), and lacked the level of stress a detective might suffer from in a more urban setting, so be it. He'd become a good friend, and at times like this, as he liberally doused me with exotic spices, he was like the brother I never had (and possibly never wanted).

"That's not going to be very tasty, is it?" He asked, looking at me as I started making the plain patties for the grill.

"Well, you wanted an American barbecue," I teased. "Seriously though, good beef doesn't need any spices. Just the grill."

"Where'd you get the good beef?"

"Stop it. And just slice up those tomatoes if you can." I passed him a knife, handle first.

You have no idea how good it was to be out of New York and in the company of normal people.

Normal?

Maybe not normal, but real.

Suitably unique and quirky, but not money and status-obsessed. Just a couple dozen people chilling on a deck in Panama.

"This is nice of you to make an effort for everyone. They appreciate it. Go say hello." He motioned towards the window where we could see everyone outside, animatedly talking in a language I had yet to know. They'd switch to English when I came out, but I didn't want to always be *that* person. "You've been here for a while. You're one of the crew."

I'd go out eventually, but I was shy. Moving to the Caribbean on a strong whim was so outside my wheelhouse that I might as well be sitting in a car down the street. I held up a handful of ground beef. "I will. Let me just get my plain patties down. Calm weekend?"

He opened a beer, taking a conservative sip. "Like bathwater. One fight at the Pickled Parrot, but that's just called Saturday at 10:30. It's been very mellow lately. Like maybe the rowdiness on Bocas is on the way out. It's going to be a very calm fall."

"Looks like it, doesn't it? There have been less people getting drunk and sleeping on the beach by Grito Mono. I agree. Looks like it's going to be calm."

Gabby walked back in the door, dropped her beer on the floor, and looked at us incredulously. "You can't say that."

"Can't say what?" I felt like I'd made a criminal offense.

She picked up her beer and looked for a towel to wipe up the liquid. "You can't say it's going to be calm. You've jinxed it."

"What do you mean?" LeGuardia stopped his smooth tomato slicing.

"It's like when you are driving in traffic, and the other side of the highway is in a traffic jam. Then you talk about how lucky you are that you aren't sitting in gridlock, and all of a sudden you get slammed. You've cursed yourself. Something bad is going to happen."

She'd gone to college at USC in Los Angeles. She knew traffic jams.

We had a good laugh.

LaGuardia had never been in a traffic jam, so I had to explain to him what gridlock was. He got the point.

DAY TWO

31

4
YOU'RE GONNA NEED A
BIGGER BOAT

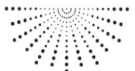

*L*ast night's party was a huge success. Driving the next morning I congratulated myself. Then I spilled a full water bottle over myself taking that terrible left onto Dirt Road to head towards Hywel's.

As one would suspect, locals get far less drunk than tourists, so last night was a pleasant evening of outstanding plain burgers, mustard slaw, and spiked Arnold Palmer cocktails. Someone had brought a red, white, and blue donkey piñata, which both the adults and kids went after like rabble-rousers in a dive bar. Though it wasn't the Fourth of July, I loved the sentiment.

I felt good. I looked good, too, having opted for a Kelly green sundress instead of the standard daytime wear of cut off jean shorts and a t-shirt. Monday mornings at the surf camp were a good part of my week. There was always a crazy amount of excitement from the new campers who were over-the-moon to get into the water and start learning how to surf.

From where I watched, I can only say thank god for ankle

straps and first aid. I was embarrassed about how horrible the wedding guests had been on my first trip to Bocas when I saw how graciously regular people checked in and explored.

People here said thank you, and they meant it.

Spilling water all over myself wasn't a big deal. It was cool upon my torso, and the sun would take it back soon. I'd be happy enough to be half soaked when the full sun rained down on me.

The cassette recorder in the Jeep was permanently out of commission, so I'd rigged up a Bluetooth speaker where a rearview mirror once sat. I enjoyed my morning doo-wop music mix, singing along as I bounced down the rough road.

Even if the stereo had been working, where would I get a cassette?

Following the road around to the left, I took a sharp turn at the Caracara Cabins, named for a local falcon breed. As if last night's conversation with Gabby was some prophecy, I was faced with southbound traffic for the first time since being on the island. And when I say traffic, I mean maybe ten cars slowly driving in the opposite direction of me down the beach. As a courtesy I pulled over to the side of the road to let the oncoming vehicles pass.

As the worried faces passed me in their convertible jeeps, I muttered to myself, "Speed racers." They were cruising far faster than the typical 10 MPH necessary for that stretch. Locking eyes with the drivers, they made no attempt to reciprocate the island's standard to wave hello..

Everyone was determined to get off the rugged East Coast as soon as possible. A wave of nausea came over me thinking about the possibility of Daisy having done something above and beyond at Grito Mono, waving a baseball bat in the general direction of Hywel and anyone else in swinging distance of her. Why else would this mini-mob be jet-propelled down Dirt Road? Like the infantry following the cavalry, trailing after the cars were the folks on bikes, followed by walkers.

Safety first. Don't ride a bike down this road.

Rental bikes were often old and rickety. I took one out when I first got there and that was the only time. Almost as if my thought was an omen, one rider toppled into another, which turned into a four-cycle pileup. I stopped the jeep in the middle of the road and ran to the injured like the over-protective mother I was likely to become one day.

The cyclists were all cursing at each other in the sort of language that I don't care to repeat, in accents that I placed as German and French. Would the two countries ever truly get along? I pulled a bike off one of the injured. The four of them moved to slightly different areas on the beach to survey their damage. "Please watch that you don't get any sand in your cuts!" Maybe I was a lifeguard in a past life. Or a second-grade teacher on a school trip.

I rushed over to a pretty brunette who was giving me big eyes and a face full of pain. I crouched down next to her, assessing her leg. I assured her, "It doesn't look too bad. You guys are probably more in shock than in pain. Don't worry. It's nothing."

Don't forget the possibility of staph infection.

Shut up, Lexie. You'll get them to the doc, and all will be as it should.

Her boyfriend limped over to her and kissed her fore-head. "I'm fine," he said in a French accent. His leg was pretty scratched up, but it looked like it was only surface wounds. I smiled (and I'll admit it, a little wistfully) as he chose to put her injuries before his. There were still good men in the world. I knew this, but reminders like this of what might be out there for me were helpful.

"Can you tell me what's going on up there? Why the mass exodus?" I asked my French patients.

With genuine concern, she looked up and said, "Shark attack…"

She said what…?

"It's not a shark attack. It's a shark sighting. *Dumme frau,*" snarked an infirm German gentleman from the shade of a nearby tree. I don't speak German, but I think what he was saying was pretty clear. Time to separate these warring factions before it became a full European conflict.

She raised her voice, "It was a shark attack."

"You saw the signs posted."

"I don't care about the signs. That too-tall surfer said to me that there was a shark attack, and to get back to Bocas Town as fast as our little feet could take us. *Homme ridicule.*"

I may be shy but I've had way too much experience handling warring factions before, and that was just as recently as April. "Ok, Germany, over on those lounge chairs on the beach. France, you stay here. I'll call a doctor, and he'll drive out here and make sure you are ok. Do you understand?"

Back to being the teacher chaperoning a school trip.

One more outburst and it's a time out on the naughty stairs.

The German man ended the conversation with the simple statement, "It was Great Whites."

Unfortunately that's the one thing they could agree on.

The promise of medical attention seemed to calm them. They sat by the side of the road as the last of the walking stragglers made their way South.

I needed to find Hywel, the too-tall surfer. Sharks? It couldn't be.

Lucky to get service, I called one of the eight numbers on my favorites list on my phone, the young Dr. Nolan. By favorites, I meant one of the eight people I knew well enough to ever call on the phone. And when I say eight numbers it's more like seven.

I never wanted to insult him by asking his age, but I sometimes doubted his MD status as he looked about twenty-five. He hadn't been accepted to any American medical schools, so he'd studied at the American University of Antigua, which he swore was equal to Johns Hopkins. I wish I'd had the foresight to have gone to a college in the sun.

Like half the island, he could have passed for a surfer but was diligent about his work. He'd been essential to solving April's murders. He was definitely awkward and desperate to be taken seriously by the island officials, but he was hanging in there, making his way.

He picked up on the first ring, "Hey, Avanti."

Silence on my part.

"Hello, you there?"

"Yes."

Let's nip this nickname in the bud.

"Sorry," he said. "I mean, Lexie! Up to no good?"

Never up to no good myself, I explained the situation to the doc, who said he'd jump into his SUV, one of the few on the island. He'd bought it in Costa Rica during the summer. "Look, Lexie. I'm a doctor. There's nothing wrong with the word Avanti in my book. I love safety! But I'll never call you that again."

I left Nolan's number with the Frenchies, hopefully not upsetting the Germans with any perceived favoritism.

I jumped back in the car and drove as fast as I could (AKA 15 MPH) up to the beach.

Sharks?

Couldn't be.

Believe you me, knowing that I was moving to a rainforest, I had researched and memorized every animal, fish, or insect that could possibly be of danger to me. There were plenty, and I don't even count poison frogs anymore.

Jellyfish, sure.

Riptides.

Don't drink the water.

There were 24 kinds of venomous snakes, which is why I preferred the beach and occasionally had nightmares fit for a herpetologist.

But sharks? You saw them fairly often, but they were completely harmless nurse sharks (or so they say). According to my thorough research from sharkdata.com, there had been only one fatal shark attack in the Bocas del Toro region since the year 1900, and there was no official record of that besides perhaps being an urban (or not so urban) myth.

Approaching my place of employment, I saw Hywel's signature light blue lounge chairs tossed in the middle of the road. There were dozens of pieces of printed paper, some taped to chairs, some scattered on the ground, stating, "DANGER. GREAT WHITES." He'd even gone through the detail of adding some shark clip art.

Hywel had traded in his monkey moniker for that of a beaver and dammed the place up. Blocking the way were his two cars, parked horizontally. One was a newish Ford pickup, the other a 1953 Ford Ranch Woody Wagon. I'd honestly thought the Woody Wagon was just for show, figuring it hadn't moved since, well, probably 1953. I think it came free with the purchase of the run-down hotel.

He'd taken what looked like black grease paint and hastily painted, "SHARKS HERE. GO AWAY," on two beach towels that he'd affixed to the cars with duct tape.

Making my way around the cars onto the soft sand of the

beach, the expanse was eerily empty. I passed the tree nailed with a half a dozen planks of driftwood advertising the snack shack, the restaurant, and cocktails such as Panty Rippers and Monkey Tails. Most importantly, though, the bottom sign: NO SWIMMING.

It wasn't a private beach, so besides the weekly tourists, there were generally a dozen people out for the morning surf. Not today. And Hywel was nowhere to be seen.

He wasn't the one attacked by the shark, was he?

No, dummy. Who would have written the warnings?

It was going to be a hot day. The huge swells were terrifying to me, but I could see that today's waves would be an experienced surfer's nirvana. I stared out to the waves, looking for any sign of Jaws or his brethren.

I walked up towards the lodge, starting to call out, "Hywel! Hywel, are you here?!"

Just down the beach, he quickly emerged from the closed surfboard shack. He looked petrified, and though it didn't seem possible, his perma-tan had faded to a shade of white. He did not smile. "What are you doing here? I left you three messages not to come to work. We're closed today."

I'd long abandoned checking my phone with any regularity. The dodgy service had reduced it to a twice a day check. Once when I woke up and once at the end of the day. Sometimes I checked at lunch if I was near wireless, on the off chance that someone needed me for a social event. "I didn't get them. What's going on here? A shark attack? Who was hurt?"

As much as I was not a fan of Daisy, I hoped she was safe.

"It wasn't quite a shark attack, but I'd say a close call."

"There's never been a Great White spotted in this area. You are the one that triple confirmed with me that nurse sharks are not a threat. You've had this camp for like ten years. What's going on?"

He guarded the door to the rickety shack. "Just go home, Lexie. The camp is closed."

"What about the guests coming in for the week?" I looked around the camp, which looked to be on the unprepared side. Oh, and the fact that he was advertising shark warnings.

His eyes were quickly shifting from left to right, scanning the beach and the lodge. "Don't worry. I called down to Pedro who's got that overflow place on Wizard Beach. It's not Bluff, but they aren't going to know the difference. I should move to a calmer location one day. Calm sounds good. Less liability insurance."

"What's going on, Hywel?"

"What do you mean?" I half expected him to grab a board and paddle out to avoid my questions like he did with Daisy yesterday.

"Just stop it. Why are you hiding whatever's going on? I'm your friend, Hywel. Let me help you. We'll figure out whatever's going on and fix it together."

Oh Lexie, do you really want to go down this road again?

What happened the last time you helped friends get out of a pickle?

He closed his eyes and took a deep breath. When he opened his them, he let out a huge petrified sigh. "There wasn't any shark. Of course there wasn't. I don't think the nurse sharks even come to the east side. But it's not good. Not good at all."

My nerves were creeping up on me. "Do you want to show me what's in the shed?"

"No."

I cautiously took a step towards him. "Come on, Hywel. How bad could it be?"

"Bad." He opened the derelict door to the dark shed, allowing only the natural sunlight in through the slats. During regular operating hours, it opened like a surfboard storage and snack shack, selling everything that someone could possibly want spend money on But not now. Now it was dark and surfer noir. He still blocked me from entering. "Just so you know… I had nothing to do with it."

I put my hand on his shoulder and gingerly guided him away from the door so I could go in.

Oh no. Not again.

When my eyes adjusted to the light, I saw it clear as day. Laid out on the dirt floor was a woman, carefully covered with a quilt blanket. And she was dead.

I took another few steps towards the body, the rays of light brightening up the shack. I was expecting to see that sapphire pixie haircut, but no.

It was Jazz.

I RAN out of that shack as quickly as my too long legs could carry me and collapsed a couple hundred feet away. I buried my face in my hands, thinking about Jazz, and how kind and patient she was with me. How beautiful she was yesterday. And how everyone loved her. I could see yesterday so clearly; pulling her hair back into a ponytail, saying *Sayonara*, and waving at me when I pulled away in the water taxi, knowing that I'd be seeing her the next night at the Red Frog Beach resort.

Hywel sat down in the sand next to me, taking my hands in his. In the bright sunlight I could see that his eyes were red and swollen. He'd been crying. His hair was all too shaggy with the morning's salt water. We sat there in silence for a while, staring out at the massive crashing waves, still holding hands.

He couldn't look at me in the eyes. "And. Well. She's not just dead. Something's off. Like dead. Like strangled. Like someone did this to her." He squeezed my hand to the point of pain.

"This can't be happening," I whispered.

"I had nothing to do with this. I swear. I swear on everything that means anything in my life." His puffy blue eyes made me believe him. Though swearing on something doesn't necessarily stand up in a court of law.

When I let go of his hands I turned and looked at him intently. "Ok, tell me what happened. You woke up this morning, went to get your board in the hut, and found Jazz. Did you call the police?"

He ignored the last question. "No, that's not how it happened. I didn't sleep well and, yes, I grabbed my board and went out to ride around 6:30."

I noted it was 10 a.m.

"Ok, what happened next?"

He squinted in the bright rays, sunglass free. "Yeah. I was out there for a while, just thinking about existential blah blah, and I caught sight of what just looked like a lump by that group of palm trees over there. I'll be honest, I was just annoyed. It's not the first time that I've woken up and found some hungover surf bum who crashed near the hotel. Normally I shake them awake, brew up a coffee or something for the stupid vagabond, and send him on his way.

"So I came to shore and walked over to the trees." He pointed. "It wasn't a passed out dude. It was a woman in a little red dress and bare feet, face down. And I turned her over." His eyes welled up again. "It was too hot. It wasn't even

7. It was her. I couldn't leave her out here. I got some blankets and rolled her on to one and pulled her to the shed.

"I was going to call the police. I was. I just needed to get my mind together. I panicked. I just panicked, Lexie. My defense mechanism chose sharks to be the monster of the moment. I don't know."

"Hywel. You can't move a body! Don't you watch TV?" This wasn't going to be good for him.

"Help me?" He pleaded.

I pulled out my phone, and as probability would have dictated, I had no service.

"Can I use your landline to call the police?"

"Call the police? Are you crazy? Can't you just help me figure this out… like you did with the wedding…" He got on his knees as if about to beg.

It doesn't look good for him. You can help, Alexandra Marino.
Are you crazy?
This is the kind of thinking that almost got you killed, Avanti…
Even my inner monologue was cracking on me.

"Absolutely not." In April, I had taken time out of being the by-the-books queen by hiding the fact that there had been a murder. I wouldn't be that person anymore. The pushover version of me was over. "You didn't do anything, Hywel. And I did nothing but flub around last time."

"The police don't like me." Hywel was not a criminal of any kind. He just had a propensity to be verbally attacked by Daisy and be part of major scenes. These blow-ups often inspired others to fight for the sake of fighting. It was hard to imagine the oh-so-chill guy I knew with an ex-girlfriend who was in desperate need of anger management therapy.

"They can help you more than I can." He stared at me with puppy dog eyes, and I took it as him saying yes. I walked over to the closest phone, up the eight steps into the deck restaurant. Detective LaGuardia's phone number was the only one I knew by heart, having said it out loud at least once a week to make sure I knew a number in case of an emergency.

If you are only going to memorize one person's number, you could do a lot worse. And though he may have regretted giving me his personal mobile number on the odd occasion, it was ten times easier to get him that way than calling the station. I filled LG in on what happened, from Hywel spotting her on the beach to me seeing the body.

It wasn't a body. It was Jazz.

"I'll head over there, but McDonough will probably get there first. He's on the way already. We have to close the beaches today. The town's gone crazy about a shark attack over there."

It was going to be a long day.

5

OH WHAT A TANGLED WEB...

*T*wo police cars and the island's one ambulance parked as close to Grito Mono as they could. The whole scene was making me feel sick.

I watched Hywel walk back and forth from the palm trees where he'd found Jazz to the surf shack with McDonough and LaGuardia. I sat in the shade on the deck of the lodge, watching from a distance. I didn't want to know about the details of what happened. I didn't want to be involved in this one. I wanted the capable police department to solve the case as soon as possible and let family and friends grieve and get back to their new normal. Once the paramedics entered to eventually take Jazz out, I was running over to the steps of the restaurant to try to look away.

There was always some mild island jealousy going around towards Jazz. With her looks, brains, and money, she was someone to admire. Envy always comes along with that. I'd heard some untoward catty whispers from time to time, but never anything that lead you to believe that someone would kill the marine biologist.

Two of the officers who I knew were casually walking towards me, with pleasant but concerned looks on their faces. They took off their sunglasses as they reached me, sitting down on a lower step, facing away from the bright sun.

How was I going to help them? I knew nothing.

It seems they had a different intent altogether, because the tall one named Rolando said, "Can we talk about the shark attacks?"

Why didn't Hywel clear this up?

He's playing at something.

Is he diverting attention?

It was getting hot, and I was starting to sweat. "There were no shark attacks. Hywel was freaking out about finding Jazz by the trees and closed the camp. Poorly. He was originally just saying it was a shark sighting. Just a self-defense mechanism. He just did something really stupid."

Rolando and the shorter of the two officers, Romeo, gave each other a stern glance.

Romeo (so not Romeo by the look of it, but hey, there's someone for everyone) said with a heavy accent, "So he faked a shark attack so no one would discover a crime scene?"

Rolando nodded. "Maybe because he didn't have enough time to move the body. Why do you think he didn't call the police?"

Romeo, wherefore art thou?

"I thought we were talking about sharks." I wished I had some water.

"Were we?"

"Yes, we were." I was getting paranoid, though I knew with 100 percent (or 93 percent) certainty that Hywel hadn't done anything. "And a great white has not been sighted in this area ever. The records go back to 1900."

Rolando smiled in a slightly superior way. "Do they? I have records going back to 1896 stating there have been 36 deadly shark attacks in the Caribbean in that time period." He was being a smart ass. Was he trying to out statistic me?

"A great white has never been seen in this area."

"Maybe so. But," he continued, "there was a fatal shark attack by a nurse shark two years ago near Curacao."

Yikes. How did I miss that one?

"Ok. Can you stop trying to out-shark nerd the other shark nerd?" Romeo looked like he was often annoyed by his partner. Understandably.

"The shark business? That was said when he was in shock." I defended my employer. "I think that if you asked him the same question now, you'd get another answer."

"Convenient." Romeo nodded his head.

Rolando, the statistician cop, stood up. "This is not something to take lightly, no matter what else is going on. We're already in the process of closing the beaches for the day, whatever might or might not have happened. No chances."

It wasn't a town that kept secrets. Gossip flew like the wind. I'm sure that the news of a possible shark attack had already spread through the islands. Especially when the police had decided that all beaches were closed, despite how ridiculous the claim was. Better safe than sorry. I could go with that one. This was going to be madness. The small police department split between trying to solve a murder and trying to control a landlocked population of shark-fearing tourists left with nothing to do but get drunk. I pitied the Picked Parrot today. "Is that really necessary?"

"Maybe you aren't concerned with the safety of the island..." Romeo also rose, the two of them standing in my sun.

"That's unfair."

"If we have any further questions, we'll have LaGuardia get in touch with you."

And they were off. It was just like Hywel to waste the police's time on a shark hunt rather than looking for a murderer.

~

LOOK. I'm not perfect. The curiosity was killing me, and I hoped that LaGuardia would be okay if I was a fly on the wall, just quietly wandering about.

If I've said it once, I've said it a thousand times: it never hurts to be friends with a detective. I walked down the beach to where LaGuardia and McDonough and my shell-shocked surfer were talking by the palm trees. Hywel looked tired and scared. They were pressing him about the extent of his relationship with Jazz.

"I've already told you," Hywel said, his voice dry and raspy. "My relationship with her was giving her two-hour surf lessons twice a week. Wednesdays and Fridays. I can check my sched to see exactly how long she's been coming."

I hardly worked on those surf lesson days.

Did I have any potential knowledge that could help? We'd all seen Daisy, the semi-stalker, lurking the periphery. I'd seen first-hand that the sapphire dragon lady was paranoid enough to suspect that every woman who crossed her ex's path was sleeping with him. She was an angry woman. Could she have done it?

Hell hath no fury like a woman scorned.

I'd certainly seen that enough to believe it.

LaGuardia was about to get back to his own questions when we all grew silent. The EMTs were ready to bring Jazz's body to the ambulance. I couldn't watch. It felt too gruesome and sorrowful. I walked further up the beach, where the shore became remote and rugged, and in the opposite direction of the scene of the crime.

Scene of the crime.

My least favorite words.

I sat on a lone lounge chair that looked like it had been dragged away from Hywel's camp. Probably by the kind of hopeless surf bums crashing nearby that he gave coffee and a kicking to. I had the vague idea that I could fall asleep, wake up, and breathe a colossal sigh of relief because it had all been a bad dream.

Hywel soon joined me, sitting cross-legged in the sand. "What do I do now, Lexie? I don't think they believe me."

"You're sitting here with me, not in the back of a cop car. That's a good sign."

For now.

"Firstly, clear up this shark business. You're just making things worse. And, listen. I've got to ask you," I said, though I dreaded the answer. "Because I believe you had nothing to do with this. Do you think Daisy could have something to do with it I mean she's strong. She's like a blackbelt in some kind of version of Kung Fu called Wang Chung or something like that."

"Daisy?" He grimaced like he'd swallowed a Giant Rhino Beetle. "God, I hope not."

"Because… well… I wouldn't go as far as to say that she threatened me yesterday, but she made it clear that if I was the one… if I were your new gal, that I might find myself regretting it. She was pretty aggressive with soft accusations to Jules about it as well."

"I didn't know she was doing that."

"Your private business is your private business, but now

maybe your business is anything but... Is there someone new? Was it Jazz?"

He smiled but was shocked. "Jazz!? No way. Look she is beautiful and smart, and sexy as it gets, but she's married material, and I don't go there. There's no one right now. I mean, if you spent as much time as I did with Daisy, all a guy's going to want is a long period of silence."

That's good.

He gave an exaggerated shrug of the shoulders. "I mean, okay, if I'm going to be honest with you, remember that gal from Ashland, Oregon, like two weeks ago?"

"I actually do remember names. It was Helen."

"So there were a couple of nights with her... with Helen... just a little you know..."

"Too much information!" I didn't need the thought of my boss and his sexy times in my head. "Unnecessary information." I had one last question. "Anything Jazz ever said to you to think she was in danger?"

He broke my gaze and focused on the sea that he loved so much. "Jazz? She was the personification of this island. Cool. Calm. Collected. A tiny bit wild. Never mentioned a thing."

I didn't 100 percent believe him on that one.

6

THAT THING ABOUT MADNESS AND GENIUS

*B*y the time it hit high noon, the police were packing up to leave, and Hywel had not being charged with any crime. Yet. Jazz's body would be taken to Dr. Nolan. Cause of death was most likely a crushed windpipe, a sign potential of strangulation.

They'd want to talk to both of us again.

But I had somewhere to be.

If working at Grito Mono gave you the idea that I live a pretty chill life; posting pictures of might-be surfers on Instagram and Pinterest, and giving final bills to the bruised and hungover, you'd only be half right. That's where my glamorous career as a professional beach bunny ends. Last call for Tiki drinks.

There were no goodbyes from the cops for Hywel or myself. The police got back in their cars. At one point, Hywel just walked slowly north towards destination unknown. LaGuardia now had the unfortunate task to track down Cam to tell him the tragic news about his wife. The detective had never been the bearer of that kind of bad news to a local before.

The black seats of Lady Luck were hot under my legs, but I wanted out of the scene pronto. Speed racing like a whirling dervish at 13 miles per hour, I was late for my other job. The one that was not on a beach. That was for sure.

I was not the only guest from April's wedding who had decided to move down to Panama. Lloyd Wilson had fallen in love with the archipelago and hadn't left since.

I worked for him on Monday afternoon and all day on Wednesdays. I was paid three times more an hour at Lloyd's lab than working for Hywel, but one and a half days were more than enough working in what I referred to as the Dark Place.

It was officially named ANANKE, which I thought was an acronym for some technical process, but no. Ananke was the Greek goddess of inevitability. Very Calvinist.

Meet Lloyd.

Unlike myself, who left the island for a few months, gathered my thoughts, underwear, and three boxes of books, Lloyd just stayed. He bought an ocean-front, five-bedroom villa by the turn-off to Dirt Road by Big Creek, and ordered some shorts, cutlery, and a formidable collection of summer trilby hats. He said that there was nothing that he could need that he couldn't simply just buy again. He had animatedly told me a story about a friend of his who was relocating to Miami, and the moving truck blew up on the trip south. He'd asked the forlorn friend, "Isn't there a part of you that is completely thrilled?" The friend thought about it and said… yes. Besides a few photos and some old letters, he didn't miss anything at all.

Of course, Lloyd had the means to set up again, as many times as he wanted.

How does one describe Lloyd Wilson? Physically, if you can imagine a slightly taller Gregory Peck as a tan vampire, you'd just about be right. He was a genius with more degrees and credentials than I thought existed, and he had quickly set up a medical research lab in the heart of the Isla Colon rainforest, which he was beginning to pitch to venture capital firms and private investors.

He was like the King Midas of his kind of medical research. I had no doubt that he'd easily raise the money, but he didn't have what you'd call a congenial nature. Part of my job was to read over material or correspondence intended for investors, and to make the writing sound, to quote Lloyd, "Less like me." By which he meant to not make him sound like the condescending logistician he was. So, less of a Grade J-Jerk.

We'd had a bit of a rough start when we'd met in April, but had come to a place of peace and, I believe, even mutual respect. He was kind enough to offer me a job when I let him know I was moving back to the islands, even after it was more or less my fault that he'd been arrested in the spring. With an emphasis on the more.

The lab was about halfway down Paved Road, just north of a small village of cattle farmers. A rugged driveway carefully landscaped with pineapple plants and banana trees lead up to a brutalist block of a small building, where half a dozen guys worked, currently researching Mucocutaneous Leishmaniasis.

You are now asking yourself if you would be at risk. Are you an adventure traveler, bird watcher, army personnel, or missionary? Are you on the inside of the island sleeping under nets treated with insecticide to fight the sand flies? Most importantly, are you currently in Bocas del Toro? It's beautiful, so stay on the beach, and if you venture far inland, protect yourself.

I won't get into the gory details, but let's just say that you could factually lose your nose. Not pretty.

I entered my security code into the door panel. They'd set up facial recognition biometric security, but one of Lloyd's employees was able to dress up a coconut enough to replicate his visage and get through the scanner, so they went back to thumbprints. Inside was sparse and meticulous, but I never ventured into most of the facility. There were enough creepy crawlers on the outside to want to know what was going on behind those metal doors with these guys.

For the first time in my life, I had my own office with a door I could close and often did. It had minimal personality, but a nice stereo and a good view of the jungle. As of yet, I had done nothing to make the place homey. I don't even know whose photo I want to put up if I owned a frame. Rebuilding a life came slowly.

Not that I disliked anyone at ANANKE, but I'd found that the best way to do my job was to go to my office and not interact with anyone. I had a paper inbox that would be full when I walked in and empty when I left. I'd say hello to everyone at some point during the day, but I pretty much kept to myself. I guess just like the real world. Starting to scan the papers on my desk, it was apparent that I didn't have the focus to be working on tropical viruses.

How could this have happened to Jazz? Twenty-four hours ago she'd been boating around the islands, happy as a clam. She couldn't have known she was in any danger, could she? She was all smiles and light of heart, but her mind was elsewhere, and cautiously optimistic. What could have happened between the time that I waved *sayonara* to her and the deep heart of night?

I walked down to the cold steel kitchen and made myself a cup of coffee. Stirring in the sugar and cream, the spoon made an echo throughout the empty room. Caffeine wasn't probably the best choice to calm myself down, but it felt like comfort food.

Stop hiding in the kitchen.

You know what you want to do.

I wanted to talk to Lloyd. Truth be told, I wanted to talk to anybody about the day, but it didn't hurt that he was the smartest person that I knew — and detached. He looked at things from a distance, which was the only way I could imagine Jazz and him being alike. Except his observations were very calculated. He'd have questions I wouldn't have answers for.

I chugged half my coffee and walked the short distance to Lloyd's office, knocking on the open door before walking in.

He looked up from behind his giant desk, made out of a Panamanian wood called Massaranduba, aka Brazilian Redwood. Though we were in the middle of the rain forest, it was a true executive office, which surprised me. It was vast and dark, punctuated by leather club furniture and framed large photographic prints of various inanimate objects, shaded by shadows of the hand of a woman smoking. I'd wondered if she was a woman he once loved. Though it was sparse, it had surprising warmth that the rest of the building didn't.

"The world has gone mad," he said, as he waved me into his office. "We need to get the facts straight."

"It's impossible," said Lloyd's guest, sitting smack dab in the middle of the huge couch.

Ew. If there was one person in Bocas I didn't want to sit next to, it was this guy. His name was Crabby Paolo, and Lloyd had poached him from the Smithsonian Research

Institute down the road, where his specialty had been slugs and jellyfish. He was called Crabby neither because he studied crabs or had a poor disposition, but because of an unfortunate incident at an open-air brothel and I'll leave it at that.

He was wearing a t-shirt with a picture of a monkey on it and the words, Saguinus Geoffroi, which was the scientific classification for Tamarin monkey. Just catching sight of him made me feel dirty. He acted inappropriately and would stare shamelessly at any woman who came within twenty feet of him. He leered so much at me the first day that at quitting time, I walked into Lloyd's office and decided to do exactly that. He pulled Paolo into his office for about ten minutes; no shouting had been heard, but when Paolo left the office he looked as if he'd seen a ghost. Lloyd had poked his head out the door and said to me, "Taken care of. I hope you'll stay."

Whatever had been said, Paolo had kept his distance since.

Lloyd pointed at a chair, offering one out of the range of Crabby P. I sat, pulling the skirt of my dress as close to my knees is it would go. "What are you talking about?"

Paolo scratched his stubbly face. It wasn't that he was a bad looking guy. He just generally looked as if he'd rolled out of bed, considering both shaving and showering as an afterthought. "It is impossible. It can't have happened."

Lloyd was the antithesis of Paolo, being the only person on the island who wore button down shirts every day, every strand of his black hair in its wavy place. "Well, that's idiocy if I ever heard it. There is nothing certain. You cannot even say with 100 percent certainty that the sun will rise tomorrow. That's the remedial basics of probability. How many millions of variables?"

Yup, that's Lloyd.

"You get what I'm saying though." Paolo was getting frustrated.

"What's not 100 percent certain?" I interjected. I'd learned early on here that if you don't butt in, they'd go on forever.

"This business going on at Grito Mono. You just came from Hywel's? It didn't happen, did it?" Lloyd tapped the desk with his finger.

"That's what I was saying," Paolo whined.

"We were talking about probability theory, not about the terrors of Bluff Beach," Lloyd snapped back.

News travels so fast. I knew he was a detached individual, but he couldn't be this callous. "That's very cold of you."

"I'm a cold person." He opened one of his desk drawers, looking for a cigarette, momentarily forgetting that he quit.

"It's a person you're talking about. You could at least pretend…"

"So there actually was a shark attack?" Lloyd's inquisitive blue eyes bore into mine. Paolo raised his eyebrows so high they disappeared under his shaggy bangs.

"No, there wasn't a shark attack," I said quietly.

"Then what am I being cold about?"

"There wasn't a shark attack. There was a murder."

Paolo spit out the water he was drinking and started coughing. Lloyd looked like he was ready for the game to begin.

"It's bad. It's really bad. It was Jasmine Belmonte."

Paolo looked like he was about to be sick and ran out of the office.

Lloyd's jaw dropped in perhaps the first display of human emotion I'd ever seen. "Jazz?" He got up from behind his desk and closed the door, returning to sit on a leather chair next to me.

"Jazz was a good woman." Coming from Lloyd, that was the highest praise there was.

"You knew her?" I was surprised. He didn't run in the glamorous circles that Jazz did. Or any circle that I knew of.

"I did," he said, wistfully. "When we opened ANANKE, Jazz showed up in her capacity as a concerned marine biologist and was quizzing me on the company's ethics. Regardless of what I can see what you are thinking behind your swollen eyes, yes, we are very ethically minded here." He took a deep breath and gazed through the window. "She was fascinating." As if he could feel that his icy exterior had cracked, he looked back at me. "She wasn't murdered by a shark then?"

"I don't think if a shark kills someone it's murder."

"You don't know it's mind."

Lloyd's brain: Everything is a possibility.

I sighed. "Well, I don't think that a shark could strangle a woman under a bunch of palm trees."

He noted something on a pad on his desk. "Crime of passion."

We hadn't had a good experience together with our last encounter with murder. We hadn't been working together – indeed he was in jail at the time, but he had repeatedly questioned and insulted my investigative skills, even referring to me as Encyclopedia Brown, boy detective. Though he respectfully corrected his actions and attitude at the end, and here we were sitting cordially in an office together, I suspected that he believed my brain was not up to snuff.

"I don't know. I don't want to be involved. I'm sure it goes both ways. And curiosity killed the cat." I watched him write something else down.

"Did it, though?"

"I guess probability dictates that it could happen." In my

running list of dangers in this world I'd never clocked curiosity as a potential cause of death.

"And what does the almost adequate police force think about it?"

"Filter, please." Since I'd been de-jerking his writing, I had become comfortable telling him when he was out of line or condescending. He thought that LaGuardia and his team were incompetent and didn't keep it a secret. I saw a bit beyond his façade. "I don't know. They spent a lot of time questioning Hywel. But he didn't have any reason to kill her. They were friends."

"The majority of murders are committed by the person who found the corpse. Second to that are spouses. What's her husband's name again?"

"Cam."

"A strange couple in my eyes. Punching above his weight. Do you know that saying?"

"He's a nice guy. Funny."

"Comedy doesn't play between the sheets." He put his pen down and gave his conclusion. "They should arrest Hywel. In my humble opinion."

"There's no reason to arrest him. I don't think they even suspect him."

"They will." He scrambled through his drawer, finding a battered pack of cigarettes and a lighter, preparing to succumb to his bad habit, ready to go outside to smoke in the wild humidity. "And putting a guy in the clink for absolutely no reason hasn't stopped them before, has it?"

He raised his eyebrows and left the room.

I DID NOT WORK for the rest of the day. I locked the door to my office, something that I had never done before, and listened to sad Spanish guitar on my computer.

The police could arrest Hywel any time they wanted. In Panama, you can detain people for up to 72 hours for no reason.

Better safe than sorry, Lexie.

Isn't that your motto?

The outcome of today's conversation was nothing certain, though I had absolute confidence Hywel was innocent. I wracked my mind for thoughts of anything I'd seen since I'd been friendly with Jazz that could be of relevance. I stared out my window into the jungle. I needed no art in my office, the giant window was enough.

What had Jazz's cryptic note to Hywel meant? Dangerous Curves? Santo Amaro? Hywel had mentioned, along with the comment that it was an inside joke. I'd have to ask him about it at work tomorrow, if there was any work to go to.

And if he's not in jail.

The camp had to open. There were twelve people arriving that afternoon who'd come down for a week of surfing lessons, now in a lodge of a questionable state of disrepair on Wizard Beach. Hopefully they could stand a day or two basking in the sun on the beach, just not in the water.

What a tangled web we weave, when first we practice to deceive.

Did Bluff Beach itself have any significance in Jazz's death? She'd always been laughing on the beach, savoring her surfing lessons. She'd loved learning to ride.

On our Sunday boat rides, my focus had generally been on the expensive silver and black fins I had purchased. With genuine care and support, I remembered Jazz being patient while still encouraging me to make one more step towards sliding into the water. She made the romance of being under the sea irresistible.

Almost.

The pleasure and confidence of boarding the boat. The relief of getting off of it. And sneaking occasional glances at Renny.

They fought out of earshot every Sunday. But they were partners of sorts. Since the wouldn't tell anyone what they were bickering about it was just dismissed as family-like bickering.

She said Renny wasn't the kind of guy I'd want to get involved with. Was that in the hope of protecting my bruised (but getting better) heart, or something more sinister? How big of a heartbreaker could he he?

Despite being a little flirtatious, we were just friends who went out on a boat ride on occasions, trying desperately to sing our favorite songs over the loud motor. Maybe to play a game of waterproof Monopoly. Fun but benign. He was still not enough of a friend to go on my phone's favorites screen, but who knew. One day. I was happy to be his friend and sometimes daydream just a little.

Sometimes a mutual stare lasts just a little too long. When we'd dock, I'd run, pretending that I had somewhere to be. Like absolutely nothing at all.

Time must have passed more quickly than I thought. Lloyd walked into my office announcing, "Quitting time. Six o' clock." He pulled one of my transparent Phillipe Stark ghost chairs up to my desk and sat.

"Hi," I said, surprised to see him. This might have only been the second time he'd ever been in my office. And to Lloyd quitting time was merely a suggestion.

"This Monday ex-pat shindig you've been going to…" He

frowned at the thought of it. He wasn't a fan of parties. "I'm going to come with you tonight."

I was shocked for several reasons, his disdain for the masses being the most obvious. Still reeling from the fact that he'd offered me a job, he's another one I'd mistakenly imagined being buddy-buddy with when I returned. We'd shoot the breeze and have after-work whiskeys (even though I'm not a fan of the wretched drink).

For the first week, I'd go into his office at the end of the day, and talk about whatever was on my mind. It turned out I had misinterpreted any sign of bonding between us. At the end of what I considered a particularly funny anecdote about a family of stick spiders found in the bedroom of a honeymooning couple at Grito Mono, he declined an offer to head out for happy hour in town, finishing the conversation saying, "You know, this BFF thing? It's not working for me."

He certainly didn't pull any punches.

I started to shut down my computer. "I don't know, Lloyd. It doesn't seem appropriate to socialize after what happened today."

"It's a healthy thing to do. People need other people when a tragedy like this happens, don't they? Booze brings people together."

I'd seen it before. I guess there was a need to be with other people. To not feel alone. To touch people. To be alive. "Are you sure Lloyd? You don't particularly like humans."

"A necessary evil."

He gave me one of his rare smiles. "I'd say that I'm interested in the tenor of the attitudes. I'm curious to see what people are whispering about tonight. You might not want to be involved, but let's just say I have a vested interest."

7

BACK TO RED FROG BEACH

*L*loyd and I drove Lady Luck to Bocas Town, a short but rather uncomfortable ride. The battery on my makeshift Bluetooth stereo had died, so we drove in silence - if you don't count the racket of insects and howler monkeys. Nervously wanting to fill the quiet, on occasion I'd point out an interesting fact about a random island beetle that I'd learned about, but it didn't spark any conversation.

Once we parked the car, there wasn't much of a line to get a water taxi, but supply was sparse that night. When I asked the driver about it, he said that based on the shark incident, many of his associates decided to take the night off. He didn't believe it at all, having lived in Bocas del Toro his entire life without ever encountering even an aggressive nurse shark. He explained the conditions of local waters were not friendly to the likes of a man-eating shark.

Like Uber surge pricing, when we reached the Red Frog Beach marina, he charged double. Fair enough. If there actually had been a shark attack, he'd be taking his life into his own hands, so outlaw rules apply.

Darkness descended over the horizon.

There was a "jungle shuttle" that transported guests from the marina to the resort and its swanky restaurants on the wild side of the island. Red Frog Beach was one of the few luxury hotels in the area, and the location of the mess of a wedding I'd been maid of honor for.

After the short drive, we walked the short distance down the tiki-lit beach until we hit the bar, *Playa Bajja Plage*, which translates into Beach Beach Beach in Spanish, Maltese, and French. Talk about identity crisis! A beautiful veranda nestled perfectly into a bed of palm trees, a couple dozen folks mingling and drinking overpriced but exquisite tropical cocktails. Half of the group were tourists from the hotel, and half were familiar faces I'd met since moving down here.

Everyone's mind was on the one conspicuous absence: Jazz. News of her death hit the island hard. Half of the usual crowd was missing, and the ones who were there drank nervously, spoke low, and seemed scared of smiling at one another.

I'd never entered an event with Lloyd on my arm. I was surprised to find that I enjoyed the sideways glances we were receiving, myself astride the Prince of Darkness himself. He was not my type in the least, but he was definitely a type. The dangerous bad boy with a big bank account and questionably mysterious past.

My association-by-proximity with him ended there, as the man who hates parties separated from me quickly. "Okay, I'm going to mingle."

Oh well. Such was my station in life.

"Guess what? I stopped calling you Avanti," a friendly voice said from behind me.

I turned to face a smiling Dr. Nolan, presenting me with a Blue Lagoon cocktail garnished with a slice of pineapple and a maraschino cherry. In flat shoes, like I always wore, we were eye to eye, so he was an average height guy. He'd recently cut his longish dirty-blond hair short, in an effort to both look older and to be taken more seriously as a doctor.

I'd seen the expression on his face before. It wasn't that he was pleased that someone was dead, but murder investigations were turning out to be the only time he became part of the gang. He'd been reading his girlfriend's cozy mysteries since summer and was ready for action.

"This is just too sad. Too wrong." He slurped his cocktail audibly. "I can't say more, but the team is on the case."

When Dr. Nolan says that he can't say more, he really means to please ask him kindly, and he'll spill the beans. I'm not sure if this particular doctor pledged the Hippocratic Oath.

As if he already sensed I was going to question him, he started to share. He took a step closer to me and spoke quietly. "It wasn't pretty this afternoon. So, Cam? The husband? He'd just come back from a fishing trip that afternoon and was at Aqua Point Marina. When the police finally tracked him down there, and when they brought him in to, you know, officially identify her, he broke down on the floor weeping. I've never seen a man cry like that. I don't even think I've seen a woman cry like that. Holy Macintosh.

"After LaGuardia talked to him, I gave him a bottle of Xanax, and Romeo took him back to their house in Tierra Oscura. Romeo said he was afraid to leave Cam alone so he sat with him until his friends arrived." He started welling up a little, which was needed to temper his terrible bedside manner for sure. "It's never going to be the same, is it?"

It was true. Besides the immediate heartbreak, the death of someone in a community of this size was going to seismically change it.

The second most likely person to be the murderer is the spouse.

"Doc, you know you can trust me. Look at the insanity we've been through." Both statements were true.

He pursed his lips as if physically trying to restrain his words. "Okay, so they're going to go talk to Cam again tomorrow, but he did say that Jazz wasn't regularly home on Sunday nights. It's a thing. She stays over at her sister's house once a week. Jazz helps with the kids, and then they watch horror movies. Do you know Bella?"

I did. Jazz's sister was a funny little thing. She was sweet as syrup, but always looked like she didn't entirely trust the veracity of what you were saying, even if you simply stated, "I find that the sky is blue today."

"I've met her a few times. Here. Even last week, I think. What did she say?"

"She said the same. Jazz came over to watch some movies, they went to bed, and when Bella woke up at 6, her sister was gone. She said it was pretty normal for Jazz to go out on a sunrise sail or a run or something. Wasn't worried." He finished his drink, which he had downed too fast.

Every Monday he got a little too sloshed, and his girl-friend would come to pick him up. As if it were part of an agreement, she showed up every Monday at 9 p.m., had one glass of white wine, and took him home at 9:45.

Between 4 and 6 a.m.? That could mean that if Hywel had gone surfing just a little earlier he'd might have been able to save her. "Did they say anything about Hywel?"

"They always say something about Hywel. He's not very popular with the police, you know? They're going to talk to him again, though. I guess some things he said didn't quite add up. You trust him though, right?"

The first most likely person to be the murderer is the person who found the body.

"He's always been good to me." I smiled at a tourist couple who'd taken up camp next to us. Dr. Nolan eyed them suspiciously and led me away from the duo.

He looked around to make sure no one was listening and said, "Okay, I'll tell you what was weird though. When I examined her, she had the remnants of a temporary tattoo, of an angel with vampire teeth. You know..."

"Daisy's tattoo?" That made absolutely no sense.

"Exactly. Everyone knows that tattoo. You know that crazy night club she runs? The End of the World? Twenty-two-year-olds running around in bathing suits. The fire breathers come around and practically force all the woman to put on the temporary tattoos. And those things take like a week to wash off. Trust me, I know." His attention was pulled. "Woah, what the winking walrus!"

Fair enough about the walrus. I followed Dr. Nolan's stare and saw Cam walking in with two of his friends. He lumbered over to a table on the side of the bar. One of his friends sat by him in silence, as the third of the trio went to the bar.

"I'm going to get another drink...on the other side of the bar" Dr. Nolan said, a little wobbly. After taking a few steps away, he turned and said, "I've said too much. Don't tell Cam anything I've said."

"That goes without saying." I smiled and watched him teeter off.

Cam was sitting with his remaining friend but none of them were saying anything. The silence continued as his friend brought a bottle of scotch and three glasses over. Slightly balding and a little soft around the stomach, he looked like a completely defeated man.

I picked my Blue Lagoon up and slowly walked over to him. I didn't want to interrupt, but I did want to give my condolences. He was slightly slumped over, stirring the two ice cubes in his scotch with his finger. I almost put my hand on his shoulder but didn't, waiting for him to feel my presence. He looked up at me, sorrowful as I've ever seen a man.

"Cam, I don't know if you remember me, but I just wanted to come over and say how sorry I was. My heart is breaking for you." That was true.

"Of course I know who you are. Lexie. Jazz adored you. She said despite your inability to get in the water, you were one of the bravest people she knew."

It wasn't my place to cry, but I couldn't help it for a moment. "I'm sorry."

"Here. Sit down." He motioned to one of his friends to give me his seat.

"Scotch?" He held up the bottle, but no glass.

"No, I've got this." I held up my colorful cocktail. "But thanks."

"Sorry we couldn't get your ball game up tonight. We'll do it soon. I promise."

In my experience, people who were grieving were always apologizing for something.

"Cam, no one is thinking about baseball right now." I almost reached out to put my hand on his, but I thought better of it.

"I shouldn't have been out on a boat. There's got to have been something I could have done, instead of a stupid fishing trip with Larry Breger. So stupid." Larry was a very cool man I was acquainted with who owned my favorite restaurant, Yarisnori, up in my neck of the woods.

"There's nothing you could have done. There's no way you could have known. You can't feel responsible."

"We'd been squabbling lately over nothing. About stupid things. About nothing at all. What if our fights are what drove her out to the rough side of the east side in that ungodly hour?"

I didn't have an answer for that, but I didn't think he expected one. I sat silently with him and his friends until I reckoned it was time to go. I scanned the room for a new person to chat with. Lloyd was looking bored, towering over a woman who I'd seen at these gatherings before.

I'd only known him as a semi-adversary at a wedding. At the time he'd had no reason to temper his Lloyd-ness to a small group of people he thought he'd never see again. Bocas del Toro was now his home and he had to play nice. The woman didn't seem to notice his apparent disdain as she kept on talking, looking up at him, both worried and drawn to him. He caught my eye and shrugged in his indifferent way. I bit my lip, about to laugh. She noticed this and took his face in her hands and turned it back towards her. Wow. I was going to leave him be for now.

Walking towards the area of the bar furthest from Lloyd, I waited for the bartender to pay attention to me. No matter how many social situations I'd find myself thrust into, it had never become easy. I always made myself go to events, even at the peril of showing up alone, because to change a habit you just have to do it over and over again.

But this dying horse still wasn't quite dead. It was especially crucial for me to throw myself to the wolves (it's just a party, Lexie, get over it) being a new gal in a new town; otherwise, my life could turn into every night on my deck with a white wine spritzer and a waterlogged book.

Doesn't sound too bad to me...

Stop it!

Plus, I needed a real job. Cobbling a living together between two part-time jobs would be okay for a while, but I wanted to find a way to make something of my own. I had a tiny cushion of money with which to go for it, but historically never having enjoyed any of my jobs, I had zilch idea of what I wanted to do.

I didn't think there was a local career coach.

My eye followed a waiter carrying a tray with three bottles of wine and at least twice as many glasses. He walked to the corner by the door, adorned with white Christmas lights and with the best view of the ocean. You couldn't see it at night, but you could hear it, big waves crashing in the dark.

Renny sat with a half dozen of the Sunday friends I'd been seeing regularly, talking seriously as the waiter uncorked the cold wine.

The waiter was pouring everyone a first glass of wine, and I cautiously put my hand on Renny's shoulder, waiting for an invitation to join. He turned around and looked at me, big brown eyes lost in the world. He was sad but glad to see me.

"I'm so sorry." I took my hand away from his shoulder. This was no time to be reminded of a silly crush. "I don't even know what to say, except... I don't know."

He looked around, searching for a chair. "Here, you can share with me." He invited me to sit down with him on a two-person bench which now would fit three.

I shared my condolences with the rest of the table before they devolved into more intimate conversations. Half off the chair, I turned as best I could to face Renny. "I know how much you meant to each other."

His eyes welled up, pressing his lips tightly together. Barely above a whisper, he said, "You were pretty close with her too. Don't think you don't have a right to grieve."

If someone else cries, I do too. It's not a pretty habit.

"She was the first person friend I'd made down here. Everyone loved her."

Not everyone.

However, I had to ask. "Was there anyone who might have wanted to... Has LaGuardia talked to you yet?"

"I went right to the station as soon as I heard. He asked me where I had been during those hours. I was offended at first but he was doing everything right. I was embarrassed to admit that I was passed out at Ned Livingston's villa here, along with that money grubber across the table. We have a monthly poker game with a bunch of guys, and they sometimes get... late. Which means pretty drunk, which I don't normally do."

"Did you know anyone who had something against Jazz?"

"You saw her. She is, was, intense. She had hard and fast rules for what she thought was right. She had no problem confronting people and giving her opinion, but she always did it with class and intelligence. People respected her. I mean, even I got into it with her sometimes. You saw us on the boat." He looked around the table at his friends.

"Just curious, now that... now that what's happened has happened. What were you fighting about?"

He puffed out his cheeks, and let the air out slowly, thinking. "Medicinal research of marine life near more newly discovered reefs." He said it almost like a question.

Though what he said was essentially gibberish to me, it didn't sound like a reason to kill a good friend.

Murder is not always rational.

I changed the subject, smoothing down my hair. "We should probably postpone our trip on Wednesday. I understand..."

"That's the last thing we should do. She wouldn't want us to stop living. This seems stupid to say, but I still want you to get in the water. I want to finish what Jazz started with you. You're so close. Just a little jump."

Would Jazz want this to continue?

She had said, 'Stay away from him, Lexie. He's no good for you.'

Was I betraying her?

I wasn't betraying her if nothing happened between us.

"I don't know if I'm ready to cave dive or anything, but I'll take one more step. It doesn't mean I'm going in the water though."

"Good."

I was sitting too close to him and stood up. I felt a stare boring into me, and I knew before turning around that it had to be Lloyd, who was now very obviously ignoring his over-enthusiastic conversationalist. Catching his eye, he cracked a wry smile, looking darkly amused.

His look seemed to express one thought that I didn't want to entertain.

Everyone is a suspect.

DAY THREE

8

THE MORNING AFTER THE NIGHT BEFORE

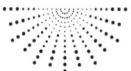

*T*woke up at the break of dawn after a nightmare. This happened more often than not.

Last night's dream had been a completely new one. Sharks on the beach, coming up through the sand as if it were liquid, snapped at my tootsies. A derelict (or even more derelict) version of Hywel's camp seemed to be the location, only it was little blue men who were surfing, and no one seemed to notice that a new species of terrain-smart sharks was on a murderous rampage.

What's *that* a metaphor for? A dream analyst would have a field day with that dreamscape. Or run for the hills.

Whether having nightmares or not, I woke up every morning a little sweaty, which was the way of the non-air-conditioned tropics. Everything I owned was a little damp, but you get used to that pretty quickly. I'd been able to fend off the mold with OCD cleaning, but I didn't resent it. To be honest, cleaning gave me something to do during the many hours that I still had free in my social calendar.

I put up my hair in a high bun, dressed myself in shorts

and a tank-top, and grabbed an ice tea out of the fridge before heading out to the dock. I had a long list of things that I needed someone to bring me from the States should I ever have a visitor, and that included Arizona iced tea and Dunkin Donuts coffee.

The previous night had finished quite unceremoniously. Lloyd walked with me to the Jungle Shuttle, letting me ramble on about the things I'd learned that night. Daisy's tattoo, the time of death, and Renny's account of Jazz being a bit of a hard nosed moralist. He listened, took it all in, but didn't get into the Jungle Shuttle with me.

I'd asked him what he'd learned, to which he answered, "Nothing of consequence."

"Really?" I tried to raise one eyebrow the way that he did when he was judging someone, but I don't think mine worked so well.

"I'm just an observer. I just watch from a distance." He let me know that he wasn't coming back to Bocas Town with me, with the unspoken understanding that he'd allowed the woman at the party to prattle on for a reason. He would not be alone that night.

Jazz. Had I learned anything of importance?

I scrambled to think of any truth I'd gathered since yesterday morning that I could pass on to Bocas PD. Of course I didn't want to get involved, but I wanted Jazz's murder to be solved as quickly as possible. Could I offer anything?

They knew most of the same things that I did. The fact that Jazz had a temporary tattoo from Daisy's wild night-clubbing world was confusing, to say the least. It was feasible that Daisy might have seen Hywel giving Jazz lessons, and accused her of being his new squeeze, as she did to every other female he came in contact with, but would she physically attack her with a temporary tattoo? She had to be smart enough to know that if you murder someone it's not the best idea to stick your logo on their bum before you leave the scene of the crime.

From what Dr. Nolan had said it seemed that Hywel was definitively on their list, but that wasn't a surprise. I had vouched for his character, but how well did I really know him? I'd only been working for him since the beginning of June. He was entertainment to his guests, with a crazy ex-girlfriend, and perhaps a penchant towards lying about sharks to get himself out of trouble. I poured through memories to see if there was anything that would help to get him off the list of suspects.

Or to put him right on the top of the list.

Slow it down, Lexie. You've helped put an innocent man in prison before.

It's a bad habit to get into.

Leave it to the pros.

The doc had said that they were on the case. They were going to talk to Hywel again, as well as Cam. They'd tracked down Jazz's sister, Bella, and had either already talked to her or would as soon as the real world woke up.

Jazz was argumentative. LaGuardia had known her his entire life, but they existed in very different circles. I'm sure her disputatious nature was no secret. But still...

I assumed I'd be working at Hywel's relocated surf camp on Wizard Beach that morning, but it was still four hours until opening time. Mornings seemed to last for eternity in my current state. Hopefully, someone had informed his guests that no sharks were lurking past the break.

It was not outside the realm of normalcy for me to text LaGuardia and meet him for breakfast. To clear his head on most mornings, he'd start his day by riding the waves over at

Paunch Beach, south of Bluff where the road was still decent. Besides absolutely everything, what was different about today?

I sent him a message and got ready for what I could see was going to be a very long day.

~

MY CAR WAS in Bocas Town, and I cursed myself for doing the right thing and not driving drunk. While taking water taxis home was a most civilized way to get around, it's not like you could call one, so I stuck my flip-flops in my bag, put on my hiking shoes, and walked fifteen minutes to Paved Road to wait for the bus to take me to Bocas Town.

The bus was a bumpy affair, and I'd learned very early in my time on this island not to try to drink anything, make a phone call, or take anything out of my bag as it might go flying into someone's head or out the window. The buses were old, and the idea of shock absorbers seemed to have eluded them. You just had to hold on tight, suck it up, and curse yourself for leaving your car in town.

I still hadn't heard back from LaGuardia by the time I got to Bocas Town, but he wasn't great at getting back to me. At first, I took offense at the fact that most of my texts weren't returned, but his wife, Gabby, had said that was just par for the course. "That means he likes you," she'd said. That logic was lost on me.

It was next to impossible to not eat healthily on the islands. I grabbed a watermelon, mint and lime smoothie, and headed towards my car. Compared to my recent ride the old junk, Lady Luck, felt positively luxurious. Next stop, Paunch Beach.

9

CIUDAD MUERTA

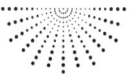

(GHOST TOWN)

*P*aunch Beach was quiet when I parked by the side of the road, the white sand devoid of a soul. It was always one of the more tranquil beaches; no restaurants or bars speckling the area. It was a unique surfing spot as the waves broke to the left and to the right, something good for both the beginners and the pros. The water was warm, clean, and clear. This early there were usually half a dozen people out on their boards, but not today.

On all the trees in the area there were still signs written with a magic marker warning against sharks. When would this great white madness stop?

As if even the waves had heard that no one would be surfing today, the ocean was way too calm, maybe informing the swells that they also could take a day off. I sat down on an old plastic lounger and checked my phone. No response from LaGuardia.

I'd learned my lesson about island service well. I restarted my phone three times, and finally a return message from him registered on my phone: *Not going to make it today. Stop by the station later. LG.*

I guzzled my smoothie through the deteriorating paper straw, taking a guilty time out to enjoy the mellow morning sun before it got too hot. No wonder the random surf bums (and drunks) didn't mind sleeping on the beach.

It was a bright new day, and I could already see things with a kind of retrospect. I smacked myself in the head for the big piece of information I'd flaked on. Whether consciously or unconsciously, I had a potential clue that neither the police or Lloyd were privy to.

The note from Jazz to Hywel.

Cuidado con las curvas peligrosas. Adios, a Santo Amaro.

Beware of dangerous curves. Goodbye, Saint Somebody-or-other.

Relative gibberish. When Hywel had been clearly amused by the note, he'd casually said it was a private joke.

I got back into Lady Luck and took the short drive north towards Grito Mono. I owed it to Hywel to ask him about the note before I mentioned it to anyone else. There was no reason to start suspicion over something benign.

Or is it?

Go away, annoying voice in my head.

The two cars blocking the way to the surf camp were still there, so I parked in front of them. The warning signs from yesterday were still hanging, damp, and with the words starting to run and blur. Some 8 ½ x 11 versions were wadded up by the side of the road.

I'd never been in the hotel when it was empty. Even in the 24-hours turnaround on Sunday and Monday, there was cleaning staff, some of Hywel's staff out on surfboards, and a very mellow bustle.

"Hywel? Are you here?" I climbed the stairs to the open-air restaurant, momentarily thrilled that my phone had picked up the wireless signal. I walked through the joint and into reception, which was dark and empty.

I knew the vague direction of where Hywel's little cottage was but had never visited. A not-so-short distance behind the lodge into the jungle lay a very cool little abode, looking more like a Frank Lloyd Wright bungalow than a beach shack. There was a clean stone walkway leading up to the door, and a well-manicured outdoor area with quality lounge furniture. The curtains were open, and it was dark inside. I knocked on the door, loud enough to wake the dead. "Hywel? Wake up. Are you in there?"

I walked around the cabin looking in all the windows. The place was really very well appointed. I would have assumed it would be a mess of unmade beds and mismatched dining room furniture, but it was showroom clean.

Correction: I never imagined this place with a living room at all, only an old sofa and some mismatched furniture, complemented by unframed posters of surfers and rock bands. But like everyone and their brother says, don't judge a book by its cover.

He wasn't there.

I returned to the beach and walked north, the direction Hywel was heading when I last saw him, but just came face to face with a rugged expanse with no man in sight.

The shade of the restaurant seemed the right place to sit and plan my next move. The bar's contents had been packed up and hidden away, with not even bottled water in sight. I started to type a message to Hywel. 'Are you here?' I stopped before I hit send, deciding to reword.

"Are we working at Grito Mono today?"

Ten minutes later, there was a reply. "Down at Pedro's dump on Wizard's beach. Show up when you can." This was followed by three emojis: a surfer, someone about to vomit, and a monkey covering his eyes. At least I think it was a he.

It was close to 8 a.m. and I dreaded the journey to Wizard's Beach. It was only a half-mile north of Red Frog Beach, but not a route you could survive. I'd have to get a ferry from Bocas Town to the bay at Old Bank, then walk a half hour over a steep hill on a dirt path to Wizard's Beach. I'd been warned that people had been robbed on the trail, so I always carried just enough money that I could share my wealth with the criminals and hopefully be left alone.

What's the rush, Lexie?

He said, get there when you can.

The quiet was too much. I half expected tumbleweeds to roll by, and the ghost of a misplaced Oklahoma gunslinger. The dreaded surf-shack where Hywel had covered Jazz's body was ominously waiting. What was the harm in checking it out?

I knew where the extra key was. It wasn't exactly high security, living in a fake rock under one of the stilted rooms. It wasn't pretty to get to, having to dodge a swarm of *chitras* and two helmeted iguanas, but I got the battered-looking key.

I was probably more scared than I needed to be. Crabby Paolo had put the fear of god into me when he told me that the island was home to a small population of banana spiders. There were supposed to be as big as your hand and the most venomous in the world. His last words on that subject were, "If you don't hurt them, they won't hurt you."

It wasn't exactly comforting. I'm pretty sure that's how I'm going to die. Not paranoid or anything.

Wiping the dirt off my hands and knees, I walked back to the surf shack, unlocking the door to where Hywel found the body. I dreaded going in there, maybe afraid that I'd be attacked those banana spiders laying in wait. Or a great white shark who'd chosen land living. Or the truth.

It smelled of old cheap wood and Mr. Zog's brand coconut surf wax. I opened the shutters as if for regular business and took a look at the place in the light of day. It was always chockablock with anything an aspiring surfer could want for - a couple dozen boards, some wetsuits that could use replacing, and a wall of folded blue towels. For sale, there was suntan lotion, snacks, a good selection of beer, and a small selection of juice and water. Nothing of interest remained. The blankets that had been covering Jazz were gone, most likely with the police. Every towel on the shelves had been gone through and hastily returned to their resting place.

I grabbed some water from the fridge and closed up shop, walking over to the group of palm trees where she had been found. I was no forensics expert, but there was nothing but the bushy base and some detritus from the sea.

Feeling guilty and paranoid about what I was about to do I sent a message to Hywel. "Send me a selfie. I want to see the place."

He immediately sent back a photo of himself with a group of frowning campers behind him, all just a smidge sunburnt. He was clearly there and I was alone in the monkey's lair.

Flip-flopping all the way down Hywel's stone path I took a moment to think about what I was doing at the door to his house. It was almost a compulsion to go inside. Because I didn't expect to find anything. Really. I didn't.

It was cool and clean, and though I knew no one was home I whispered aloud, "You son of a monkey's uncle – you've been hiding air conditioning from the rest of us." It felt relentlessly civilized, and for at least a moment I thought that the best way for me to play out this strange day would be to kick back on his comfy couch, try to catch some very missed American reality shows on his satellite TV, and make this my headquarters for the day.

I was correct when I guessed that there would be plenty of Jules' minty homemade limeade in the fridge. It was also well populated with Soberana beer, hummus, steaks, and a couple of nice looking champagne bottles on their side, ready to pop. It was a lot more upscale than I would have guessed from a man I'd never seen in shoes, but it matched the minimalist chic of the rest of the bungalow. I felt there was no problem in grabbing a bottle of limeade. After all I wasn't breaking and entering... I was just entering. That was just walking into a friend's house.

I casually strolled through the small bungalow, which looked like he'd recently employed the magic-art-of-tidying, so there was really nothing left to pick through. There was a beautiful photo of him with a group of people I assumed was his family. They were all tall and blond, aged ten to eighty, trying to get into formation for a serious family photo but having too much fun. It must have been his parents' house in La Jolla, CA. Though, to never forget their rainy roots, they posed in front of a large Welsh flag - a young boy's dream of a red dragon in a green field.

I opened kitchen drawers, but there was nothing suspicious. Eating and cooking paraphernalia shared space with a medley of tools for surfers. The only impression that I could gather was that he was clearly much better in the kitchen than I was. In the very near future, maybe we'd laugh about my time ripping through his drawers while I was trying to keep him from getting arrested. We'd throw any bad feeling away when he offered to share a dinner of duck confit and fondant potato. Soon.

He continued to impress me with his clean bathroom and quality of product choice available. Dark slate floors gave the place a slightly spa-like feel. The place smelled somehow peppery. Or maybe it was nutmeg. The only thing that looked out of place in the very metro bathroom was one women's bathrobe. It was short and pink, and made of quality cotton.

Could be Daisy's?

Could be anyone else's?

This one garb of femininity did not shine a light on anything else. Looking through the bathroom and the two bedrooms, there was no extra tooth-brush, or socks, or nighties. No wadded up panties stuck into the back of a drawer fighting for their right to stay at their boyfriend's house. No eyeliner, hairbrush, or zip-lock bag full of lipstick and eyeliners. The pink bathrobe was on it's own.

Poking through the drawer of the one bedside table unearthed an amazing amount of nothing: blue-tac, what looked like a two-year old California lottery ticket, a flash-light, and a completely blank journal. He had a Christmas McDonald's coupon book, which would be a good thing if he was ever looking to go an hour off island. Still, it was the thoughtful gift of some niece or great-grandmother some-where that had meant enough that he hadn't throw them away.

There was an expensive looking bottle of aromatherapy spray and a handful of promotional material for Grito Mono. All innocent enough, but just in case I delved a little deeper. I opened a drawer and came out with half a gallon bag of smaller bags of Sugar Babies (of which I took three, because who's going to know?) sitting on top of a black envelope.

I grabbed the envelope (along with the sugar babies and

the mint limeade), straightened up anything that I might have messed up, and sat down on the modern couch in the cool air.

The envelope contained a small pile of pink post-it notes; unique keepsakes. Examining them, it was clear that I was looking at love notes of sorts. There were dozens of the adhesive reminders - stick figures of a man and a woman mostly next to or on surfboards, kissing and expressing their love for each other. They were all drawn with some humor, but with a heart's worth of emotion. The surfboards were made of x kisses, or a walk up the beach, hand and hand with a setting sun made of x's and o's. The artist had left her easily identifiable signature in the bottom right corner of the sheet: JZ.

I didn't have to be Einstein to figure out that Jazz had been leaving the funny love notes, featuring a way too tall shaggy surfer and a regular size (at least in the world of post-it art) woman with wavy long dark hair. They were having fun. The one of them diving warmed my heart, the two stick characters avoiding treacherous sea predators and speech bubbles of what looked like short Spanish curses.

Underneath the post-its was a folded and refolded reef map of the Bocas del Toro Providence. He'd been checking off the ones that he'd been visiting. Correction, I suppose he'd been checking off the ones that they as a couple had been visiting.

Then came the kicker. It was simple really, just a photograph of the two of them. I snapped a picture of the map, and of the photo of Jazz and Hywel, and put the envelope back where it came from before I left.

Jazz had been cheating on Cam. Had Cam seen this picture as well? Had he already known about Hywel? It's the kind of betrayal that could send a man over the edge.

The couple never made sense physically, but they seemed happy enough. They seemed to laugh a lot. But never smiling like she did in this picture. Sweet Cam. Being presented with this information could drive a man to do most anything.

Walking back to my car, I looked at the picture of them again. It made me incredibly sad to see her looking so vital and so happy. They weren't doing anything more serious than sitting together, looking into one another's eyes with the hope of new love, but one thing was clear. It was no selfie. They hadn't taken that picture. So who had?

Though I got a full pass on punctuality it was time to migrate to Hywel's relocated camp. It wasn't an easy jaunt. Hywel had questions to answer. Just another day in Paradise.

DEAR CUPID, NEXT TIME HIT US BOTH

I sat on the hood of Lady Luck near Palanga, the ferry terminal in Bocas Town. There was one big passenger ferry that came in from Almirante on Panama's mainland every morning and left in the afternoon. The rest of the time it served as a local ferry service with ten-minute voyages to Old Bank and the Red Frog Beach Marina. A ferry that went to Isla Solarte with much less frequency.

It's also where you could count on picking up a water-taxi at all hours. The difference between water taxi and small ferry wasn't much. The former was a little more swanky, and could hold as many as eight or ten passengers. The latter could carry a few dozen passengers, but they were in a worse state of disrepair, and you could definitely count on a brawl or two after certain hours.

I was more partial to the water taxis. They were still inexpensive at a few bucks a ride, but every so often, I decided I was being an unreasonable ferry snob. I'd ride with the drunks (didn't matter what time of day) until something would put me off for the next foreseeable future.

From where I sat on the scorching roof of my car, I could just see the dock of the Bocas P.D. Bocas Town was tiny, so I was also virtually just past the end of the runway that brought their two flights in and out on a daily basis. I was on my second Sunset Beach smoothie, deciding whether to get on the ferry to Old Bank to go to work, or to visit LaGuardia and tell him about the note, and the photos, and the very endearing series of post-it notes.

It's not that Bocas PD was not a good police force, they just didn't have that pesky need for probable cause that might keep a questionable man free while they dotted their i's and crossed their t's. There had never been any rumors of abuse or mistreatment, but it still made me worry that in a poker game gone wrong a friendly foe could find himself on an undeserved three-day holiday, all expenses paid, courtesy of the government of Panama.

The sound of a turboprop airplane in the vicinity gave a boost of energy to the sleepy port, and the machines started coming to life. I took the short walk from where my car was parked down to the tiny terminal. Though I couldn't pass through into the arrivals area, hanging out at the nail salon/bar was a fun way to waste a few minutes (it could never be too long of a visit, as the biggest plane carried less than 60 people).

Like I've said, my favorite thing about island culture was waving. Too many years in New York City will rob you of that pleasure. There are simple niceties in life, like a wave, a hello, and a new visitor ready to get sunburnt and sloshed.

A charter Cessna-206 six-seater had landed bumpily (they all did) and a handful of folks disembarked, taking their luggage with them. Catching a familiar face, I turned away for a moment and blushed and breathed in like a thirteen-year-old girl just caught staring at her movie star crush in the eye.

"Well, ain't you a sight for sore eyes?" The handsome man said as he smiled wide, passing the length of the nail bar, headed towards security. He blew me a light, whimsical kiss and said, "Don't move," as he hurried through security.

I wouldn't be going anywhere. Migs was the wedding photographer who I'd made friends with way back when. He was local-ish to the area, and when he wasn't doing underwater photography for National Geographic someplace impressive, he did parties and weddings from time to time… for a price worth his reputation, making him probably the only photographer making any real money in the equatorial belt. iPhones and digital cameras had ravished an entire industry of click-click-clickers, but he stood tall. I'd like to think it had nothing to do with his curly black hair and fairytale green eyes.

Returning to the tropics, it's not like I had a lot of friends to check in with, and he'd have been an obvious call. But I had become shy and never reached out to him. I was very matter of fact in the reasons that I didn't let him know of my change-of-address. He didn't technically live on Bocas del Toro. He lived a short plane ride away in a sweet little town called Manzanillo on the Caribbean coast of Costa Rica. I say sweet little town since I'd heard it was quite nice and a little less rough around the edges than Bocas. I'd never been.

He could have taught a master class on flirting with kindness and dignity. Though nothing had happened between the two of us when I was last down, he was a solid sounding board, a concerned friend, and the best example of snake hips I'd ever seen. He never made it a secret that he was wide open to getting involved with me, but the last time I was down here I picked the wrong guy and it subsequently didn't work out.

Also, how seriously can you take a guy as handsome as Migs, who's saying the right things while staring into your soul with his green eyes, knowing that you'll be flying away on the upcoming Sunday? That's not an invitation to a relationship. It's a five-day fling.

So there was a particular reason I didn't reach out to him, and it's called self-preservation. Maybe one day. There is also one straightforward way to say it: he is simply out of my league.

I checked myself out in the dark scratched glass in the bar; no mishaps yet today. My hair was still in the same messy bun that it lived in, my outfit was covered neither in smoothie or mud, and I was looking alright. Changing up a diet of NY cheeseburgers, French fries, and cannoli, in exchange for smoothies, octopus tacos, tuna tataki and a whole lot of H20 changes your body pretty quickly. I fumbled through my bag searching for some semblance of lip gloss and my coolest pair of sunglasses before walking over to the waiting area directly outside immigration.

Not thirty seconds after getting his passport stamped, he had his arms around me, swinging me through the air. "Lexie Marino! What are you doing here? Don't tell me you're down for another wedding, god help us all."

"No, no. No wedding. I moved down here in July."

He looked pleasantly amused. "You? Faithful subject of the kingdom of New York? Moved here?"

I nodded. It definitely felt like I had done the right thing.

"Please don't say you moved down here with that boring intellectual dude? Kill me now." I could never tell if his enthusiasm was a put on.

"No. No, Josh didn't work out. Sometimes when you

almost drown with someone, it's easy to mistake it for true love. It wasn't."

He laughed heartily. "Someone's got to make a motivational poster out of that one."

"Are you here for an event?" I asked. He wasn't packed for a long trip. He had a small, gorgeous, but battered Louis Vuitton duffle bag. Suitable for four days maybe, but not as long as a week.

"You've been down here for months and you never reached out? I would have flown over to see you in a heartbeat." He looked around at the seemingly innocent crowd and said, "Let's find a place we can talk a little more quietly." He threw his bag over his shoulder, taking my hand as we exited the airport.

There was a hotel called Tango Vista just a five-minute walk from the airport. It sat on the water and had a nice breakfast menu. Like many of the waterfront hotels in Bocas Town, there were very attractive seafront restaurants on great decks, deceiving you about the not-so-quality rooms inside the building. We were shown to a wobbly table at the edge of the dock looking towards the tiny Isla Caranero.

We said little until we got our coffees. As soon as they were served, he ordered a Soberana beer, and I remembered that not so lovely detail about Migs. He was a serious drinker.

"So what brings you to Bocas Town today?" I put piles of sugar in my coffee.

He pouted, "It's sad really. Very sad. And I wished I had known you were here – I would have come sooner. But, did you know a woman named Jasmina Belmonte?"

I felt my eyes welling up. "Jazz..."

"Yes. I don't even know where to start. So you know... of

course. Her sister, Bella, called me yesterday. I can't believe it. I still can't believe it. I don't want to believe it."

"I was still really getting to know her. She's been so cool with me. So much fun. She had really gone out of her way to be my friend."

His beer was served, and he pounded half of it. He noticed me noticing. "Welcome to the tropics."

"How did you know Jazz? Were you the photographer when she and Cam got married?"

"Thank god, no. I've known her since we were teenagers. We were all from... Our families had a little more money than a lot of the people around here... we were all at boarding school outside of Panama City. Renny, too. Have you met Renny?"

I casually agreed that I may have made his acquaintance.

"When I was younger and needed money, I'd do underwater photography on their charters. But a week spent drunk with a dozen dentists from Kholer, WI gets really tiring. Plus Cam never liked me. Over the last few years, since she's been doing these projects on the newly discovered reefs, I've been doing some work for her from time to time. No dentists invited. You're not going into dentistry now, are you, Lexie?"

That was the question for the ages. Not if and when I would be pursuing my DDS, but what I'd be doing to make a life at all.

"I don't know what I'm doing, Migs." Looking down at the table, I quickly gave him the rundown of my hodgepodge of jobs, my doubts about the future, and the fact that I could identify over three-dozen different spiders.

"It sounds like you're in the middle of a mid-life crisis. A little young for it, but... I've got faith in you though, Lexie. You'll figure it out." He pushed the chunks of local fruit around his plate, reluctant to bring a bite to his mouth. "But this… *murder?* I couldn't understand half of what Bella was even saying when she called. What happened? Does anyone know?" He surveyed the landscape from the extreme left to right. "And why isn't anyone in the water?"

I made the decision not to address the last question.

Migs was a person I'd trusted from the minute I met him back in April. It had never been a wrong choice, but I didn't feel like I could trust anyone at this moment. Truly a fish out of water, I was going to hold all my cards close to my chest.

At this point, was bringing up a photo of Jazz and Hywel going to do any good? Or why did he need to know that Daisy's tattoo was brazenly temporarily branded on Jazz's butt? For all I knew the police had arrested the real criminal, Hywel's name had been cleared, and all of this was for naught.

So what are you doing to help, Lexie?

Sitting around doing nothing...

I was biding time over fruit and coffee while sitting on info that I had to either share with the cops or confront Hywel with first. I committed myself to action.

"I'm going to need to get to work soon. I should have been to Hywel's camp a half hour ago." I didn't offer up the fact that Grito Mono was temporarily displaced and shacking up in an old camp on Wizard's Beach. I found myself praying that there was actually running water and a working kitchen for the new 14-guests at shark refugee central.

"Where are you staying?" I asked curiously, not suggestively.

He bit his bottom lip in that way that made me sure that he really was Migs. "Is that an offer, tall girl?" Thankfully he hadn't been around long enough to hear about Avanti.

"No." I blushed. He was good at making my cheeks turn red. He wasn't even annoying in his supreme confidence that it was merely a fact that every woman on earth was drawn to him. That was annoying in its own right. I didn't need to explain further, but I did. "I'm very sad about Jazz. She was teaching me how to snorkel. She was good to me."

"I don't doubt it." He smiled sadly. "I'll be staying at Bella's. She's got a nice guesthouse that I stay in when I'm over here just to hang. This time it's emotional support. That Belmonte family is well off. They owned half of Isla Bastimentos at one point. Chocolate plantations. So much has been sold off, but from what I hear there's still plenty. I know a lot of people said she married Cam for money, but she probably had more than that *puta madre* did."

"Sorry if I'm intruding at all, but you said that Cam didn't like you? Why was that?" I was hoping that Jazz wasn't a serial cheater and that Migs wasn't one in a list of many. Or in a select category of his own.

"That guy has a temper. She's out of his league on every level. He wasn't abusive to her at all or anything. He put her up on a pedestal. But he wasn't a fan of men around her. Maybe it's because I was hired for a project that took her attention away from the charter business. Maybe he thought something was going on with us." He cleaned his sunglasses with his comfortably worn t-shirt twice, not finding them clean enough the first time.

I didn't want to know but I had to ask, "But nothing was going on between the two of you?"

"Jazz? Never. And never with a married woman. Not available, not interested. It's like a switch goes off when I see a ring on someone's finger. Besides, maybe I'm waiting for someone special."

I met his eyes after that statement, green and almost playful. Forget about surf camps – I could start my own resort to teach flirting for tourists with all the local experts from this crazy Flirtsville Island. We could teach classes. Run seminars. "You don't give up, do you?"

"No, I don't." He peeled at the paper label on his beer, and I realized I hadn't seen that it in quite some time. Back in high school, that signified that you were nervous around someone you were crushing on.

"But Cam could have thought that you were… maybe?"

"I don't know. That guy is unreadable to me. Treated me like the help after meeting him a few times." He shook his head. "Doesn't matter now. But when Bella called, I jumped on a plane, and I'm here. I didn't even think about having to see him. Poor bastard, whatever he's going through. Come with me tonight to Bella's? All her friends are getting together to talk and think about… Cam's intense."

He looked really nervous. He wasn't hitting on me with the odd request to go with him to a get-together of mourners. He was scared to show up alone because of Cam.

"Cam? All I've seen of him is a big goofy guy. I believe you, but I can't picture it." He'd always been a friendly guy, making self-deprecating jokes, then fixing anything that went wonky. I still couldn't picture Jazz and Hywel together either. Half the world is in the shadow of secrets.

"He's not a goofy guy."

"If you want me, I can come. I can meet you after work."

He put his hand on mine. "Thank you."

"Why don't you meet me at the restaurant by the ferry at Old Bank, Ugly Martha's Snack Shack?"

"Is that what they're calling it now? That's terrible."

"It is."

It was a little terrible on the inside as well, but it was awfully convenient. I always busted out my travel pack of anti-bacterial wipes for the seats and the table. I had a momentary light bulb flash above me, with a thought to start bringing my own drinking glasses.

We agreed on a time and tried to retreat into a more pleasant conversation. I regaled him with tales of the current shark attack craze on the island. When it was time for me to leave, I brushed crumbs off my lap, wishing I'd worn something nicer. Before I walked away, I asked, "Are you okay?"

He bunched up his face, earnestly replying, "No."

He stared out at the water, thinking about better times.

11

THE OTHER SIDE OF PARADISE

*M*oments after the ferry took off from Bocas Town, I knew I'd made the right choice about going to work before checking in with LaGuardia. I sat at the very back of the boat as we departed, gazing off at nothing in particular. My smooth sailing was disrupted by a sudden change in intensity of the current.

Someone at the front of the boat shouted, "Shark!" Everyone laughed. A good sign that people were hopefully getting back in the water on that scorcher of a day.

No, it was not a shark, but a luxury speedboat approaching the police station at a breakneck speed. All the passengers moved to the port side of the ferry, weighing it to one side. The captain yelled at everyone to calm down, after taking an extended glance at the action.

Cam and two other men got off the 33-foot boat (I'd been on it once, I'd been told the length), and whatever state of extreme grief that the police had observed the day before had been replaced with sheer fury. I'd known Cam as the comical, slightly goofy, widget-king; soft around the edges in a dozen ways. Today? Not cuddly.

This was a Cam I hadn't seen. Maybe I'd never seen him stand up straight. He seemed taller, his broad chest puffed out, looking more like a Bensonhurst gangster than benevolent charter magnate.

Cam was muttering as he walked right into the station. The purpose of the two men was obviously to be back up to the bereft visitor, but my guess is that they knew their friend well, and would be quick to act if needed to pull a warring Cam off of one of the cops.

I didn't envy anyone involved in the conversation that was about to go on in Bocas PD. Hopefully one, if not both, sides of the situation had new information to share with the concerned group.

Or is Cam turning himself in?

Does he look like a man ready to go anywhere without a fight?

I double-checked the clips on my safety vest. There are some things more important than trying to look pretty.

Aren't there?

GETTING off the boat at Old Bank was always an interesting adventure. It was a rowdier and more remote area. It was popular for many reasons; cheap rents for locals, and plenty of hostels for the twenty-something crowd.

Backpacking had morphed a ton from what it had been twenty years ago. Now it was bikini-clad gals looking to party into oblivion for a week before moving on to the next place with a cheap mosquito netted bed to lay their heads. Usually, these college-age girls came with their friends, had a week-long relationship with their anonymous male counterparts, then split as quickly as they came together. Not my scene.

But Daisy's bread and butter.

Wizard Beach was hands down one of the most stunning beaches in the area, pristine with perfect surf conditions. And empty. Why? Because the only way to get there was that dread-inspiring, 30-minute walk up the steep hill on a dirt path.

It could be muddy, and various nettles could grab your ankles at any moment. I hadn't seen any banana spiders, but that didn't mean they weren't ready to pounce. I'd been told that every few months a new group of men would start hiding on the side of the road, performing their version of highway robbery. The police always snagged them within a day or two, but the road got a bad rep. That was warning enough for me. This was only my fourth journey to the other side of paradise.

There had been one case along the treacherous paths that took the police weeks to crack. There'd been an elusive flasher, displaying his wares to women walking solo or pairs. He'd always run off very quickly, nasally yelling, "*El mundo tiembla*," The World Shakes. People seemed more entertained than threatened by him, and I half expected for him to come back in a new role as a tourist attraction. He and a smoothie stand were a recipe for success.

At the very least, the one thing I knew I could do was run very fast. Especially from *El Mundo Tiembla*. I had my trusty oh-so-hot Merrill hiking boots to get me through the sludge. Reaching the top of the hill before descending to Wizard Beach was a beautiful scene out of a movie. I cleared the muddy jungle and came upon a wild expanse of blue sky, white sand beach, and hardly a beach bunny in sight.

The area was known for being one of the best surf locations in the islands. There were no restaurants, no snack shacks, no bathrooms. Occasionally a local would make the journey from Old Bank, with a little red wagon of coolers, full of room-temperature (whatever that was in the tropics) water, which would sell like hotcakes. It would have been a great business model, except that you couldn't count on it. Sometimes there would be fifty people on the beach, but just as likely there would be three.

Once upon a time there was a surf camp not too unlike Grito Mono called Waxy's Surf School. But the location was just too much of a pain in the posterior to keep it in competition with the dozen others on the archipelago. Who and where was Waxy? No one knew. It had been basically abandoned, except for the occasional disappointed Airbnb group who arrived at the genuinely-described rustic lodge. Rustic in this case meant dilapidated grandeur without the grandeur.

When I'd been on the phone with De Sousa, one of Hywel's surfing staff yesterday, he'd said that there was indeed running water, but it was cold. There was a hypothetically workable kitchen, and Jules could set up a bar faster than you could say, "fraudulent shark attack."

Hywel was full in view doing what he often did; putting the wet suits, surfboards, and necessary accessories on display, but no one was in any hurry to get in the ocean. The guests all lay on towels on the beach in a haphazard semi-circle listening to De Sousa tell them something engaging. Hywel couldn't have run the camp without him. Most of the guests looked like they'd accepted their fate for the week, and they weren't happy about it.

As soon as I hit the sand, hiking boots were off and flip-flops were back on. Quickly walking towards Hywel, I was thwarted by Jules pulling me out of the way and back up to the shabby deck. "This is going to be the worst week of my life. It's only Tuesday. Can it really be only Tuesday? How many days..." She counted off on her muddy looking fingers. "Wednesday, Thursday, Friday, Saturday, Sunday... Lord help us all, five more nights.

"They wouldn't go to bed last night, cranky as all get out. I ran out of booze and they really went to town. De Sousa had to run down to *Playa Bajja Plage* because you can't get a water taxi at two in the morning. Or more aptly, never at this craggy old beach. He begged the night porter for whatever he could grab out of the kitchen, which was four bottles of whiskey and one Malibu Rum. What are you going to do with that except beg them to drink water as well and hope they pass out sooner than later. I got the itchies like crazy from sleeping here. I live at Bluff. I'm definitely going back tonight. I think I have a rash."

"Oh, Jules. I'm so sorry." I gave her a quick, clammy hug.

The chef was sitting around with nothing to do. Jules gestured towards him. "And he can't do anything until the runners from Old Bank show up. The guests have been living on the fruit that we nearly killed ourselves carrying over that cursed hill this morning."

I glanced over at a hungover group of non-surfers waiting for their day in the sun. I was pretty sure that my social media manager skills would not be put to use today. "Is there anything I can do?"

She shook her head.

"But by now, Hywel has to have told them that the shark business was a hoax?"

"He did! He did this morning. But now they think he's trying to pull something over on them. They think that there is a shark and that now he's lying to them. Hopefully they'll start believing him eventually. After we get some food and a couple of Bloody Mary's into them, De Sousa's going to take them down to the zip line at Red Frog Beach. That should take up a few hours. I told Hywel he should rent a villa there for the night so this bunch could get a hot shower. But you know how tight he is…"

Because he's spending all his money on his secret luxury bungalow.

Jules wiped the sweat from her brow. "The police were out hdre yesterday. It didn't come to anything, but it certainly wasn't great for customer relations… They said they'd be back."

I glanced over at Hywel, who was arranging the boards in a particularly artistic way. "Is he okay?"

"Who knows with that one… At least Daisy hasn't tracked down our alternate location, knock on wood." There was no lack of wood to knock on, and we did so heartily. "Hopefully they'll get back in the water and the rest of the week will be saved."

I walked down the beach to Hywel, approaching with a soft hello.

He almost jumped out of his bare feet. "Sheesh. You scared me."

"I have to talk to you, Hywel." There was no point in beating around the bush.

He looked exhausted. The dark circles under his eyes made me think he'd been tossing and turning all night. "I'm not in the mood to talk. I've talked myself to death over the last twenty-four hours." He started putting coconut wax on the board he just finished working on. Take two.

"This is not funny, Hywel. Not funny at all. There is some serious stuff going on that you aren't being honest about again."

"What are you talking about? I'm an open book. Always have been, always will be."

"I know, Hywel. I know what's going on. And you better come clean or you'll be getting yourself into serious hot water."

He looked at me in a rather dismissive way. "Honestly, Lexie. It's like you're talking Swahili."

Growing very annoyed, I raised my voice, almost yelling, "I was in your house. I was worried about you. I saw the picture of you guys in the envelope, Hywel."

He looked serious, deep in thought, like he was weighing his options. And then, as if I was Daisy, he grabbed a surfboard and ran into the water.

You're kidding me.

He paddled out quickly having perfected a very successful self-defense mechanism.

I cupped my hands over my mouth, yelling, "I'm trying to be your friend, Hywel!"

He pretended not to hear. He lifted his arms, stretching while he sat placidly on his board. He'd forgotten his sunglasses, so he covered his eyes, squinting to assess the incoming waves. Not that he was going to ride one in or anything…

What was he thinking?

"Fine!" I spoke to no one in particular. "You leave me no choice."

And I did the unspeakable.

What's that, you ask.

I marched back towards the shack and when I was pretty sure no one was looking, I stripped down to my underwear and wiggled into a wetsuit. I'd almost drowned once before, but ultimately didn't. This time I had a beach full of people who'd be watching me, most likely folks who didn't want to see me die.

I grabbed a Chilli Rare Bird board that I'd been told time and again was user-friendly with a good 5-fin round tail, whatever that meant. It was heavier than I thought, but I'd been watching people take surfing lessons for months. I had no aspirations for shooting any curl, but could do what all guests could do two hours into their week with Hywel: paddle out.

"Hold on just a minute, Friday," a voice called out from behind me. I turned to see De Sousa running across the beach to me. He was a cool enough guy, always picking up the slack for Hywel, and sometimes that was quite a feat.

He was a taller guy who shaved his head and wore a different t-shirt from some international surf spot every day. I had never seen the same one twice: Hanalei Bay, Montanita Beach, Jeffrey's Bay. He didn't talk a lot, but would always start the day with a short and humorous anecdote about his time at one of the places. Could he really have visited 365 surfing spots?

Why was he calling me Friday? Did he mean Avanti? Then it dawned on me. Because when someone takes off their clothes, there is always someone watching.

My mother had given me a packet of Monday to Sunday underwear before I traveled down here. Wrong day. Oops.

She had cried and cried and cried when I told her I was moving to Panama. I reminded her that she could take a five and a half hour flight from Boston to see me. I was going to Panama, not prison. She'd dramatically left the room saying, "Maybe Christmas. Paolo, deal with your daughter." He was Paul, but Paolo when she was putting on a show.

Maybe Christmas.

"No, no, no, Lexie," De Sousa said, without a smile.

"I have to go out there." I continued to carry the board towards the water clumsily.

"You don't."

"There's no shark. I'm in on the scam."

He shook his sheared head. "Look at those swells! This is not water for beginners." He pointed out towards our howler monkey on a surfboard. "Look, he'll come in eventually. He has to. Don't risk your safety."

Usually I'd be thrilled that someone else was using the word safety, but not now. "We don't have time to wait. I don't know much about what's going on about Jazz's murder investigation, but I'm trying to keep that big baby out of prison. Maybe he can hide from his problems with Daisy sitting out in the middle of the ocean, but he's not going to be able to hide from the police out there."

Even if Hywel could paddle halfway across the world, LaGuardia was every bit as good as a surfer as him.

De Sousa started walking away then thought the better of it. "Hold on." He grabbed my Rare Bird, repeating, "Hold on." He walked away and returned with an old school long-board. "I'll paddle you out."

Oh my god.

I'm starring in Gidget, the movie.

Only it wasn't quite like Gidget. I walked three paces into the ocean, felt the riptide, and turned to my surfing partner. I wasn't as brave as I thought. Or maybe I was just doing the right thing. "I can't do it. I just can't do it."

De Sousa was still heading out on the board. "What do you want me to tell him?"

I had to break it down to reality. "Dude, you're going to jail. She needs to talk to you before that."

De Sousa reached him quickly. Hywel wildly looked around. I don't know if he was looking for a police boat that was coming to grab him or some secret door that would take him far away from this madness. They shared a conversation I'd never be privy to and head it.

I have no idea how he could balance enough with two hands in the air. The waves were rough, and potentially fatal. They paddled towards the shore.

Some of the guests had made the trip over to the boards and were putting claims on them should they ever decide it was safe enough to venture into the blue yonder. Getting out of the water, De Sousa took the opportunity to lasso the rest of them over and try to rally up some interest for tomorrow. He wouldn't take them out today after they'd been drinking like they had. They could wake up early and try again. It could still be a vacation they'd always remember... in a good way.

Hywel dropped his board on the sand and walked up to the makeshift bar in the lodge. I followed him, dripping wet with no towel to dry my hair. I grabbed my bag that I'd left on the beach next to my dress. Except for Jules, the restaurant was empty and somehow looked grungier than it had a half hour ago. "Jules, I need a coke, and then I need you to go away."

Jules brought me water and then teased the coke above his head. "I'm sorry, Hywel. Not sure that I heard what you said."

He wasn't in the mood but gave the requisite reply. "Jules, I need a coke, and then I need you to go away. *Please*."

"That's more like it," she replied, wiping her hands on a towel. "Have fun with this one."

Hywel looked around the shabby surroundings and shook his head. "This place is a real den of iniquity. I'm going to sleep back up at Bluff tonight. Wizard Beach makes me itch."

"Will you bring everyone else up there?" I squeezed some of the water out of my long black hair.

"No. No. They'll be fine. I'm sending them all to dinner at *Playa Bajja Plage* down at Red Frog tonight. I need to be alone. That'll be fine, right?"

"Hywel, let's forget them. You've got to tell me what's going on. You've already lied to the cops, and I've heard they aren't particularly fond of you anyway."

"They've got a problem with Welshmen."

"No more joking. I've seen the photo of you and Jazz out on a boat."

He deflated like he knew he was out of time. "I'm not going to get mad at you for going into my..."

"Stop it, Hywel!"

"I don't care that you went into my house, but does anyone else know? Does anyone know about that envelope?"

I noted that he said envelope and not picture.

"I didn't tell anyone. Because I'm leaving that to you."

He looked out at the group of guests who were all standing around De Sousa smiling, probably being entertained by a bonus story of the day. "If I tell the police, they're going to throw me in jail."

"You didn't do anything. Why would they throw you in jail? If you don't tell them it's really going to look suspect. Who knew about you and Jazz?"

"No one. I don't think. I wouldn't have cared, though. Hell, I would have been proud, but she was super-secret about it. I don't make it a habit of sleeping with married chicks, but Jazz was, you know, Jazz." He downed the coke and crushed the can on the wood table.

"I'm sorry, Hywel. I'm... no words. But did she ever say anything? About someone who might have wanted to do this?"

He got up and walked behind the bar grabbing a beer out of the cooler. "No."

"How long were you guys…together?"

"A couple of months or so. I'm not good with time. It was right after your crazy wedding party. Everyone was talking about how ridiculous… the island was bonding over the wedding experience from hell."

"So, you and Jazz were serious?" I got up and walked over to the bar, sitting on one of the wobbly stools.

"You know, Lexie, I don't know. It just was. It was nice. We just had fun. She understood me. I don't think anyone knew. Jules might have had a word with me about too much flirting with her, so we used to go down and grill and stuff at one of the houses my buddy, Jake, rents out when he can be bothered. Just down by Playa Escondida. I'm an excellent cook, you know. Just don't get any chance…"

"When did you last see her?"

He travelled somewhere else in his head for a moment, maybe remembering her alive for the first time since he found her yesterday. "Last Thursday. After the lesson."

"And she didn't say anything?"

"Not a lot of talking," he responded, almost smiling at a fond memory.

I wondered if this group had the pleasure of seeing him howl at the non-existent moon.

I took my phone out of my waterproof bag and nervously found the photos I'd snapped of the contents of his envelope. He scrolled through a few of the post-it notes, the map of reefs, and stopped at the picture on the boat of him and Jazz.

"Who took that picture?" I asked.

I believed him when he replied, low enough I could hardly hear him, "I don't know. It showed up in an envelope last week, slipped under my door." He looked at the photo of them in obviously happier times, then promptly went and deleted them off the phone. "Sorry, Lex. I'd just rather they weren't around."

He got up, tossing my phone back in front of me as he walked away.

12

THOSE LAZY, HAZY, CRAZY DAYS OF DAISY...

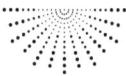

*T*his time at least Hywel hadn't grabbed a surfboard and distanced himself to oblivion in the middle of the Caribbean ocean. After getting him to drop the silent treatment (I can't see that having worked with Jazz…) we wandered up and down the beach for about a half hour until we found a location with enough service that we could reach LaGuardia. Predictably, Waxy's was without wireless. I knew better than to take Hywel's word that he'd get in touch with the detective and brokered the deal myself.

We let LG know the basic facts, that Hywel had been having an affair with Jazz and had not come clean with the cops. We arranged for the two men to meet down at the Red Frog Beach resort, and Hywel would answer any and all questions. Honestly this time. I'd done my duty – saved my friend the best that I could while not obstructing justice.

My next stop after work, the meeting with Migs at Ugly Martha's, was hours away. On that thought, I became conscious of the fact that I was sitting in a wet suit that covered only wet underwear that proclaimed the wrong day of the week of all things. I needed a change of clothes. I was going to Bella's for a memorial of sorts, after all.

Jules lent me a black, one-piece bathing suit under a black cotton sundress that had seen better days. My hope was that I could at least buy a pair of black flip-flops when I walked back to Old Bank, which I wasn't looking forward to.

Though our previous quest for cell service on Wizard Beach was a Herculean task, when I reached the entrance to the path back to town, magically, I had four bars and a clear 4G signal. A text message popped up, *ding*, clear as day. It read:

'What do you know?'

That was unsettling. I returned with:

"Isn't the question, what do *you* know?"

There was no response for a good five minutes as I waited by a sign that said, in all seriousness, 'Don't lick the frogs.'

Trust me. I won't.

But that's a story for another day.

The text was from an unknown number. I felt like I was being watched. I looked around for some lurker hiding just feet into the rainforest. *El Mundo Tiembla* shaking his stuff. I shuddered at the thought and wrote back:

'Who is this?'

The person on the other side of the exchange was playing psychological games as the conversation repeated itself.

'What do you know?'

'Who is this?' I wasn't enjoying this.

'What do you think you know?'

I'm starting to get it.

'Who is this?' I typed furiously, taking out my frustrations on my phone.

'How many people have your number, Lexie?'

No need to be insulting. But probably eight. More like seven. Six?

'Who is this?' I wasn't going to give up on my question.

'Who do you think this is?'

Lloyd.

'Pick up the phone and call me like a real person... Lloyd.'

The phone rang immediately. "Can you just act like a regular person for three minutes?"

"How does that make a murder investigation at all interesting?" His voice was so monotone, but filled with friendly condescension.

"I don't have time for this, Lloyd."

"Intriguing. Why?"

I put on my best impression of the Prince of Darkness. "What do you know?"

Because he knew something.

He wouldn't fire me. Not now. I took a deep breath, laying down the gauntlet. "You first."

"This isn't a contest."

"Isn't that what you are making it already? If you have any information, you have to call LaGuardia. He's investigating this, not me." Time was ticking on, and I wanted to get to the small port town with time to search out the best black flip-flops they had.

"I've got more faith in you." High praise from Lloyd.

"Do you have anything you want to share with me? I don't have time for this riddle-of-the-sphinx game right now."

In the first instance of defeat that I'd ever seen the mad scientist experience, he replied, "I'm working on it. Like I said before, I have a vested interest."

That and a dollar won't get you on a water taxi.

"And what does 'vested interest' mean?"

Silence from Lloyd followed.

I'll just say I wasn't in the mood. "I'll see you at 9 a.m. tomorrow. I simply don't have time right now." Then my apologetic, don't-make-a-fuss gene kicked in. "I'm sorry, Lloyd. I don't mean to be coy. I don't know much of anything right now, and I really do have to go. Please understand."

Did he understand? He hung up the phone.

Filter. Missing.

But he still got the last word in his termination of the call.

Vested interest? Could he have anything to do with this? Doubtful. Playing psychological games was one of his favorite pastimes.

As I started walking up the hill on the path to town, I became very conscious of the dangers of the rainforest flanking me. When I'd rushed to Wizard Beach a little while earlier, I'd been determined and not thinking about anything but wanting to help my friend. With some time to breath and more fodder for rumination, my body remembered that there was a killer on the loose.

It's a calculated murderer. Not a mad man.

True. What would I do and where would I go if I killed someone? Truth be told, I'd probably run to the police about three minutes later, overcome with regret, guilt, and sorrow... I wouldn't be lurking in the rainforest ready to pounce. Or maybe I'd be at home, at work, at a café, playing it like a regular day, hoping that I'd tied up all loose ends. Then just watch the drama play out from a safe distance...

I turned the corner and ran right into a couple of college-age kids walking in the opposite direction. I screamed. They screamed. We laughed at the joke. I told them that that they weren't far, and they went happily on their way.

I caught my breath, bending over, hands on my knees. I felt flushed and realized that I hadn't reapplied my SPF 50 after going in the water. I pulled my bathing suit strap aside and saw that the sun had already started doing its damage. Only I, Avanti, would stop in the middle of the rainforest, still half terrified out of my wits, to rub sun block carefully over my body.

I'd check in with LaGuardia when I got to Old Bank where I knew I could find wireless, but all my thoughts on the murder were coming around to Hywel. I still believed he wasn't Jazz's killer, but it was all too clear that he was stingy with the truth. Now the question of the hour was if Cam knew about the affair? And for how long? The more immediate question made its way instantly into the fore: Did Daisy know that Jazz was Hywel's new something-something?

"Well, dip me in mustard and call me a hot dog. Hey, girl-friend." A sweet voice greeted me.

I screamed. You don't hear a lot about thirty-five-year-old women having heart attacks due to shock on creepy rainforest paths, but my heart was pounding like a drum solo, so it wasn't outside the realm of possibility. I'd check it out when I got back in front of a computer.

If you make it.

Stop it, Lexie.

Like her namesake, fresh and innocent looking, Daisy stood before me, perfect tan glowing in the late afternoon sun. She'd died her hair since Sunday and was now sporting a blond-ambition platinum coif. She wore a strapless A-line mini-dress. White eyelet with a little daisy pin off to the side. She almost looked like a casual beach bride except for the fact that she accessorized the look with a pair of black Hunter Wellies, transporting the quasi-bridal look to that of a rocker at a rainy British music festival. I'd wait to give her fashion advice on another day.

Perhaps the killer was a pixie maniac. Maybe she was this madwoman, waiting, ready to take out all female associates of her lost love.

"Sorry I scared you," she said. All trace of Sunday's antagonism was gone. She kind of glowed divinely.

Quickly I reminded myself that as strangely charismatic as she currently seemed, she had a tattoo of an angel with vampire teeth. They call it a wolf in sheep's clothing, I think.

"Just a bit jittery with everything." Rethinking the logic in talking to her about Jazz, I added, "You know, with the shark attack."

Fast thinking, doofus.

"I think that you're probably safe on top of a hill in the rainforest." She fiddled with her dress, hitching it up her body, which, as we all know, is a constant battle when going strapless.

"Not if you go by Lloyd's logic." I looked around, hoping for some more folk to come around the corner.

"What does that mean?"

"Private joke."

"Okay, whatevs." She pointed at a narrow path deeper into the rainforest. Sticky and sweet as simple syrup, she beckoned. "Anyway, Lettie..."

"Lexie..."

"Love it. Anyway, Lexie, very stoked I ran into you here, as I did want to apologize for being a bit muggy with you on Sunday. And maybe some other days too." She slapped a mosquito on her arm quite violently.

I wondered if I could outrun her. Yes, my legs were infinitely longer, but I didn't doubt that she might have superhuman strength with her karate master status. "It happens. I understand. Like I told you on Sunday, I broke up... split up... with someone not too long ago. We all go a little crazy."

I calculated that I had to be ten inches taller than her. Too tall for a head butt.

"Yes! See? You see! I've been a little cuckoo, but not truly outside of the realm of normalcy." She pointed to the tiny path. "I bet you didn't know that there's a little lounge just down this path. It's called Cloud Cuckoo. Whatevs on the name." She made a spiral gesture with her pointer finger. "Can I buy you an iced coffee or an alcoholic cocktail?"

I peeked down the path, wondering if this could possibly be true.

She took me by the hand. "I don't bite. Much." She laughed. Wolf in sheep's clothing indeed.

Narnia? Through the looking glass? Track Nine and Three-Quarters? I decided it was better to go along with her than to make her angry. Especially with her Wang Chung experience.

She wasn't lying. After a nettley two minute walk which scratched my calves to hell, we came upon a surreal oasis that made me wonder if I was dreaming. "Pinch me quick." And she did. Surprise, surprise... "Ouch!"

I found myself in front of a sweet little joint, which looked like it should have been seaside. Chic bistro tables with happy people drinking colorful cocktails.

This has to be Daisy's secret vampire angel lair.

It was positively civilized. Like a movie, there was one perfect little table with two seats dead center waiting for us. A pretty, red-headed waitress came over to take our order immediately. Without asking me, Daisy ordered for both of us. "Dos dragones en duelo, por favor."

I'd left New York City to get away from toxic people like

Daisy. I took myself out of a circle of terrible friends for a new start in a world full of kinder people. However sweet she was going to be to me, I'd never succumb to her drama queen tactics.

"It means dueling dragons. You're going to love this."

True enough. When it came, it was an impressive drink in a huge glass. It looked like a red slushy sitting on top of a blue raspberry slushy. What the what is a blue raspberry anyway? Besides umbrellas and paper monkey straws, there was plenty of fruit garnish topped with three sugar cubes. The proud waitress lit the cubes on fire and walked away. I quickly removed the paper straw, fearing a mini explosion in my ridiculous dragon extravaganza.

"I just came from my Wing Chun class. Do you know that kind of Kung Fu? I'm a black belt. It was Bruce Lee's thing. A dueling dragon seems the perfect way to cap off Kung Fu mornings." She motioned with two quick karate chops before she focused on her cocktail.

She proudly stood up, excited as all get out. "Wait. You're going to love this one." She raised her leg almost as high as her head and then down to shoulder height. She brought her knee to her chest and then kicked out at that level. "How about that? I once kicked a guy sitting in his car through an open window just like that. I felt bad that I gave him a concussion, but what can I say? I don't know my own strength."

Maybe I'd be her friend after all. For self-preservation only.

She collapsed into her chair. "Very advanced. That takes like five years to learn. It's insane."

I couldn't tell if she was looking at me with kindness or a kind of expression of a practical joke. "Let me show you. You've got the body of a very tall kickboxer in my humble opinion."

Having worked out twice in the last six months, I didn't know how well this experiment was going to go. She pulled one of the chairs away from the table. "Alright, leg up, lady." I kicked my leg up as far as it could go, which wasn't very far.

"Ok, then." She grabbed my leg, bringing it up another foot to rest on the back of the chair.

I needed to get to the gym.

She put my hands on her shoulders. "Just in case you fall. Now pull that knee back to your chest… geez you're wobbly… and kick straight out."

I did my best, taking myself down to the ground, and Tiny Dynamite with me. "Sorry."

She scowled at me. "It's a process. You are very inflexible. Work on that." She dusted what she could off her cute white dress and sat down, ready to change the subject. I pulled the chair up from the ground and sat. My borrowed dress couldn't get any grungier.

"Needed a drink!" She delicately sucked half the drink down through the straw. "I love these so much that I tried to serve them at my club nights. What a catastrophe. One and only time. You have to do trial and error sometimes, but we have a menu that works, so I'll stick to that. Beer, rum punch, margaritas, and a 'Bitch on Wheels' shot. It was named in my honor."

Honor?

"What's a 'Bitch on Wheels'?"

"Malibu, Jager, pineapple juice and a little tequila top up should the bartenders be short on something else. Rumplemintz. Mateus. Just throw it all in. It's disgusting if you ask me, but it's popular with the chicky-doos."

"Sounds like a hangover waiting to happen."

"I only care that they're having fun that night. The next

morning is their own business." She sipped her drink while swaying just a little to the mellow reggae.

I took a small sip of the drink and coughed loudly. Besides being the ultra-sugar bomb it was, pure vodka hid behind the façade of colorful crushed ice. "Oh my god, that's strong."

"Should have mentioned that." She adjusted her strapless dress again. "*Este vestido va a ser mi muerte.*"

"What's that mean?" I shivered in the sizzling humidity. My Spanish vocabulary was still dreadful, but I understand that *muerte* meant dead. When you've been around a few Bocas murders, you pick that one up.

"This dress is going to be the death of me."

"I like the new hair." I needed to lead the conversation in a different direction than flaming cocktails and binge-drinking tourists. "The blond suits you. Of all the colors I've seen I like this the best. Not that your last color of blue wasn't divine."

"I'm not blue anymore, as in my mood isn't. No more singing the blues, at least for now. And everyone knows that blonds have more fun. What do you think the happiest color hair would be?"

A question I never thought I'd be asked in my life. "Cotton candy pink?"

"Could be, Lexie. Could be. Do you want me to order some guanabana dip?" She was non sequitur city.

"No thanks, Daisy."

She changed the subject again. "So you were coming from Hywel's temporary surf squat? It took me a while to figure out you guys were over at Wizard's. I was curious to hear about the shark attack at Bluff. Such a traj." She reached her hand out at me like a tiger mauling its prey.

How could Hywel have put up with this hot mess for two years?
I distanced myself from the terrible drink. "There was no shark attack." How do I explain this without murder implications? "There was a crazy scuffle between some Germans and French and they misunderstood each other and now the islands are at DEFCON 1 over imaginary sharks."

"Int-er-est-ing." She raised her hand to summon the waitress and pointed at her empty glass. It was understood.

"So blue to blond?"

She winked at me. "Well, gentlemen prefer blondes… right?" She did a little shoulder dance along with the music.

Is it true? Probably. I redid my frazzled bun into something that hopefully screamed 'Not having fallen in the dirt.'

She ran her hands through her short hair. "I feel like hair color is an expression of your emotional state. Ya know? I was seriously singing the French dog blues because of obvious reasons. But circumstances have changed."

Jazz.

"What circumstances?" The waitress put another Dueling Dragon next to my almost full glass.

"Lovely Lady Lexie, you don't know me very well. Yet. I'm a gal who is honest to a fault. I don't believe anything bad is ever going to happen to me if I speak ill of… the dead in this case. *Je suis* not an idiot. She…as in Jazz…was not a good person, despite all the worldwide genuflection towards her. As if. Nothing happens on this island that I don't know about when it comes to Hywel." She howled at the sun, like Hywel did in better days, but painfully off-key. "Why did I confront everyone and their *hermana*, threatening them if they turned out to be his latest squeeze? Because someone would know something and be like, 'It's not me, it's this other *puta*.' And that's exactly what happened. Flies on walls come to me.

Plenty. I knew about him and Jazz. And I knew that it wouldn't last. I just didn't think it would happen like this. I didn't like her, but I will say rest in peace. Or who knows, she could have gone south."

This unsettled me to no end. "Who told you that Jazz and Hywel were a thing? How do you know that's true?" I wasn't going to confirm this for her. Even though I was already clammy from the humidity, my nerves added another level.

"Because I know. And, I've got my own ten commandments. And one of them is… keep all secrets."

"What are the other nine?"

"Boils down to…Thou shall stay away from my man."

Now it was my turn to down half my drink in 30 seconds flat. I knew that I risked getting a right hook to the kisser, but there were questions to be asked. The lack of even a grain of remorse was missing. "Have you talked to the police yet? You probably have some information that would be helpful."

"I don't have a phone or email or an address anyone knows. I just float around like a dream." She swayed her finger like she was conducting an orchestra.

"You know they're probably going to ask you where you were in the early hours of Monday morning." I didn't want to get kicked in the head, but I had to ask.

Like a nightmare.

"Interesting question. I guess I'll have to check my calendar. Let me think. Maybe I was visiting my parents overnight in Limon. That's Costa Rica. Or was I at my all night knitting circle? Was that it?" She over-dramatically tapped her temple. "Probably in bed, binge watching My Name is Earl. Karate retreat in Isla Solarte? Like I said, I'll have to check my calendar."

She was worse than my NYC toxicity circle.

She's not even pretending to be decent.

"May I ask you another question?" I was about to betray Dr. Nolan's trust. On the other hand, he had probably violated his vow of confidentiality fifty times since I saw him last night. Was it only last night? Any chance she'd be honest?

"Open book," she said all cool. Though you could tell she was beginning to get on edge.

"Swear on Hywel's life?"

Her eyes locked on mine, dead serious. "Like I said, open book."

"So, Jazz died. We know this. But when she was examined by the doctor, they found the temporary tattoo from your club on her butt. Do you know how that might have ended up there?" I poked at her incendiary tattoo.

She scratched her upper lip, wondering if she should lie or save her love's life. "I think you'll find this a funny story."

I don't think so.

"I knew she knew I knew. We don't exactly play in the same circles, but I'd mentioned my suspicions to just enough people who knew the people that she knew... I think you'll find that people find me rash and don't want to leave things to chance with me. Hywel is a secret she didn't want to get out. She's not going to throw away that big cash cow of a husband."

She said 'knew' five times in a couple sentences. She didn't know it was Jazz who didn't need his money. "So you started telling people that you thought Jazz and Hywel were sleeping together?" I made sure that I put the word 'thought' in there.

Though she was playing this all very calm and matter of fact, when I mentioned the intimate nature of what might have gone on, I swear her vampire teeth almost appeared. "I did not tell anyone. I planted the possibility in some choice people's minds. There was something that I wanted to happen, and it did."

Of course she wasn't going to confess to killing Jazz while we were sitting here potentially getting smashed on Dueling Dragons, was she? Did that mean I was next, cleaning up any loose ends? "What did you do?"

"Do? I didn't do anything. I let that *pagano* come to me. She showed up at End of the World on Saturday night without the secret password. One of my security guards came to get me, and I played a little game. I told them if she wanted to come in, she had to do what everyone else does. Pay for her entrance fee and put on the temporary tattoo. Generally very good for Instagram, but in this case, *eres mio.* Branded."

This woman was cold. Like the East Antarctic Plateau cold.

"What did she say to you?" No more flaming cocktails for me.

"At the club, I always stand up on one of the platforms overlooking the chaos." She waved hello at an adorable couple entering and passed them two flyers for her party.

"Opens again tomorrow. Wednesday through Saturday. It is the place to be. *Adios!*"

Overlooking? Like a sniper...

She looked back at me. "I had her brought up on the platform, and she asked me what I was playing at. I'll give the woman credit – she'd stand up for herself. I'd had about three margaritas too many so let's call it seven total.

"I don't remember the exact words, but she was telling me to butt out of her business, and I was telling her to stay away from my man. She very coolly said that nothing was happening between them, and could I please stop spreading lies. Whatevs. The convo wasn't going anywhere. I gave her two free drink tickets. I don't think she used them. Snob."

"Was she threatening you?"

"I'd say that there may have been some strong-arming on both sides. I respect her for sticking up for herself. But I'm not sad she's gone."

For some crazy reason, I thought there was a shred of truth in there, but there was no point in getting into it with her now. A good woman was dead, and Daisy was the only person I'd encountered that had a bad word to say about her. I'd tell LaGuardia what I'd learned and that she was currently playing hide and seek on Bastimentos Island. How much of a 180 could I do? "So, what brings you to the road less traveled?"

She smiled, wickedly raising both of her over-plucked eyebrows. "When you've got a soul mate, things like this happen. So I got mugged off for a while! Someone might stray, but they come back. You set them free, and you know, they come back. Do you know that saying?"

She looked around to make sure we weren't in earshot of anyone, not that I think she would have cared. "So believe me when I say that it shatters me to think that my Hywel is sitting around with a broken heart. That's 100 percent true. I want to be there for him. But it was nice to stop to have this lovely Double Dueling Dragon delightful break with you." She rummaged through her bag and pulled out two knackered envelopes. "In the hope that you and me will be on better terms in the future, here are two free passes to End of the World for tomorrow night. That's normally ten bucks a ticket. And I'll give you all the free Bitches on Wheels you want."

Double entendre?

She held out her hand for a fist bump. "Girl code, right? I know we're going to be great friends one day."

"Sure." What else could I say? I was glad to know that Hywel wasn't where she was going.

"Ok, cracking on." She winked at me and twinkled down the path as if she were Dorothy skipping down the yellow brick road. She turned around to remind me, "Remember blonds have more fun. You should try it."

13

ANALYSIS PARALYSIS

*T*here were three hours until I had to meet Migs at Ugly Martha's and not much to do in Old Bank. I poked around the few stands selling various souvenirs and smoothies and ended up in an oceanfront restaurant called Minxy's Hideaway. It was cute, mellow, and almost as hidden as Cloud Cuckoo. Just a little off the beaten path, it remained a place of general calm (if you don't count the infamous bamboo stick fight of 2013. Notorious!).

I bided my time, picking at excellent grilled fish tostadas full of cobia fillets, Caribbean salsa, and coconut shavings. Like I said, it is almost impossible to eat poorly in Bocas del Toro.

I smiled for the first time in a while. This strange beach community had become my home. It wasn't a vacation where I had to absorb everything in six nights and then rush back to the rat race. Like Jazz had said two days ago, "Such an easy slide." I'd snorkel in her honor if it killed me (statistically it was unlikely unless you wore one of the newer, full-face masks. I wouldn't.).

Interrupting my 'Wicked' level of Sudoku, which had been vexing me for more than twenty minutes, was a text from LaGuardia. I was surprised. Usually it was the other way around; me bothering him about something or other. I tried to reach out to him as minimally as I could, but he was the best friend I had on the island.

'I'm going to need to talk to you about what just happened with surf-boy. Where can I find you?'

Oh, Hywel, what did you do now?

Not expecting to hear back from Hywel, I texted my surfer boy the same question.

I let LaGuardia know where I was and went back to my wicked level Sudoku. I could do the so-called breeze level in two minutes flat, but this was making me feel like a grade-A idiot. By the time the detective showed up, another 30 minutes had passed, and I was feeling sick from my obsession with the game. He joined me at my high-top table, and I let him know what was going down. "This Sudoku is making me insane."

"You think that's bad, try Calcudoku." He motioned to the waitress to come over.

"I'm nauseous just thinking about what that could actually be."

It was always interesting watching LaGuardia walk into a joint because everyone knew who he was, and the staff usually thought he was there to shut the restaurant down. When they realized that they were safe he was treated like the King of Panama. They'd bring over plates of their best food, plus whatever he wanted, and then they'd tear up the bill at the end. I hoped that they'd add my tab to his today!

He'd accept the generosity at the time, and then send the proprietor cash in the mail. He didn't want to be in debt to anyone, even if it were just for a fish taco and a Soberana beer.

While he took the first sip of his sweating beverage, I started to recap my latest adventure before he'd had a chance to ask me anything besides my success in logic-based Latin-squared games. Crazy Daisy and her new blond persona had been skipping down the path to Wizard's Beach to create who knows what kind of havoc. "She said she might have been at an all-night knitting circle or perhaps binge watching 'My Name is Earl.' When you track her down, she's not going to give anything away easily."

"She is the scourge of my existence. The End of the World is close to the point where it's giving me as much trouble as the Pickled Parrot. And don't even get me started on her fire-eaters. I should just shut her down." He pretended to knock his head against the table. "Ah, Lexie, don't let me become that terrible third-world Latino police officer cliché. I've never had such a hard time tracking down anyone unless you count *El Mundo Tiembla,* and I'd rather not." He got on his phone, which seemed to have magnificent service, and instructed that some officers get to Wizard Beach and try to track the blond bombshell down.

He'd already heard plenty about Jazz and Hywel after some officers went to try to find Daisy at her club. Though she wasn't around, she'd hardly been as discreet about slipping that info to people as she led me to believe. Her beef with the deceased was no secret to anyone who'd been within a hundred yards of her.

I threw in my two cents. "She can kick a man through a car window. I don't doubt she could crush a windpipe, knitting circle or not."

He took a deep yoga breath and let it out slowly. "Hywel

was not as forthcoming as you'd let on he was going to be. I'd say he wildly contradicts himself."

"What do you mean? He promised me he'd be straight with you."

He pulled a pad of paper that looked like it had been dropped in the ocean one time too many and flicked through the pages, rolling his eyes before he started talking. "He said he knew that he had a conversation with you, but he couldn't remember it clearly. He was taking in circles."

"Consider yourself lucky. If he doesn't want to talk to most people, he takes his surfboard and heads into the ocean." I leaned over to see if I could make out anything he'd written.

He snapped it away from me, smiling. "It's all *Espanol* anyway, tall girl."

"What does that mean that he doesn't remember our conversation? It was just a few hours ago."

"He doesn't deny that they he had intimate relations with Jazz, but he said it was a one or two time-time thing after a surf lesson. Months ago. Then the story changes to a few weeks ago. He can't remember his made up story. And he's telling me facts that I don't think you'd get out of a one-night stand." He grabbed the last tostada off my plate and scarfed it up.

"Hey!"

"Don't worry, I'll order more." He shook his head. "I don't know how that man manages to run a business. He's coming down to the station at six, so we can talk to him away from the beach. It's going to be as on the record as it could be. It's like he's been sniffing surf wax or something." He signaled the waitress for more of the same on the food. "Don't worry. It's on me."

The bill always ended up on him as he was fully aware of

my non-stellar financial position. Thirty-five years old and nothing to show for it but the proceeds from a gargantuan Harry Winston engagement ring in my bank account. And it hadn't even been my engagement… "I'll figure out my life soon, LG. It's been a tough year."

"You'll figure it out. Don't be so hard on yourself. You've been here for, what, not even half a year? You're a smart coconut. Give yourself a break." He comically knocked me on my skull. "Sorry that's not more specific at the moment. You're going to be brilliant…"

"Between Grito Mono and trying to make Lloyd Wilson sound less harmfully combative… I'm tired. Not normally." I shook it off. "Anyway, I don't understand. Is it better or worse if Hywel did or didn't have a relationship with Jazz?"

"What do you think? Who do you think he's telling the truth to? Anyone?"

"I think I'm asking you if you think he did anything bad?"

"He's high on the list, Lexie. Don't be naïve about this."

"I know Hywel is acting like a massive ding-a-ling, but this is not a man who could kill someone. For the love of mike, when he gets threatened, he runs into the ocean. Fight or flight? He might as well be a macaw."

I had to be careful about what I said. LaGuardia was my friend, but he was also a police officer investigating a murder. If you examine my previous behavior when it comes to homicide, I've had a bad habit of sticking my foot in it, of implicating someone innocent when I was trying to get them off the hook. Well, I wasn't always wrong, thankfully, but there was a propensity. "He's a good man but he's a man-child. You need to put every man you have on a task force to track down Daisy. She's *loco.*"

Hey, look. I spoke Spanish!

After taking a moment to pat myself on the back symbolically, I continued. "Daisy said she'd accused someone, I don't know who, of fooling around with Hywel. She's saying that someone who got scared for her life tipped her off about Jazz. And what about Cam? I saw him stomping full force into the police force. That wasn't a grieving man. That was an angry man."

"Cam has a pretty solid alibi. He was out on a two-day deep fishing trip with Larry Breger who owns Yarisnori. He corroborated it. Now Renny…"

No way that was possible, was it? They'd been bickering, but it was all in front of us. "He was at a poker game with half a dozen people. He told me. They all passed out or went to sleep and woke up at 7 a.m."

"Exactly. Everyone was passed out so who would notice him sneaking in and out? We've been able to track down a few of the other gamblers, but not all of them. Those hours aren't clear."

Impossible.

Right?

Due to the 4 p.m. ferry arriving, a group of sunburned tourists with a Lonely Planet guide wandered in. They sat down at a table for eight, thankfully not close to us.

Tuesdays would normally be a tourist's second day under the island's equatorial sun. The burn would turn to tan in a few days, but today's rays had done their damage. The group was ready to grab some shade and get three sheets to the wind, if they weren't halfway there already. One of the guys started singing Sweet Caroline, and before their first pitcher of sangria showed up, they were happily swaying and singing as one.

"Boston." I guessed. "I apologize for my people."

"You get used to groups like that very quickly." He passed on another beer for water, frowning.

"Are you allowed to be talking to me about this?"

"Probably not. I need to look into an honorary deputization."

"Cam. I get that he's got a great alibi. And he has every reason to be furious. His beautiful wife was murdered, but what was he raging about?"

"He was yelling at us, telling us we don't know how to do our job because 24 hours had gone by without us tracking down the killer. You know how Americans love to scream at us about incompetence. After he insulted most of the locals on the island, he got around to asking why Hywel hadn't been arrested. I've never seen Cam that way."

"So he must have known about them?"

"He only found out very recently and has no idea how long it'd gone on for. There was a picture he showed us of Jazz and Hywel looking a little more than comfortable on a boat. It was taken from a distance. It wasn't someone on the boat with them."

"I've seen that picture too! Hywel got the same picture last week." I hurried to get the picture up on my phone before remembering that Hywel had promptly deleted any evidence of what I found in his house. I'd leave the deleting detail out. "I thought I had it. I don't. Do you have it?"

"It's in evidence. Cam says it was left for him in the galley of one of his boats the Aqua Point Marina." He started doodling on his pad. "It came to Cam. It came to Hywel. Cam's had no note with it. Did Hywel's?"

"Hywel said that he didn't know who took the photo, but a note didn't come with his either. There was nothing in the envelope I found it in. He intimated that it was only at some point last week."

"Someone was trying to send a message."

"Daisy." Whether it was blackmail, or her confrontation

with Jazz, or just getting Hywel back, this crime has vampire angel written all over it.

"We still have an extended list of suspects. We won't leave any stone unturned." He was making sure that he was taking care of the investigation, and that was peachy keen with me. "We've almost got the basis of a timeline, but it was like she disappeared. We talked to her sister, Bella, who said that they had their regular Sunday night sleepover like they always did. Jazz comes over and she watches the kids while Bella has a long bath, and they watch horror movies after the kids go to sleep. This time it was Halloween III: Season of the Witch, god help us all. They went to bed around midnight after some white wine, and when she woke up around 6:00, Jazz was nowhere to be seen."

"I'll be seeing Bella tonight," I volunteered. "I'm going to a gathering at her house in a couple hours."

"Are you?" LaGuardia perked up. "How did you get an invite to go over there?"

"Do you remember Migs the photographer?"

"Everyone remembers Migs."

I blushed. "Bella called him about Jazz, and he got here this morning. He was the one who first told me that Cam had a temper. Migs didn't want to chance being in a room with him, so asked me to come along. I think Cam's threatened him before. I guess I'm his safety blanket for tonight."

LaGuardia changed his tone to that of the closest thing to girly BFF that I had. "Do you really think that's what you are? A safety blanket?"

"Yes. He was scared of going. And he's just a major flirt. It's like a necessity in Bocas. He and I are just friends."

"Then why are you blushing?"

I'd be a terrible criminal. My face would give everything away. "He's cute. He's nice to have on your arm. He's charming. But he could have anyone... I'm only a challenge because I say no. He's a major player."

"I'm not going to get too into it with you, because I think you're fishing for assurances. He's taken pictures here, on and off, for maybe twenty years. He's never come off like a major player. A heartbreaker maybe, but not a player." He drew a picture of many hearts in his notebook.

This is not where my heart has time to go right now. My priority was settling into this community, no attachments. I couldn't have the pressure of having the sexiest guy I ever met *maybe* liking me a little and going for it. "How about we make a deal, LG? Let's bring this up next spring when I've had a chance to really acclimate to just being a normal resident. I want to associate this place with home, not heartbreak. Is that cool?"

He held out his hand to shake. "I promise. But don't you go bringing him up if you hear he's coming to town and need someone to help you pick the best outfit. You're on your own on that one."

We shook. And then I pushed the idea of Migs right out of my head. Friendsville, not Flirtsville. "I appreciate it. I need friends more than romance right now."

We engaged in some light conversation until I had to go: about advanced Sudoku, low point Weight Watchers salads, and next Sunday's get together. Something to look forward to.

I didn't look great, but I at least had some lipstick in my bag. "Ok, I dramatically go into the night, whenever night may fall."

LaGuardia scarfed down the last fish taco. "Like I said, I'll be seeing Hywel in an hour at the station, so hopefully we can get some things straight and start putting facts in some kind of order... but it wouldn't hurt for you to keep an ear to the ground at Bella's. No one seems to be able to talk honestly to me on this one. Just let me know if anything… you know what I'm talking about."

As we left the restaurant, I realized that I'd unofficially been made deputy.

14
STICKY AS THIS

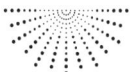

J'm only human. Yes, I know that now wasn't the time for me to date, but crushes are a normal thing. They remind that you are human. They give you a reason to put on a pretty dress and lipstick and hope that someone notices. On a grey day, they make the trudge to work worth it.

Only it wasn't a grey New York day, I was in the Caribbean. And it wasn't really a pretty dress.

Despite LaGuardia's insistence that he wasn't going to be my go-to-guy on wardrobe approval, I did drag him to the few shops that had some potential. I was able to shove Jules's threadbare dress in a bag and buy a crisp black dress that was almost appropriate. There was a small pattern of happy flamingos around the hem, but it was the best I was going to do in Old Bank. I found a good pair of black flip-flops with a hint of glitter that almost complimented the ensemble. And yes, LaGuardia ended up being reluctantly great in the accessorizing department, finding some things like a black beaded necklace and some matching bangles. As I paid for my new purchases, I almost said to my detective friend, "Louis, I think this is the beginning of a beautiful friendship." But I didn't. It was a nice break from reality, and I left only $18 poorer.

The impetus was gone when he said, "Never again."

Someone like Migs made you feel like you were the only person in the room when he was talking to you, but I think he has that effect on everyone. Whip smart with green eyes and snake hips, he was the kind of guy you'd want to have fall in love with you. Note that I said 'fall in love with you,' not fall in love with. Like a teenage dream...Whether an almost-crush meant me going on a morbid non-date with Migs or getting my weekly dose of Sunday flirtation from Renny, I couldn't beat myself up about it.

But flirting was fun in Flirtsville, possibly being the official pastime of the island. Why wouldn't it be? Fully dressed down here meant wearing a beach cover-up, the scenery looked like a movie, and we lived in an endless summer. I put on my black glitter Kaleos sunglasses and walked towards Ugly Martha's.

Predictably on the inappropriate side, the chalkboard hanging outside the dive bar was advertising a shot called the Shark Attack, which to my eye looked like blue Listerine with some gummy sharks thrown in for good measure. With the advertised price as $1, there was a large group of back-packers in front of the place, complete with blue lips, tossing the candy at each other. Oh well.

I had to make my way through a packed group of drinkers who were suffering from whatever the Shark Attack blue version of red wine mouth was, little blue lines forcing dizzy smiles. The crumbling bar was dark and dank. I don't know why anyone would want to be inside instead of on its enviable deck with unobstructed views of Isla Solarte and tiny Isla Carenero.

Migs was sitting as far away from the backpacking crowd as possible, at the end of the dock, waiting for me at a dingy white plastic table with matching white chairs. He'd gone through the trouble of getting us some beer and a shot each.

I sat down and rummaged through my bag. "You're going to like this." I pulled out a packet of wet-wipes and cleaned the table.

"I was going to laugh at you for that, but I'm actually relieved." He kissed me on the cheek. He was looking very smart, in a black, short-sleeved, skinny fit, button down shirt and light cotton pants. I noticed he was also wearing flip-flops, so I felt a little more comfortable in my choice of footwear. He raised his beer to toast with me.

"Lexie Marino in Bocas del Toro. My mind is still spinning. Not that I thought you'd really be able to stay away from yours truly, but wow. What happened to all your friends who were down here with you? I knew I'd cross paths with you again one day, but I never thought it would be at the Bocas del Toro Isla Colon International Airport. What are you doing? How do you spend your days? Blowing. My. Mind." He smiled that smile of his.

"It's a very long story for another day. My friends? Well, they really weren't very good friends. And going back to New York to work in theatrical marketing in a cubicle in a room with twelve other people? It never appealed, but when I got back even less so... I thought maybe there was a better life for me out there. And Bocas seems as good a place to start as any."

I hadn't even considered anywhere else. Back in New York City, I'd been sitting in my living room window every night, overlooking the Hudson River, daydreaming about the sun and dolphins. Everything became very clear.

"Bet you had a bash to end all bashes when you left that awesome city…"

"Not so much." My party had only been with my office mates, out at a theatre-land pub, where my boss paid for two hours of drinks and vegetable crudité. Then we were on our own. I picked one of the blue gummy sharks from the shot and ate it. It left my fingers sticky.

"But seriously, Lexie, you call me whenever you need. This area is too small town for me, and I grew up in a suburb of Panama City. Keep an eye out for yourself. You can go *loco* in a small area like this. Paradise isn't always what's it's cracked up to be." He held up the Shark Attack. "You aren't going to make me do this alone, are you?"

I held the shot glass up. "I guess there's no reason not to."

"Wait!" He reached into my drink, fishing out the remaining gummy sharks. "I've seen a few people inside almost choke on the candy while shooting these. Ugly Martha wouldn't be pleased… This place is even grosser than last time I was here."

"I think it's the proximity. Location, location, location."

His eyes were still sad, but his charm sang through. "You look pretty. Not like that's news, but you look great."

A lesson that I'd recently learned from Jazz was to just say thank you. Regular me would have pointed out the ridiculousness of my flamingo hem, or disparaged my three dollar glitter flip-flops, or made fun of the cloth black flower that LaGuardia had found last minute to tuck behind my ear. 'If you get a compliment, it's because you deserve it,' Jazz had casually said. I looked across the table at my handsome companion. "Thank you." It was that simple.

"I'll be honest. I'm getting cold feet about going tonight. I got a call a few hours ago that this get together is going to be at Jazz and Cam's, not Bella's. It's not in neutral territory anymore. I'd feel terrible not going. Cam lost his wife and I want to support the family. I just don't want him to... He's got enough to deal with without me making his blood boil."

I wanted him to be safe, but I equally wanted to live up to my deputy status and uncover something that LaGuardia could use. "Tell me more, Migs. When did he get mean with you? And how long ago was this?"

We were momentarily disrupted by an unhappy looking waitress in cut off shorts and a bikini top, who was trying to get us to buy more of the Shark Attacks. She had a tray full of plastic shot glasses and extra gummy bears everywhere. Migs gave her two crumpled one-dollar bills and grabbed drinks off the tray. "I'm going to need all the courage I can get tonight."

"Was it that bad? How he was around you?"

"Being treated like an employee wasn't a big deal. I'm never surprised when that happens, but there were a few times that he made snide comments. He'd yell at me for nothing that had to do with Jazz, but some boat issue.

"Again, all of this was stuff I could easily deal with. Generally photo clients aren't known for being the kindest people in the world. The weird thing was that he had ways of showing up at places that he would never be otherwise. Showing up at the reefs Jazz was studying. Finding us at restaurants with the crew that he was never told about.

"Was he paranoid? Sure, she's beautiful. And she hugs everyone. It wasn't what he said, it was the look that he gave me. Like I said, just a little off-putting. That particular gig with Jazz was coming to an end, so three days later I was out of there as quickly as possible. I turned down the next couple of jobs she tried to hire me for. I shouldn't have."

"But Cam never accused you of anything directly?"

"Nope."

"I'll be honest with you, Migs. I don't think his anger is going to be pointed towards you tonight. Sometime last week, he found out that Jazz was cheating on him with Hywel from the surf camp. There's a mysterious photo of them together that started making the rounds last week. I think you'll be no more than an afterthought right now."

Even though I'd seen Cam storm the police department this morning, it was still hard for me to picture him threatening anyone. Or worse. Last week, at *Playa Bajja Plage*, he had everyone in stitches pretending to have electrocuted himself while figuring out a way to rig satellite TV for the beach restaurant. He didn't pay me much mind, but he always felt like a fun father figure, not a violent man.

"Jazz? With that surf guy? Of all the guys she could have picked…"

"He's a better man than he comes off." I was hardwired to stick up for Hywel-at-the-moon. "I've been working for him a few days a week and he's a good man."

"I would have guessed she'd make a more sophisticated choice of secret lovers." He put his sunglasses on and downed his shot.

"I'm going to skip mine, so drink it if you like." I was a bit of a lightweight. After already imbibing half of a Dueling Dragon, and a terrible Shark Attack, I could pass on a second mouthwash concoction. "I'll take the gummy sharks though."

He handed over the candy and drank mine as well, as I knew he would. He never made a fool of himself, but I don't know how he stayed so lithe with the amount he drank. I'd imagine that he was no stranger to the gym.

He held his hand out to help me up from my chair. "Ready to go?"

He helped me out of my chair and walked arm and arm with me through the madness of Ugly Martha's.

We were right at the dock as the ferry arrived. Migs led me away from the line for the ferry. "I've worked too hard in my life to take ferries with drunk college kids. I borrowed a boat from Bella." Lo and behold, he had; a small but beautiful speedboat. "My lady…" he held out his hand again, helping me on to the boat.

It wasn't a date, but was I going to ruin the illusion with a safety vest?

Leave it off for Jazz?

Don't mix up loyalty to her with just wanting to impress a guy, Avanti.

I'd hold it close. Just in case.

The sun was just beginning to go down, the slight pinks and purples slowly taking over the bright blue of the day. I put my sunglasses back on and got ready for the ride. Migs turned the ignition on and took off with as much ease as if it were the car that he drove to work every day. It felt very special to be riding into twilight with him.

I'd never been to *Tierra Oscura*, which translated to The Dark Earth, so the route was new to me. Though it was part of the Bocas del Toro province, it was also technically part of the mainland of Panama. The better-off people in the area lived there and liked their little private enclave.

It was a good 30-minute boat ride from town, so epic compared to my dozens of ten-minute rides around the island. Quickly, we were away from most of the boat traffic and cruising south. It felt comfortable to sit in silence during the trip, and I sat back and relaxed.

I mean, there is relaxed and then there is relaxed. I was emotionally relaxed but still very cognizant that though the water was amazingly calm I wasn't wearing my life vest. All to impress a man…it never gets old.

Arriving at Jazz and Cams' house was more like showing up at a five-star boutique hotel, but much nicer than any hotel I'd come across in the rest of the area. We docked the boat, and gentlemen were on hand to help us out on the landing, leading us over a long dock to the huge property. The house was built with a dark caramel wood, lit and warm with soft lights on the outside. There was an enormous covered terrace where a few dozen people had gathered. The get together was larger than I had imagined. We weren't close enough to make out who had arrived to pay their respects.

"Are you ready?" Migs had taken off his sunglasses and his green eyes looked mystical in the night. He was nervous though. That much was obvious.

"Are you okay?" I asked, and wondered if I should take his hand.

"Sure." He spoke in an octave higher than usual. "Let's get this over with." He grasped my hand and started heading towards the party. Once we got closer, I could see the terrace was dotted with people I was semi-familiar with. They sat on expensive-looking, rattan lounge furniture accented by various shades of red and purple cushions.

It was a wine and whiskey night from the look of it. People were there to feel alive next to the warmth of loved ones. Together but anonymous. You could sit with your arms around friends, crying and laughing, or you could sit in the corner with a Jack Daniels straight up and all would be ok. It's whatever you need at that moment. The journey of going through grief starts the next sobering day.

I felt safe metaphorically (or literally) clinging on to Migs. He didn't mind… yet. Bella came up to us right away and hugged him like her life depended on it. It was no time to be jealous, but he'd been around the islands enough that it was feasible that they'd been an item at some point. After all she was Jazz's sister, and though not the 10-out-of-10 of her older sibling, she was a solid eight herself.

I kicked myself for not nixing that bad NYC habit of judging everyone and their (not so cute) brothers on physical appearances.

After they finally separated (was it an hour? Felt like it), Bella turned to me. Blurry eyed and without the slight condescension I'd seen from her before, she gave me a quick hug. "Thank you for coming. You were just getting to know my sister, but she talked about you a lot. She was happy you moved here. You made her laugh a lot."

That was humbling. "I'm so sorry, I thought she was great."

"Can I get you anything? Wine?" She was looking for something to do.

"You, my love, can't get us anything. What can we get for you?" He was always the gentleman, even if there was a suggestive tilt to it sometimes.

I don't know what I would have said if I w left alone with her, so thankfully Migs guided me by the elbow to the wet bar. From there I could see the expanse of the place, over-looking an enormous pool with enough lounge chairs for a pool party every day of the week.

I was very used to the conspicuous consumption of wealth that plagued the Big Apple, but this kind of wealth was still intimidating. It was more genuine. People were enjoying it, not taking it for granted and wondering how they could make their own homes more impressive than this one.

Migs was pouring the wine, and I was looking around the

party at no one in particular when I came eye-to-eye with someone who'd been staring already. Renny.

Like the cliché, our eyes met across the crowded room... I gave a startled look, and he shot me an intense smile. Boy, when it rains, it pours.

He started to make his way through the gathering. While I was thinking of something witty to say when he reached me, I felt a pair of strong hands on my shoulder, gently moving me to the side. Standing next to me was Cam, pushing through to get to the bar.

Migs almost dropped the bottle as Cam looked at the selection of wine in the giant ice bucket on the bar. I don't think that he even recognized the photographer, which made me wonder how many men he'd lost his temper with over the years. I raised my eyebrows to Migs as a nudge to be the better man.

"Cam, I'm so sorry for your loss." Migs was almost shaking, making me wonder what Cam had really said to him all those years ago.

"Thank you. Thanks. I can't believe I'll never see her again." Cam grabbed a huge glass meant for red wine and emptied more than half a bottle of rose into it. "Lexie, thanks for coming. Nice to see so many people here." There were dozens of people on the terrace and by the pool, subdued and still shocked. He took a few steps away from us, then turned to Migs. "You'll excuse me if I'm a little frazzled. How do we know each other again?"

The stress melted off of Migs like ice cream in the sun. "Migs. Miguel Araya. I photographed some of the reefs for her and Renny."

Cam's face soured just a little at the mention of his wife's partner's name. "Miguel. Of course. It was a big project for her. A labor of love. Thank you."

That did not sound like the voice of a jealous, paranoid, or angry man.

"Yeah, man. It was a pleasure. I have some pictures of her from that… I'll get them to you." Migs polished off his glass of white wine and poured another.

"She loved those damn reefs," he said, as if they were a particular affront to him.

"Well, I'm sorry." I'd never seen Migs mutter before. "Really sorry."

"And yet life goes on." Cam grabbed a beer instead of his gallon of wine and headed aimlessly back into the crowd.

I turned to Migs, who was leaning on the bar, steadying himself. "Are you being completely honest about what happened with Cam threatening you back then? Cam seemed to hardly clock that you existed."

But Migs had been practically shaking.

He leaned in and beckoned me to . We were close enough to kiss, not that I noticed. "I'll tell you more another time, but his threats were pretty specific. He said to stay away from Jazz or he'd have my equipment destroyed. And if I didn't, my pretty face would be merely a thing of memory. 'You're a photographer,' he said. 'I'd take a picture of how you look now if you want to remember your stunning looks in the future.'"

"And be truthful - nothing happened between you and Jazz?"

"Not anything more than a kiss on the cheek. Renny had warned me about Cam's jealousy. Never jealous of anything between him and Jazz. I don't think. I think Renny had seen it with other guys over the years."

The King of Greater Houston. Could it be? Was Hywel not her first dalliance? Or had his unsubstantiated jealousy pushed her into the arms of another man?

"I'm going to get some air." Migs grabbed his wine and headed towards the dock. I wasn't invited this time. He needed to be by himself.

The place was teeming with secrets. It was time for me to step up to the plate and see what I could learn.

15
WHEN YOU GOTTA GO, YOU GOTTA GO

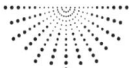

*A*lone at a party. My least favorite activity. I glanced around for a friendly face, and found none available. Renny was nowhere to be seen and Bella was crying into the shoulder of someone I didn't know. Cam was sitting on a pool lounger, talking to Larry Breger, and two other men who I didn't know. All I knew was that the pool was not the direction I'd be heading this evening.

Deputy Doofus, reporting for duty.

Like always, the group of Sunday divers were sitting together at a table in the corner. I didn't know all of them well, but well enough to know that they wouldn't kick me away from the table. They'd made my Sunday mornings a delight. Small victories…

When I got closer, I was greeted with "Hey, Avanti," and room was made for me to sit. Niceties were exchanged, and then they slipped back into Spanish. I nodded my head and laughed whenever they did.

They were a great bunch, and all tried their best to speak English to me. The drunker they got, the quicker the Spanish would return. It wasn't their fault. I was their guest, a stranger in a strange land.

LaGuardia was right – he wouldn't have been welcome at this party (I say party for lack of a better word) for a minute. Not that the detective couldn't go wherever he wanted to, but no one was going to talk to him at a shindig like this. Whatever or whomever might have known, they'd be keeping it to themselves.

How many people here were afraid of Cam? How many men, even at the table where we sat, had been the recipient of his anger? Based on Migs' reaction, maybe Cam had no problem with her regular crew. The fear of god was certainly not present at this table.

I'd have the new news about Mr. Jazz's paranoia issues to tell the detective in the morning. Paranoia and jealousy certainly pointed in one scary direction. But to what end? He was off in the middle of the ocean with Breger.

I was tired and wanted to go home. I'm not sure how much more there was to discover tonight, especially if drunken conversation was going to consistently fade into Spanish. Tomorrow promised to be another doozie of a day. I was going to find my green-eyed companion and get a water taxi home, even though it might be quite a wait for a boat all the way out in The Dark Earth.

Migs liked to party. Even if he wanted to drive me home, I wasn't going to get in a boat with a drunk captain. Maybe I had less chance of a head on collision, but I definitely had a better chance of capsizing while the King of the Flirts did the boat version of wheelies. Not that he wouldn't come to my aid if we took a spill… but I wasn't going to play out that fairytale nightmare right now.

"*Dónde están los servicios, por favor?*" My Spanish lessons had not been taken completely in vain. I was bilingual enough that someone could point out the ladies' room to me. Yay, me!

The table was pleased and surprised by asking my question in Spanish. They patted me on the back and started speaking quickly and incoherently, as if all of a sudden, I was fluent. My squished up face gave me away, and they switched back to English, pointing me through the open main doors of the grand house.

It was an immaculate home, befitting the five star hotel it resembled. Uncharacteristic for the area, the ceilings were high, better-suited for somewhere like Panama City than the remote province of Bocas del Toro. I passed a beautiful blond in bare feet who told me which one of the eight closed doors was the entrance to the bathroom.

I knocked on the tall door and got a response from a man, "Someone's in here." That was followed by a giggle from a female.

It's going to be a long wait.

There was a chair nearby, and I sat down, wondering if I should tough it out and wait, or try to get a water taxi immediately. I crossed my legs and waited for what was beginning to feel like a very long time.

"Hey, Avanti," one of Jazz's crew called out while walking down the hall. "Waiting for the head?" Sailors will be sailors.

"There's someone in there. Plural from what it sounds like. Do you know if there's another ladies' room down here?"

"There's probably a john for every person here tonight. I'm going to run up to the one at the top of the stairs, but just walk down the hall to the very end. The one on the right is... was...Jazz's office. There's a bathroom through there." He slapped me on the back for no apparent reason and bounded up the stairs, two at a time.

Is this an investigative opportunity or a bad idea?
Or a very needed trip to the bathroom. Get over yourself.

My heart was beating faster as I walked down the hall. Half of me hoped that the door to her office would be locked, but it wasn't. The room was illuminated by the bright moon shining on the sea, an enviable view by anyone's standards. There was zero need to turn the overhead light on thankfully, because I was feeling very conspicuous.

The room itself was gorgeous with beautifully framed underwater photos of her beloved reefs. She was happiest down there.

There were enormous windows and glass doors that opened to a private deck. The deck looked comfy, but the office itself was sparse - a large Mac on an enormous glass desk and uncomfortable looking modern furniture around the room. No photos of anyone on the desk, just underwater reef dwellers.

It's a cliché to say that a rich person's bathroom is bigger than a NYC West Village studio apartment, but I do not exaggerate. Honestly, if someone tried to rent this to me when I was still in the city, I'd have jumped on it, throwing a single mattress in the giant bathtub and hoping I could get cable TV. As long as there was good wireless.

I had a friend who once paid $1300 a month to rent a bedroom that doubled for the laundry room in a couple's Tribeca apartment. Her double mattress perfectly fit in the space between the machines and the window overlooking the building shaft. She said it wasn't that bad unless she decided to do a late night dry. What can I say? I was glad to be out of NYC.

There were pillows and light blankets folded and stuffed on a high shelf in the bathroom. It wasn't that the bedding was messy, just out of synch with the rest of the office. Had

Jazz been sleeping on the couch in her office? It wasn't like she didn't have an embarrassment of riches as far as guest rooms went. Maybe she was like me when working from home; a good nap when procrastinating was always welcome. Maybe things had been less than perfect with Cam for a while.

It was then that I decided that it would be a good idea to lock the outside door to the office. It was no different than locking the actual bathroom, right? A woman needs her privacy when visiting the powder room.

It wouldn't surprise me if she was the kind of eco-conscious person who operated on a strictly no-paper agenda. The whole province dictated that seldom would you see a house without solar panels. There also seemed to be an unspoken rule to not turn on lights before 5:00 p.m. I felt guilty every time I threw out a piece of paper. I tried to make good use of it first, scribbling on the back of a one-sided anything. An old receipt would become a lipstick blotter.

I stole a quick glance out the window and its unspoiled view of points north. There was not a soul in view, like she probably preferred. Unlike the office, the bathroom had plenty of drawers. Nothing gave away any potential useful information, but it was where she kept her files. Strangely, that made sense. Drawers full of files would ruin the aesthetics of a glass desk.

There were letters from what looked like various oceano-graphic organizations, all in Spanish, so that did me no good. Another drawer was filled with expensive beauty products. The drawers seemed to alternate. You'd have a giant one filled to the brim with softer towels than I had ever touched, and below that would be a deep pile of seafloor mapping documents. Jazz had explained these to me as topographic maps of sea floor reliefs, also called bathymetric maps. I had her write that one down, as it was more foreign to me than Spanish, and I spent some time googling her life and love. She'd let me know that mapping a new reef was not without its challenges.

Unlike the drawers, the shelves were empty except for the pillows and sheets that had been stuffed onto the highest level. Shaking out every sheet and blanket, I found nothing but incredible smelling crisp white sheets.

Sometimes tall is good. On my tip-toes and peering into the now empty shelf, I could see a red leather envelope. It was larger than the one I found in Hywel's bedside table. I reached for it, tossing it next to the sink, then folded all the sheets and blankets that I'd pulled out of the wall unit.

I'd hardly opened the envelope when I heard frantic turning of the doorknob, following by aggressive banging. "Why the hell is this door locked?" Cam's voice bellowed from the other side.

Had I done anything wrong?

Of course you did.

With Cam screaming on the other side of the door, I was never going to have the chance to rifle through that room again. No invitation to return would be pending. If there was anything to find, it had to be in that leather envelope. I'd left my bag back at the table on the terrace and had nowhere to slide the goods into.

"One second! Someone's in here!" I yelled, just like the couple in the bathroom that I probably should have waited for.

"Open this damn door!"

I pulled my black dress over my head. Still wearing Jules' tight, one-piece bathing suit, I shoved the letter size document into the suit, trying my best to conceal the uncomfortable leather document holder like a belt. It looked a little lumpy under my dress, but concealable. I smoothed my hair down and tried to play it cool, not my forte.

I tried to casually open the door, as if I didn't know I'd done anything wrong. He looked like a bear. I must have never comprehended the true expanse of a fully standing Cam. He was taller and wider and looked like he could swallow me whole. Shark attack indeed.

The people standing near the entrance to the house had now stopped to watch what was going down. He wasn't going to belt me one, but I'm sure he could see my nerves. "What the... what were you doing in there? And why was the door locked?"

I grasped the envelope around my stomach, playing as if my tummy was giving me trouble. "I'm sorry, Cam. The other bathroom – there was a long wait. Someone sent me down here and I just locked... it was just like what you do. I didn't want anyone to walk in."

I don't think the core of his anger was directed at me. His short fuse was on serious display. I just needed to play stupid enough for him to walk away and for me to get out of there. "You aren't supposed to be in there. No one is supposed to be in there."

"I'm really, really sorry. I didn't know I was supposed to... let me just get back to the party... get back outside and get out of your hair."

Cam's face was growing red. "Why would you lock..."

"Wait, wait, wait." Renny was quickly walking towards us. I was still cowering in the dark of Jazz's office, while Cam was fully illuminated in his fuming glory for all to see. "My bad. My fault. I told her to come down here. I was outside when Carlos told me your old friend was in there. The one down from Florida, you know how he... with the ladies... it seemed like it was going to be a while."

Money didn't seem to matter when people got angry. You could be in the most elegant place in the world, and there would still be a respected adult acting like an inappropriate sixteen-year old.

Renny put his hand on my back. "I should have sent her upstairs. Jazz's office was just close."

Cam didn't want to back down, but it looked like I'd done nothing worse than using a bathroom and locking the wrong door. He didn't know me from Adam, maybe didn't know I worked for Hywel, and hopefully didn't know that I was buddy-buddy with a police detective. Regardless of who he thought I was, it was time to get on a boat and get out of there.

Cam was looking at me accusingly, though he didn't know what it was I'd done. Was he wondering if I killed Jazz? But what would my motive have been?

His breathing was heavy when he pivoted and stormed down the hall, yelling, "Where is that Boca Raton bastard?! Does he not realize my wife just died…"

The timid and small scattered to just outside the house, but close enough that they could still watch the action. Cam starting banging on the door of the other bathroom. "C.J.! You've got about 90-seconds to open this door or I'm going to blow it down, little pig, little pig."

Renny took my hand in his. "Hey, Lexie, he's all bark and no bite. I think. You okay?" Renny turned my petrified (as in Pompei) body towards him. "I got you. Okay?"

"I don't know what happened. I was just using the bathroom." I hated lying. Renny was making me feel safe, smiling at me with concern, and subtly placing himself between myself and the big man.

He assured me, while still keeping an eye on Cam, "He's just grieving. You know he's a big widget king softie. His

Florida buddy is going to come out of his bathroom, and the two will just dissolve into a crying hug. Just watch."

Cam repeatedly knocked on the door until it slowly opened. Florida stepped out of the bathroom smiling and promptly got sucker punched in the jaw.

"Or maybe we should leave." Renny turned us around and navigated to a back entrance. There was a well-laid stone path that would take us to the dock of the house. "There are boats waiting to take people home. I'd take you home myself but I've had a little bit too much to drink."

I surprised myself by feeling a tiny bit rejected that he didn't want to follow me home in my chauffeured boat.

You're not ready, ding-a-ling.

He's grieving.

It's not all about you.

"I should say goodbye to Migs." We rounded the corner, back at the covered terrace. Scouring the crowd, I didn't see my photographer friend. "We came together so I should just check in."

"You came with Migs?" I may have been wrong, but besides the surprise in his expression there might have been the smallest amount of jealousy.

"Not like that."

"Well, if I've had a little too much, Migs has had way too much and then some. I saw him passed out on a lounge chair by the pool. The chitras won't be his friends tonight, but that's the price you pay for oblivion." He stopped at the beginning of the walkway to the long dock. "I guess I get off here."

"Thanks, Renny, for... saving me." Despite his lack of an airtight alibi at Red Frog Beach, I found myself asking for a little more. "I bet you've got a crazy week coming up."

"Too sad. I'm taking the week off. You're still coming out

tomorrow, right? We can go out to Dolphin Bay. Cool reef and calm as Xanax. Just to… be."

"I just wanted to let you off the hook if you wanted to be alone… I understand." I awkwardly held my hand out to shake, and he did not let go of it. Neither did I.

"I don't want to be alone. I want to go with you. Like we've done before. Why do you feel like you want to back out?"

Firstly, you might be a murderer.

Secondly, I'm still an insecure fifteen-year old.

"I don't know. It seems like the world has changed since yesterday."

"It has."

"Sorry to be weird. It will be an adjustment getting used to the new normal."

He let go of my hands and stuck them in his khaki pockets. "Well said."

"I have to work in the morning. Would the afternoon work?" A morning with Lloyd wasn't the most appealing thing, but a job is a job, no matter what kind of a surprise I would be walking into.

He didn't look lustful or disrespectful. "Double up on your sunscreen and bring your fins. Meet at the deck at Tango Vista in town at 2 p.m.? I'll bring lunch."

"Can I bring anything?"

"No." He smiled intensely. "No, you can't. I'll see you tomorrow."

I watched him walk away, remembering Jazz's warning about him.

He's not the kind of guy you want to get involved with.

Why did Jazz say that?

It was just a boat ride. Just a nice boat ride. We'd done it before.

I had a slight spring in my step as I walked down the softly lit dock towards a number of waiting boats. I felt my torso. The envelope hadn't moved from where I'd stuffed it.

I was having a hard time explaining my final destination to the guys with the boats. Pointing a finger north wasn't exactly specific enough to let them know the location of my blue cabin; it could have been Cuba for all they knew.

Note to self: Double up on the Spanish lessons ASAP. I was always terrible at languages, but had struggled through French and then German in high school.

I should have listened to my father's practical suggestions. First, why would I not take Spanish? And, second, follow your dreams, but also get a degree in computer engineering...

I turned back towards the villa, ready to seek out one of the many bi-lingual speakers at the party, but there was no need. Bella was running down the deck at a speed too fast to be safe. By the time she reached me she was short of breath.

"Bella, are you okay?" I put my hand on her back as she wheezed and caught up with herself.

"Yes. Yes, I'm fine. I just... I told you before how much Jazz liked you. It struck me that she'd really like you to have this book." She smiled with tears in her eyes and handed it to me with two hands.

I looked down at a new hardback version of 100 Trips to Take Before You Die. It was a nice gesture, but I couldn't imagine it was a gift that truly came from anyone's heart. Maybe Jazz had visited each and every place.

Bella explained my location to the driver and he helped me into the back of the sleek boat. I had lost my safety vest somewhere along the way and was too tired to mime that I needed one. Maybe today was a sign that I needed to rip the Band-Aid off and live a little more freely. Murder would fly in the face of that theory, but I was grasping for logic on this crazy day.

We took off through the dark, quiet waters. It would be a good half hour voyage, and the air was heavy with humidity. It hadn't rained in quite some time, and we were just about due. I looked back at the dock, Bella staring after us. She didn't wave.

After ten minutes without phone service and more than half the journey left, I turned on my phone's flashlight to look at the book that Bella had gifted me. A thick cardstock peeked out of the top of the book. It was a beautiful monogrammed piece of personalized stationery with Jazz's name and a short message:

I NEED TO TALK TO YOU IN THE MORNING. I'LL COME TO YOU. BELLA

DAY FOUR

16
WHAT'S THE STORY, MOURNING GLORY?

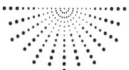

I didn't go to bed until sometime around 3:00 a.m. but I still woke up at 6:00.

My dreams had been like a black and white damsel-in-distress movie, where I'd been cornered by a steaming mad Cam in what looked like the throne room of an old castle. There was loud music, and though his lips were moving, no sound was coming out of his mouth. I had blocked my face with my hands and arms, expecting the worst.

And then Renny came and saved the day. He pushed through a mighty iron door, fighting off the pink giraffe guards (look, it's a dream, and I certainly don't know what *that* means), and eventually he took out Cam with one strong punch. Not unlike Cam and his bathroom friend last night.

I raced into the arms of my savior, who had morphed into Migs (not that I need someone to save me, thank you. I do fine on my own…), and right before he brought my lips to his, I woke up.

Isn't that always the way?

Well, at least it wasn't land sharks.

How had Renny become a thing over the past few days? Coincidently at the same time Migs stepped off that airplane. Migs would be heading back to Costa Rica soon and there would be no Sunday morning outings with the crew anymore. I'd throw myself into some kind of work and be busy for all mid-week jaunts with Renny. I'd be safe from temptation for the foreseeable future.

I hadn't left the light on the dock on (okay, I know it's not eco-friendly to do so, but I'm a woman living on her own in a rainforest), so I'd had a precarious walk to my front door in the moonlight. This time I'd been worried about more than the possibility of a banana spider climbing up my leg. Exhausted, I'd laid down to get my thoughts together for a minute and fell asleep.

I woke up clammy under the quiet but inadequate ceiling fan. My morning routine started again as usual - hair up in a messy top bun, a search for my favorite flip-flops, and a very large cup of my imported Dunkin Donuts coffee. When I got to the kitchen, I wrestled the envelope out of the too tight bathing suit I'd fallen asleep in. Not the most comfortable night's sleep with a leather envelope stuffed next to my sweaty body.

I hadn't dared try to look at anything last night while on the boat. Firstly, to get to it would have required me taking off my dress, and that would have been more than strange. Secondly, precious documents could have easily been lost to the bay.

Instead of heading straight out to the deck, I sat down at the kitchen table, where I spread the contents across the table. I'm not sure what I'd expected, but it turned out not to be the crime solving treasure I was looking for. There was the same picture of her and Hywel, but no threatening letters of black mail or violence. Nothing readily shed any insight into why she'd been killed.

Besides the snap shot of mysterious origin, what I had was a stack of unfinished bathymetric seafloor maps, of locations I had no way of identifying. The same pink post-its she'd used to draw Hywel her little love notes were in use here, but they were scribbled with frantic notes in Spanish and arrows pointing to things I didn't understand.

There was one map that I did recognize; that of all the reefs in the area. It was the same one that was folded up in Hywel's house with similar notations, only hers was the original document. More notes, more post-its, more earmarks of frustration.

I texted LaGuardia: 'Are you surfing this morning?'

I could go meet him at Paunch Beach and bring him this pile of paper. He'd at least be able to make out the Spanish.

It was barely 7 a.m. when I heard a boat at my dock. I walked out to see Bella peering up from her sleek little blue bowrider. I'd learned how to tie a boat up to the dock, so I was able to help her out. In a society of flip-flops and cut off shorts, she always looked surprisingly put together. Her straight dark hair was in a smooth pony tail, and she wore the preppy uniform of khaki shorts and a navy polo shirt. Her sneakers made a lot more sense than the flimsy sandals that everyone lived in. "Sorry I'm here so early. You saw my message in the book?"

"Of course I did. I've been thinking about it all night." I lead her up the short wild pathway to my deck. I didn't remember where she lived, but I'm sure it wasn't filled with cracked pathways and overgrown greenery. I felt very conscious of the down and dirty bungalow I was inviting her into. It wasn't that Bella was judging me: I was judging myself. It must have rained last night, as the deck furniture was damp. "Do you want to come inside? The furniture looks a little wet."

"Sure." Like Jazz, she was a person that took in everything. She clocked all that she saw, looking at every detail from the rickety dock to the wet furniture, to my yet to be well decorated home. This is not to give you the idea that my house was in shambles, but I moved down from New York with very little. I did well with what was around, but had not yet the time to go shopping for creature comforts to make the place really mine.

She passed on the offer of coffee or tea, but opted for a glass of water. I grabbed a bottle from the small fridge. It seemed silly to waste time with small talk when matters of such gravity were hanging out there. "I was pretty surprised by your message. What's going on, Bella?"

She looked at me with big, sad eyes. "You're friends with Detective LaGuardia, right?"

I nodded my head. "Is there something you need from him? Because you can always call…"

"No, I can't always call. And I told my husband I was just going for an early morning ride to clear my head. When we were all at the station Monday, I didn't tell the detective the whole truth. Or any of the truth really. With Cam in earshot of the room I was in, I just… there was a loyalty issue to Jazz going on. I didn't know how to fix it, but then you were at the house last night, and I thought you could help."

"Whatever you have to say, LaGuardia will be understanding. It's hard to lose someone and…"

"I don't think it would be good for me to be seen going back to the police station." She made a hand gesture as if she thought I'd understand. I didn't.

"Why are you afraid of Cam?"

"He wouldn't like what I had to say."

She might not have needed caffeine, but I sure did. I went to brew another cup. "Are you sure you don't want any?"

"Ok, sure. Milk and five sugars."

I smiled at her, a woman after my own heart. "Bella, your message seemed really dire. Why don't you just tell me what's going on?"

"Cam had told the police that she stayed over my house every Sunday night to help with the kids and watch movies. That's what he's always been told, so in a way he's none the wiser.

"When that detective, McDonough, asked me about it, I said yes, that's what we did every Sunday. That it was our sister bonding time. I told the police we went to bed at 1 a.m. and when I woke up, she was gone. Exercise." She checked the door and the windows to see if anyone had overheard. This was a woman on edge. "Well, she wasn't with me on Sunday night."

"She didn't stay over this week?" This brought everything to a whole new level now that all of Sunday was open for possibilities.

You could tell she was the kind of woman who seldom spoke ill of anyone. "How do I best say this? Truth. I do see her every Sunday. We spend the afternoon together and then she leaves before dinner. My husband flies to Panama City on Sunday afternoons for a few days of meetings, so he's not around. It was an easy cover up. But I didn't see her this week. She sent a message that she wasn't going to be able to come by early and she'd explain all next time we saw each other."

"What was she doing on Sunday night?"

She held onto the coffee mug like she needed the warmth. "For her and Hywel. Jazz and I usually had lovely Sunday afternoons together. She'd swim with the kids, shower, and get excited for whatever they'd be doing that night. Then I'd see her some time during the week. No one ever asked.

"I couldn't say it in front of Cam. You've seen his temper. He'd ride out to wherever that surf camp is and rip the poor guy's head off."

"Has Cam ever done anything? Why is everyone so scared of him? Why are you so scared of him?"

"Because I'd never heard his anger until recently, and I don't know what it meant. I just needed to keep those Sunday nights for her. I thought it was easy."

Sunday nights. Both Jazz and Hywel had said it and I missed it. Jazz had said she was looking forward to her one night off, and Hywel said that after guests checked out on Sundays, he took that 24-hours for himself. That he wanted silence from the storm that was Hurricane Daisy struck me as a very valid reason to want to be alone. I never put two and two together, even after knowing that they were a couple of sorts. "How long was it going on for? Do you know?"

She counted back on her fingers. "I think it was December when she first confided in me. I hadn't seen her so excited about a man since she was sixteen-years old. She said it was nothing, but... it doesn't matter what it was, she was happy."

December? I hadn't even been to the island yet. As far as I'd heard, Hywel was still with Daisy at that point. The inconsistent surfer had ponied up to admitting anything between five months and a one-night stand, but this was teetering on almost a year.

"We had it all planned out though. We had picked a horror movie to say we had watched together. I for one would never watch Halloween III: Season of the Witch, but it was cracking her up. Her message said she'd been dealing with a couple messy things but it looked like she was out of the woods. She never told me much about what went on with Hywel... but she was happy. Troubled for the last month, but still strong, and still Jazz."

She got up and walked slowly around my kitchen, looking at the few photos I had of my family, my old friends best forgotten, and various places I'd travelled over the year. Why did I bother keeping the pictures of people I no longer wanted to associate with?

She looked at the books on my shelves and pulled an old Agatha Christie book out. "I liked this one. I like your home. It must be very calm to be gone."

I'm not sure if 'calm to be gone' was a linguistic difference or if she was longing for something else. "Bella, do you want me to talk to Detective LaGuardia. Is that what you are asking?"

"Can I borrow this?" She held the slightly tattered copy of Evil Under the Sun to her chest.

"Sure." It pained me a little to say yes. Borrowed books have a way of never coming back. Not that I couldn't replace it for a buck...

"Thanks." She put the book on the table, but kept standing. She had too much energy to sit still. "I don't want it to look like I'm going to the police. I want them to come to me. They can talk to me at home or bring me back to the station, but I don't want it to look like I'm offering any information up."

"Are you afraid of Cam, Bella?" I got up and sat on the edge of my table, looking at her directly. She looked tormented beneath a very smooth façade.

"Promise me that you'll tell LaGuardia one last thing."

"Of course."

"I'm not telling you about her Sundays with Hywel

because I think he had anything to do with her death. That's not it at all. I think it was three Sundays ago… when she left, she said to me, 'I think I may be in trouble. Don't answer any questions about me. No matter who asks. I just need to take care of a nasty little issue.' She said it was something that she was going to have to deal with, and that we all just had to keep quiet about her for a while."

"So you think this could be more than someone furious at the two of them for the affair?" I still refused to think that Hywel was capable of murder. My suspicions were split between crazy Daisy out of jealousy or strong-arm Cam out of sheer anger.

"I think that being down at the station with Cam, and how the police can be made me absolutely terrified. If I had said something about their Sundays together, Hywel would be in jail right now. I truly do not know more about what was going on in terms of being in trouble, but I've got two kids and I'm scared. Could Cam have done it? I hope not. And Hywel? I really hope not. I need this to be over."

"You are going to be okay, Bella." I had no way of knowing that, but it's what you say, isn't it?

"I have to ask you, she said that she thought she was in trouble. Did she give you any hints about why? Or mention anyone at all? Even in passing?"

"All she does is take people out on snorkeling trips and map newly discovered reefs. There isn't much danger involved in that, is there?"

"And Cam?"

"Cam's a jealous idiot, but they had a good life together. They had a good time. I think the romance had run its course some time ago, but they'd been together for almost twenty years. He's the type of man to make a fool of himself, but if it went any further, I would have heard. You know."

She checked the time on the beautiful, waterproof Tag Heuer watch that I'd seen in magazines and had been fantasizing about since I'd come down here. She couldn't have anywhere to be – it was only 7:30. "But when he gets the idea of a fight in him it can get a little... uncomfortable."

"He never threatened anyone?"

"I never said that. I never knew what would set him off about a particular guy who might have been working with Jazz at times over the years, but every so often he flipped. And before you ask me, no, she had been loyal to Cam up until now, as far as I know. I would have thought she'd have picked someone a little more elegant, but it's her life, not mine. It was her life."

A wise woman once said to me, "Keep a secret and one day it will keep you."

"Can you look at something for me?"

"Sure."

I grabbed the envelope with all Jazz's papers, wondering if Bella was going to give me a hard time as to how the envelope came until my possession. "Does any of this mean anything to you?"

She smiled at the envelope. "Hermes. Beautiful." She carefully took out the papers and looked at them quickly, one after the other. I was praying that she'd be able to tell me what I was looking at and how it might fold into this case. "Sea floor maps? Coordinates in question? There are a lot of words I don't understand. I was a primatologist before I got married, nothing to do with water. Once the kids are old enough, I'll go back to work..."

She looked through the papers again, holding up the map with the marked reefs that both Hywel and Jazz had in their possession. "The only thing I can tell you about this map is that some of those places I've heard of and some of them are new to me. Sorry." She neatened the papers up and slid them back into the envelope, going the distance of locking it. "You should ask Renny. He'll be able to tell you what you're looking at."

"I'm seeing him later today. I'll be able to show it to him then." I believe I spoke a little too enthusiastically.

She looked me directly in the eye, questioning my last statement without making a particular expression. That was the Bella I'd always know and made the point of avoiding. "Are you, then?"

I became very self-conscious. "Just for a boat ride. Just for nothing really."

She put her sunglasses back on, which in Bocas meant that the conversation was coming to a close. "Be careful with that one. He's a little bit like someone maybe you wouldn't want to get involved with."

"Jazz said the same thing to me. I'm not planning on getting involved with anyone, but what about him makes everyone want to keep him at an arm's length."

"He's a good man and a smart man, but he's been having problems with Jazz. I don't know about what. She said that he was trying to push her into decisions she didn't want to make. She'd be livid. Other times? She'd just stew about him. Everything with Jazz was a secret over the last few months… Renny's not a rich man, you know. Maybe that's part of it. Some kind of jealousy. But if she said be wary, then be wary."

"It's nothing but a boat ride." I hadn't done anything wrong. Why was I feeling like I had? "Do you think those papers could have anything to do with Jazz's death?"

"I don't know, Lexie. But I still can't put any belief into thinking that Cam or Hywel did this… they are both buffoons in their own way, but they both loved her. And Renny was her partner for so long. We've known him since we were kids." She softened and gave me hugs and kisses, now repeatedly telling me exactly what I needed to tell LaGuardia. "You'll tell him, right?" She asked for the dozenth time.

"We all want this solved as quickly as possible. And I don't want Hywel arrested either. I'm seeing LaGuardia a little later, so stay at home and he'll to come to you."

"Thanks. You're a good woman, Lexie." She made no move towards taking the red envelope. She did take the Agatha Christie novel. Her last words to me were, "I'll bring it back."

But they never do.

17

IF SURFING WERE EASY IT WOULD
BE CALLED BASEBALL

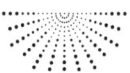

*Y*et again my car sat waiting for me in Bocas Town, after taking the boat home from Jazz and Cam's. I'd forgotten that fact until after Bella had left on her beautiful new boat. But we'd had an intense conversation and bumming a ride to town would have felt somehow inappropriate.

I took the brambly walk to Paved Road and waited for the bus to arrive. I was certainly getting in better shape with all the walking, fish, and smoothies, but my legs had never looked worse. I was still rocking a scar from an injury from my first visit, and the rest of the cuts, scratches and bruises just ruined any possible image of an adorable beach bunny.

There were only two people on the bus at this early hour - an American couple happy to hear my friendly accent. They asked me how I was doing, and my caffeine high launched me into a ten-minute diatribe about the pros and cons of having a car if it was always going to be parked in Bocas Town. They nodded along politely, obviously wondering how long the trip to town could be. Truth is you never knew; depended on the bus, the potentially insane passengers, and the outside possibility of a sloth crossing the road. I ended my monologue by saying, "You see, I can't swim."

The woman looked at me quizzically. "I'm sorry but I don't understand. What does that have to do with your car?"

"Good question," I replied, and turned back to watch the scenery.

We were just about to pass Itsmito Beach, close to the final stop in Bocas Town. I'd get my smoothie, try to remember to charge my Bluetooth semi-stereo, and head off to Paunch Beach. LaGuardia had texted me to say he'd be surfing this morning and to meet him as soon as I could. I had a big back-pack, as I had my fullest day yet planned. Regroup with LaGuardia, work a half-day at Lloyd's, then a quick boat ride with Renny before going home. It would be an early night for sure. Thankfully, parking in Bocas Town was free.

The shark scare seemed to have faded away, saving the week for the visiting sea lovers. It was a nice return to normalcy to see a surfer or two out on the waves as I drove the short distance to meet LaGuardia.

I was stuck on something that Bella had said. Just very off the cuff, she said that Hywel loved Jazz.

Why would a man kill the woman he loves? In Cam's case, it was easy if he knew about the affair. If murder was ever easy. Maybe if he couldn't have her, no one else could.

But Hywel? If he was the object of Jazz's affections, the last thing he'd want is her gone. It's the first thing Daisy would want, though.

It all seemed so out in the obvious.

The note! Crickety crackers, it was three days into the case and I still hadn't mentioned the note to anyone. No wonder murder investigations are such a mess when you've got a flibbertigibbet like me forgetting clues. I pulled the car over and did what I used to do at jobs in the past when I was in a particularly flaky state of affairs; I took a blue Sharpie out of my bag and wrote on the inside of my left forearm: "Dangerous Curves." You can't forget it until you next get in the shower, and if you haven't taken care of it by then, well, you get what you deserve.

Hywel, and Cam had received a picture of the loving couple this week. Who sent it to them? And how long had Jazz had a copy?

When I parked at Paunch, I watched LaGuardia for a while before he clocked that I was there. I envied the skill to surf and the freedom that it allowed to those in that world. There was that look that surfers got when they were out there. Whether it was LG, Hywel, or any of the dozens of other great surfers I'd seen over the months, there was nowhere else that they'd rather be. One of my snarky friends from New York had snidely commented on the level of commitment from surfing detectives, which I took particular affront to. "What's the difference between surfing and taking a run? Or yoga? Or going to the gym?" It was because people on waves were more likely to look like they were having fun.

At that moment, I swore to myself that by the end of a year's time I'd be up on a surfboard. Maybe I'd be no better than the folks who came down for a Bluff Beach week, but I made the promise to myself. Step one, getting in the water. With delusional ambitions of Pipeline.

I waited for LaGuardia on firm sand, and he quickly made his way to shore. As I waited for him to towel off, I saw a police car drive north. That could only mean one thing - something was going down at Grito Mono. I passed a coconut strawberry smoothie over to him. The only way I ever was allowed to pick up a check was by bringing him something. He quietly thanked me as we watched a cop car driving slowly to points north.

"Why are they going north? I thought you talked to Hywel last night." I hadn't technically proved that he didn't do anything, but I would definitely put him way down on the list. Hywel would just say something about the police not liking him in general, but I knew it was more than that.

"He didn't bother showing up at the station last night. We waited until 8 p.m. I know people have a way of losing track of time down here, but we were crystal clear when we had the conversation at Red Frog Beach that we'd be having an on the record conversation at the station. Very clear – be there at 6 p.m., wearing shoes, and ready to go over his story as many times as we needed."

"You're not arresting him, are you?" I panicked. Hywel knew better than to be this stupid.

"I'll just say that any polite courtesy ends here. Not showing up for a conversation is grounds for arrest. He's not illustrating very wise judgment. We're not his ex-girlfriend who he's trying to avoid. We're the police and this is a murder investigation. He doesn't want to man up, that's fine, but being cordial doesn't seem to have done any good, has it?"

"He's not even up here. They're at that dilapidated shack on Wizard's Beach." Hywel had told me that he'd planned to sleep up here last night, but I was learning that it might be just stupid for me to trust anything my boss had been telling me as of late.

"McDonough took a couple of officers down to Wizard Beach. We're both going in at 9 a.m. He can come with us, voluntarily or otherwise… and if he's not at either place, then he's really in trouble."

I thought of Hywel's charming luxury bungalow just ten minutes' walk from where we were. He was probably comfortably passed out from too many cheap drinks and air conditioning. "Maybe you'll find him here after all. He said that Waxy's gave him the itchies and he might be coming back north. I'm sure you'll find him up at Grito Mono. He said he needed a break and was going to come back up here." I laid out the events of last night's strange gathering, but both of our thoughts kept coming back to Hywel. "I'm not a police officer, so obviously there are a million reasons why a person might kill someone, but I don't get it. I can understand why Cam would want to kill Jazz – his wife was having an affair with someone else. Daisy, as well – she seems to be capable of violence towards anyone who gets within a hundred feet of him, and did you know she has a black belt? I wouldn't doubt she could hold her own with any of the big guys on the island. She's like a tiny Tasmanian Devil. But Hywel? It turns out that they might have been in love. Why would he want to kill her?"

"Like I told you yesterday, we've got both visual confirmation from Aqua Point that Cam and Larry Breger went out on a boat Saturday afternoon, and then returned on Monday. Larry's story matches up. We've got a photo of him with a marlin and Cam with a tuna. I really don't understand the allure of fishing.

"And we'd know a little better if he actually spoke with us. Or showed up. Maybe Jazz told Hywel it was over? He crushes her windpipe in a wild fury. Lexie, your downside is that you take what people say at face value, and people aren't... well, people just usually aren't that honest or well-intentioned. Forget homicide. Even if I'm dealing with robberies or bar brawls, truth is something you just don't hear very often."

"I'm always honest with you, LG."

"Well, you're not a criminal, Lexie."

Wasn't I? I'd told little white lies many a time over the past few days just to make sure that I stayed out of harm's way.

LaGuardia went off to change out of his wetsuit, which I know sounds a bit strange out of context. But what the island lacked as far as cellular service it made up for in little places to change your clothes. People were constantly getting in and out of wet bathing outfits so the makeshift changing rooms made sense. Sometimes they were no more than a couple of bamboo sticks. I would be that LG had a gun. Though I'd never seen him with one. Am I wrong to assume?

He returned wearing shorts and a polo shirt, morphing into his official identity of police detective. "You can come with me." We walked over to the newest vehicle in the Bocas PD arsenal - a brand new hybrid Mitsubishi Outlander. As soon as he turned the ignition, I blasted the air conditioning, looking forward to my ten minutes of 68 degrees and zero humidity. Between passing on instructions from Bella and trying to recall any tiny detail from last night that might be important, LaGuardia didn't get a word in the entire ride.

Pulling up at Grito Mono, I grabbed his hand before he got out of the car. "If all three of them got a copy of the photo? Jazz, Cam, and Hywel… Could that mean that one of them was being blackmailed?"

"We don't have any evidence of blackmail yet. Cam said he received the photo with no note, no information, nothing. And I guess we'll have to ask Hywel what he actually knows about the picture, because as of now I don't believe a word the bum says." He put his shoes on and got out of the car.

The news was bad already. Hywel was nowhere to be seen at the beloved lodge we stood in front of. Rolando-the-statistician cop called down from the deck of the usually buzzing bar, "Doesn't look like anyone's been here. We checked in with McDonough down at Wizard and Hywel isn't there either. The other guy at the camp says he never came back last night. His mobile's been off since we started calling last night."

I caught up to stand next to my friend. "There's one other place he could be. It's just a few minutes from here."

LaGuardia instructed the guys to take another look for anything suspicious. "Find something! Anything!" he yelled.

"He doesn't stay in the lodge himself. It's early. He's just sleeping it off in his bungalow back there" I told myself, quickly walking deeper into the rainforest. Last night's rain was making my ankles muddy, even along the manicured path to Hywel's oasis. The window shades were closed and the lights were off. "See? He's just sleeping." I knocked on the door, happily calling out to greet my friend. I turned the doorknob, which had been unlocked yesterday, but it didn't budge today.

"Ok, I'm getting tired of this." LaGuardia firmly knocked and made his voice known, "Hywel, let us in. You're in enough trouble already."

"I know where he might keep a key." I walked back towards the hotel to rummage around under the terrible porch.

No need it seems, as I turned back towards the bungalow when I heard the glass in the doorframe shatter. I quickly returned, following LaGuardia into Hywel's house.

"You didn't have to do that." I turned the lights on, illuminating the same view I saw yesterday. It was a very clean, very elegant place of residence, smelling slightly like lilacs. But he had been there. Someone, at least, had been there. "Clothes are gone." I went back to the drawer that housed the envelope with the photo and love notes, finding everything gone. "This is terrible. Someone's taken Hywel."

At the moment I was saying this, LaGuardia crossed wires with, "Looks like he's fled to me." He looked through the empty drawers a second time. "If that's not a confession of guilt, I don't know what is."

WORD WAS out across the islands: apprehend Hywel Lange, wanted for murder. For an area whose police department was called on more than one occasion for help with sloth road crossings, they now had a legitimate Public Enemy *1.

My efforts on his behalf was going nowhere, and I'll admit that I was starting to have a tiny doubt or two. They were intent on tracking him down, but not up for my theory that some nefarious entity might have him in their grasp. Couldn't the murderer want to knock off everyone?

There were a number of restaurants and hotels just south of Hywel's where officers would be questioning staff and guests. Nothing in the world worse for tourism than a police investigation, but priorities needed to be set. McDonough had left an officer on watch over at Waxy's in case he came back, but there would be no further investigation needed there. It was a beach with no hotels, no facilities, and no visitors for the most part.

I at least knew where the hidden keys to the surf shack were, so I was able to get water for the cops who'd been here for the last few hours. I borrowed a flashlight so I could scare off my nemesis banana spider, should he come looking for me. It was only a matter of time.

The lock was more symbolic than anything. Anyone with the strength of a five-year old child could have ripped the flimsy door off the hinges altogether. But I did my due diligence and opened the door the proper way. I grabbed one of the mesh bags hanging by the fridge and filled it with bottled waters, not wanting to spend too much time in the dark kiosk. The memory of Jazz, laid out gracefully on the floor would be seared into my memory for eternity. Something, however, was missing.

I took a step back to the entrance, taking in the contents as a whole.

Various size wetsuits all hung by size and gender on their rack. Just for reference, wearing rent-a-wetsuits was one of my least favorite things. But it helped beginners to be just a little more buoyant. I had purchased a half dozen shorties that were currently doing nothing but eating up storage space in my tiny home. One of mine lived here, in the room that had been taken over by Jules, but had seldom seen daylight.

The surfboards were usually set out in front of the shack for his guests to use, and to rent if there were any left. That was it. Hywel's prize board was missing - a red Mark Phipps One Bad Egg seven-foot board. It was easily four times more expensive than anything else he sent his beginners out on.

"LG!" I yelled towards the lodge, where the vexed police team stood. "Can you come down here?"

He finished his conversation and headed my way. Since April's murder, he'd been making an effort to look more like an official man of the law, but giving up flip-flops was something that he was not going to do. "What's going on in there, Lexie?"

"There's something I don't see. Hywel's board is missing."

"Are you sure it's not down at Wizard?" He peeked into the shack, the place they'd removed the body from just two days ago.

I handed him a water. "I don't think so. Yesterday when he ran away from me on the beach, he was on one of the same cheap boards that everyone else rides. And I'm pretty sure I saw it here yesterday, after everyone had already relocated."

"Interesting. Do you realize that all you are doing is making it look like he's fled? See what I mean?" He took a cursory look inside, taking inventory of all the boards, and helping himself to some Sticky Bumps Surf Wax. He addressed my concern before I could bring it up. "Don't worry. I just need wax. I'll leave you a fiver." He glimpsed at the price tag listed on the bottom. "Woah. He really is fleecing these tourists. But that's the nature of the beast."

"Please accept the Sticky Bumps, courtesy of Grito Mono." I weakly smiled.

"Don't bribe officials. It's a bad habit." He stuck the wax in his pocket and leaned against the palm tree next to the shack. "Lexie, why do you always find incriminating evidence against your friends during murder investigations?"

"Lloyd was never my friend." But he was right about the bad habit. I'd grow so excited to find something, anything, that I'd hurry to report it like a faithful bloodhound, not stopping to think about what or who it might implicate.

"Put yourself in my shoes listening to you, Lexie. Why is his surfboard missing? Do you think a criminal would break into Hywel's bungalow and ask him to pack a bag and grab his board? Maybe in case he wanted to shred some waves before his inevitable end?"

"Well, that's morbid."

"We're talking murder, Lexie. It is morbid." He could see the hurt creeping across my face and regretted his dismissive tone. "I'm sorry. But please just take a few minutes and look at the situation from the point of view of someone who doesn't have an interest in proving her friend didn't kill the woman he was having an affair with. Can you do that?"

I can. And it doesn't look good.

"A smart killer would take everything. Make it look like Hywel was guilty, so they'll be free and clear and in Nicaragua by the time he's found dead." I couldn't believe what I had just said. Did I believe that Hywel dead was a possibility? In my heart, I knew he wasn't. My mind had decided that he was being held somewhere by a dastardly villain, like Cam in my dream last night. And yes, maybe he'd let Hywel bring his surfboard. But the inevitable outcome being the same... "We need to find him before it's too late."

LaGuardia wasn't on board with my Perils of Pauline theory, but did agree on one thing. "Too late for who and what, I don't know. But we've got to find him." He glanced back into the shack for other potential items to put on his tab.

"Hey, it's not a free for all in there. You take it, I end up paying for it."

"Just let me grab that fin key ratchet tool." He went back in and grabbed it, tossing it in the air before putting it in his pocket. "And before you get any idea about corrupt Panamanian cops, here..." He took his wallet out of his back pocket and handed over $25.

I'd learned a lot since I last saw the detective. "There's one last thing..."

AFTER I TOOK my anti-bacterial wipes to a table in the ghost town of a bar and grill, I sat down with LaGuardia and Rolando and presented them with Jazz's red leather envelope. I was hopeful, but just like when I had shown the contents to Bella, it had no easily identifiable value to the cops. The same photo that had been delivered to Cam and Hywel offered no new insight. The maps were incomplete and the post-it notes weren't even cryptic enough to raise an eyebrow. The map of reefs, some known and others yet to be known, offered nothing as well.

"I am going to have to keep this." LG slid the envelope to his side of the table.

"Yeah. I know." I hoped that they had some way of analyzing the contents and finding a new path. That they could call on someone. Anyone.

"But let me get this straight. Bella did not give this to you?"

"No." I knew where this was going.

"So how did it come into your possession?"

I didn't need to recall how I was using Jazz's bathroom and stuffed it into a too tight black one-piece. "I took it from Jazz and Cam's."

He hit his head three times with his palm. "Rolando, can you get an update from McDonough, please? And leave the envelope." He watched the young officer walk out of the room, then turned his attention back to me. "So, you're a burglar now? Turned to a life of crime…"

When you put it that way…

Again, I was playing the faithful dog, only happy that I had brought something good to its owner. "Am I in trouble?"

"Next time you find something that could be helpful, call the police to take a look. Call me, for crying out loud."

I reached for the envelope. "I'll take it back from you then."

"You'll leave it right there. If it was mysteriously dropped off at the station, no one can say anything." He rolled his eyes at himself.

"Just let me look at it for a few minutes. You don't know what it means. Bella doesn't know what she's looking at either, but she did tell me to ask Renny... I'm seeing him later..."

"You told him about this?"

"No, I had made... plans with him for today. I'll be seeing him this afternoon."

"Plans? What kind of plans?" LaGuardia looked at me suspiciously. It looked like I had indeed inherited the older brother I may or may not have wanted.

"Boat plans?"

"For someone who doesn't want to date, you seem to be on a bit of a bender." He got up, stretched his arms and sighed. I'm going to walk away for 90 seconds. "Look at it again, fine, but leave it, ok? And be careful with that guy. As I said before, he's got a decent alibi, but it's not airtight. You have to remember that the other players we've tracked down confirm they played late into the night with him, and had breakfast with him. But that break of dawn chunk of time can't be confirmed."

I called after him, stopping him in his walk. No time for secrets anymore. "You haven't talked to all of them? I think there were six or so."

"Lexie, you're a very smart woman, but you don't have to tell me how to do my job. All of this is in process. It's not as easy as New York City to find someone, based on phone service at the least."

"Sorry."

"No harm, friend." He continued out of the restaurant.

As soon as LaGuardia was out of sight, I opened the envelope, quickly photographing a few of the maps and the list of reefs and the photos. The sound of flip-flops returning across the deck let me know my time with the envelope was up.

I hadn't even got my 90 seconds from him when he walked quickly back to me. "Based on what you've learned today, are you sure you want to get on a boat with Renny?"

Did I?

18

NOT MY MONKEY, NOT MY CIRCUS

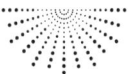

I wasn't going on a date, despite what LaGuardia intoned, and certainly not on a bender. I was going with the flow. Wasn't that the island way? And like LG said, I've got the advantage that I could chat with people about things he wouldn't be privy to.

Checking my phone before I left the lodge, I saw that I had a message from Migs. Reading the quick note, I became pretty sure last night wasn't any kind date.

'Sorry for conking out last night. Bella said you were ok. I'm pretty much dying right now, but lunch later in the week?' An offer of a mid-day meeting was not a date with a suitor. We were back to the buddy-buddy reality with my stunningly handsome photographer friend.

It's chill.

You never say chill.

Shut up brain, it's the island way.

The 48 hours of shark scare seemed to be over, so we were back to some kind of normal. The southern area of Bluff Beach was populated once again. Things were looking like they were starting to get back to normal. The shark warnings that Hywel had made had hung onto the palms and his cars for a bit, but last night's rain had taken care of the last of them. Business was open.

I had a surprising new thought: I was looking forward to going to work at Lloyds. I'd bet $1000 (maybe) that he was the smartest person living in Bocas del Toro, with a deductive mind that could solve problems very quickly. But only if he only would share that knowledge with others. He had a way of making you feel stupid, but ultimately, he led you to formulate the questions and come up with the answer on your own.

There's one thing I should tell you about Lloyd in case you weren't completely sure. He may or may not be a serial killer. I was currently leaning towards not, but that could change on a dime.

Back in April, I'd learned that when he was studying at Washington University in St. Louis, one of the schools that were considered the Ivy League of the mid-west, there was a string of young blond co-eds who had been murdered. Lloyd had been of interest to the police and had been questioned thoroughly on a number of occasions. He was let go, but the case was never solved. The murderer was still at large, twenty-two years later.

I believe that Lloyd liked carrying around this mystique. During the last investigation, he had listed the probability of himself being the murderer at 6 percent. "Would you believe the veracity of my statement and alibi?" He had asked.

Yup. Lloyd in a nutshell. I needed his help though. I'd grown confident enough in my own intelligence over the last few months, but he was smarter. It wasn't an opinion or me beating myself up. It was a fact.

Lloyd's facility was the only place on the island with

reserved parking spaces. Comical in its way, as I'd yet to see a visitor. I pulled into my allocated space, grabbed my stereo so I could charge the battery, and headed into the building.

The usually silent workplace was downright rowdy when I walked into ANANKE. I didn't want to know, so I still followed my regular routine of banging a quick left, going into my office, and beelining it to my inbox. It was devoid of any of my usual work and today's memos on official letter-head (boy was he a stickler for the good old days), were all marked URGENT. It's like he was thinking in overdrive on paper about the murder, positing questions, situations, and theories. Some familiar, some novel, and some just ridiculous.

'A faux shark attack is a great cover up for a real shark attack. AI.'

'I won't be sordid, but self-autoerotic asphyxiation.'

'Hell has three gates: lust, anger, and greed.' –Bhagavad Gita

'Sunken treasure.'

The case would be the priority that day. Whatever mad scientist thing they were doing in their subterranean labora-tory would be put on hold until the case was closed.

On Monday, he had said to me that he had a vested interest in finding her killer. What did that mean? I'd asked him twice with no response.

I turned on my computer, which was my greatest chance of being connected with the world on a regular basis. I had wireless service at my house, which generally was so frus-tratingly slow that I gave up and read a book or stared, daydreaming, out the window. At least I was retraining my attention span that had been decimated by too many years of social media and New York City. Constant need for stimulus.

Slow it down, Lexie.

Speaking of scattered, there had been information overload this morning coming from every angle. I didn't know what I was hearing or how to piece it all together.

After a short period of peace in my office, my hypothesis became clear. Daisy was in my sights. She had a clear motive in wanting to break up the couple. She was crystal clear about knowing about the love affair yesterday. Daisy could sniff out Hywel's location like a bloodhound. It wasn't outside the realm of possibility that she'd somehow taken that picture.

Trouble? Daisy's middle name. Wing Chun and the ability to physically crush someone twice her size, she was nobody's fool, no matter how foolish she acted. She'd be able to crush a windpipe with the ease of a Cyclops flicking a mosquito off his shoulder.

I looked up The End of the World on the internet one more time. I'd seen it in passing on a few occasions. It was on Carenero Island and was a massive firetrap between two of the bigger hostels in the area. The island was less than a five-minute boat ride from Bocas Town, but not my scene in the slightest. It was also home to the infamous Pickled Parrot, which I'd been dragged to on occasion by Hywel and Jules. The only time I'd ever really socialized with Dr. Nolan and his girlfriend, it had been there, and it was the moment that had inspired me to travel with antibacterial wipes. I needed to keep that fact closer to the chest, lest my nickname be expanded to Antibacterial Avanti. It's the little things.

Daisy's club was opening for the week tonight, and I had two free tickets. Did I dare? A journey towards the End of the World. The website didn't reveal much except prices and a dozen photos. Fire eaters, and women in bathing suits doing shots out of what looked like test-tubes. Groups of men holding plastic cups of beer up to the camera. Of course, the fanged angel tattoos were omnipresent.

I guess it wasn't going to be an early night after all.

I had just started to research Daisy herself when I heard the sound of breaking glass and raised voices. I grabbed my stack of memos (not eco-friendly) and made my way to the lobby of the building.

Besides Lloyd's office, the entire building was cold and stark. Brutalist architecture came to mind. Distressed metal framed couches with tight black leather.

Mad scientists had the reputation of being a messy bunch, writing indecipherable formulas on chalkboards and brewing potions on Bunsen burners (at least according to my high school chemistry class). Not these OCD maniacs.

A couple of the guys were standing around Crabby Paolo, who looked positively frazzled. There were broken booze bottles up and down the hall.

Lloyd, towering above all (he seemed to tower higher when he needed, I don't know how he did it) appeared in the door frame of his office. He held a half empty bottle of Blue Curacao out in front of him as if it was a dead mouse he'd found in the corner. "This one is yours too, I can only assume." He looked around the room, waiting for a response that never came, so he smashed the bottle on the concrete floor. As it shattered, he coldly said, "Oops."

He turned around and headed back into his office. "Lexie! I'm going to need you in here."

His office was humid and hot, not the constant comfortable 71 degrees it usually was. He had doors that opened out to a large stone terrace that I'd never had the pleasure of visiting. Lloyd paced instead of sitting down behind his desk. I took a seat on the sofa, placing my memos carefully next to me. This new environment of chaos was completely not what I'd ever experienced working at Lloyd's, and I knew when he got mad (or just a little irked) he had a propensity for condescending nastiness. So, I waited quietly for him to start the conversation. I'd never seen him lose his temper, but I could imagine it would be the basis of a recurring nightmare of many future nights…

He finally rested, sitting on the front of his desk. "Are you familiar with a French philosopher named Jean-Paul Sartre?"

Are you kidding me?

"Lloyd, remember that part of my job is to tell you when you are being insufferably rude?" At the very least, he'd ceased from being completely sarcastic with me since I'd moved down.

He skipped that part where a normal person would apologize. "Then you are familiar with the quote, 'Hell is other people…'"

"Yes. Anyone particular who's dragging you through the nine circles or all of us humans?"

"Very nice literary allusion." He walked around his desk and sat on his luxury desk chair. Opening the top drawer, he pulled out his bad habit, a pack of cigarettes, and lit up. He was certainly looking his part at the moment, vampire porcelain creeping through his tan.

I thought it was very human of him to have quit smoking, so I felt confident saying, "You ever hear the saying 'Kissing a smoker is like licking a dirty ashtray?'"

He gave me that old look that always chilled me. "No complaints yet." When he slowly and elegantly exhaled the smoke, I looked away. "Someone's tetchy today…"

"I apologize." I had a bad habit of saying sorry when I was the one in the right, but it was something I was working on fixing. "Why did you break that bottle?"

Lloyd pointed to the terrace. "It seems that our idiot

savant of a shuddersome herpetologist has been getting the capuchin monkeys drunk. There's a troop of monkeys that sometimes spend their days on the terrace. They seem to like the day-old dinner rolls one of the guys brings from his sister's restaurant. They're also fans of eating the right kind of frogs, which you'll appreciate. So Paolo decided to have drinks on my *private terrace* last night, and now I'm dealing with a bunch of hungover monkeys. You don't do that to monkeys."

He'd have been amused if a person had been hurt, but here he was, protector of the primates. "Are you sure? I know that they sometimes assault our restaurant at Grito Mono and drink the leftover rum punch they knock over."

"Well, we've run the security footage from the last month, and this wasn't an isolated incident. Seriously, you hire the smartest people in the world, and they end up getting monkeys crocked. Do you think I need a secretary?"

"The correct term these days is executive assistant. And do you want one?"

"I don't know. This simian mess has me on edge."

That seemed like a pretty serious offense, intoxicating creatures of the rainforest that we all shared in peace. I don't know if his employees had contracts at all. I knew that I didn't, but they were some serious group of guys doing highly confidential work. However, any contract lawyer, anywhere in the world, wasn't going to have the ridiculous foresight to put a clause about a drunk barrel of monkeys into any agreement. "Are you going to fire him?"

"No, of course not. He may be morally ambiguous, but he's a gifted individual. I'm just going to scare the University-of-Michigan-at-Ann-Arbor education out of him. I've done pretty well so far." His anger had receded. He was back to his natural state as psychological games master. "But there are far more important things to talk about than monkeys drinking cocktails. Riddle me this – what did you find out about Jazz?"

An extension of yesterday's strange phone exchange. Could I even compete at his game? "I'll throw that back to you. What do you know? You kind of left me for dust on Monday night on your own investigative quest with that lady."

"Turns out she was a dead end. She claimed to be good friends with Jazz. She wasn't. And I made the mistake of passing on my phone number the next morning. Women. I'll have to get a new number. I calculated that in a 10,000-person province there are probably only a couple hundred women in my aesthetic and age preference, so I've got to be a little careful. Beautiful women here? It's like shooting fish in a barrel."

"Do you remember when I started working here, and you told me that the 'whole BFF thing' wasn't going to work for you? Really, it goes both ways...TMI." There's nothing I'd less like to be privy to than the romantic dalliances of the Prince of Darkness.

"Fair enough. What do you know?"

My brain was frazzled, but spilling it out to Lloyd, I knew he'd process it into something workable. Like I said, I hated my old nickname from him, when referred to me, not in a flattering way, as Encyclopedia Brown, Boy Detective, first published in 1963. I hoped that had passed.

I talked a mile-a-minute, updating him on everything I'd experienced since I'd seen him on Monday. From the info from Dr. Nolan to Hywel's inconsistencies, to Daisy's strange hilltop cocktail oasis (which I was still not sure wasn't a figment of my imagination), to Migs' stories about Cam's temper tantrums, to Bella's visit to my morning with LaGuardia.

Take a breath.

It's going to be okay.

Let the fallen angel help you work it out.

He stared at me in uncomfortable silence for which must have been a minute but felt like an hour. He didn't break my stare when he asked, "What do you have written on your forearm?"

Dangerous Curves.

"Jazz gave me a note to pass onto Hywel on Sunday." I took a deep breath, remembering the happy moment that Hywel had translated. "Beware of dangerous curves. *Adios, a Santo Amaro.*"

Lloyd went slack-jawed. "Santo Amaro? This certainly throws a wrench in the works."

And here it was. Something that I'd had knowledge of for three days and kept forgetting. I needed to bring a sharpie, on a necklace around my neck to use my body as daily reminders at all times. "Yes, Santo Amaro."

"And you are sure she wrote *adios*?"

"I don't know a lot of Spanish, but I do at least know how to say goodbye!"

"Why would she say goodbye to Santo Amaro?" He was speaking aloud but under his breath, not towards me.

"Can you tell me what Santo Amaro is?"

He ran his hands through his black hair, staring into space for a short while. "Santo Amaro was a 16th century abbot who sailed across the Atlantic and found an earthly paradise that he was not allowed to enter. It's a legend not a fact, but on his way, he fought monsters, found a land of beautiful people with a 300-year life span, and supposedly survived the Doldrums. But that's neither here nor there."

"What does a saint from the 1500s have to do with Jazz's note?"

"It was her obsession. Not the man. It's another possible fiction unto itself. There's a local legend that a small pirate ship called the Santo Amaro sunk somewhere off of Bocas del Toro. There are versions of the story that have the boat going down anywhere between Colon and Limon, but it's generally accepted that it was in this vicinity. Local pirates raided a ship leaving from Cartagena filled with stolen Columbian emeralds, and gold coins mined in Peru. Some even say Incan gold."

"Wouldn't everyone be after that?"

"You'd be shocked to know, I know that I was, that it's estimated that there are over three million undiscovered shipwrecks laying in the bottom of the sea. The story says that this particular pirate crew of the Santo Amaro was about as sharp as marbles and took off to destinations unknown in hurricane season. Not the smartest, but… Never to be seen again." He gestured as if he was a magician making your watch disappear.

"What does that note mean then?"

"What do I think?" He paused, contemplating telling me what he knew. "I think she found the shipwreck. We'd started talking about it after her first not-so-friendly visit when she was grilling me on the ethicality of my practices. That would be my guess.

"We weren't close, but she was a brilliant marine biologist. We'd talked here four or five times since I set up shop. The last time she was talking about the questions of legalities around the treasure if it was ever uncovered. Jurisdiction questions – what country does it belong to? Countries have the rights, but in instances like this, everyone claims it's theirs. There's Panama where it sunk, Columbia where the treasure departed from with theses emeralds, and Peru with the Incan coins. "She wanted to do the right thing. It wasn't about the money; she doesn't need any. She was a good person."

I was a tiny bit envious of his rare praise for brains and goodness. Probably because she kept secrets as closely as he did. She was just not someone to play games with. Jazz had her own secrets while Lloyd collected everyone else's. On the other hand, he probably had enough skeletons in his closet to fill a storage container.

"Wow. That's motive for murder that I'd never have guessed in a million years." Where to go from there? "Can we just go over some of your memos?"

Lloyd nodded, wide-eyed in anticipation.

I ruffled through the memos, typed on fine paper. Looking at them a tad closer, it indeed seemed like an old-school typewriter had been used. Finding the one I wanted, I asked, "Can we talk about 'lust – anger – greed?' The current situation is that she'd been looking for new reefs. I guess, really, it's more likely she's been looking for Santo Amaro. Can I show you this scribbled-on map? It's got to mean something."

I brought my phone over to let him scroll through the envelope I had perhaps illegally procured last evening. He scrolled the wrong way, catching a few teenage fan club pictures of Migs.

"Don't look at those."

He scrolled the other way and came across the photo of Hywel and Jazz. He raised an eyebrow. "Well, well. Jazz was a little naughtier than I thought. Clock that expression she's got next to that surf boy of yours. Baby, baby, baby. Put him in the lust category."

"Look at the map."

Let's keep on point, brainiac.

He sent the picture to a printer, which quickly allowed us a poster size printout. He spread it across his desk for both of use to look at. My right thumb had been blocking part of Bocas Town in one photo, but so be it. "I know a lot of these dive sites. Crawl Cay. Hospital Point. I was just at Grandma's Garden. The check-marks are all with different pens. Like she'd started at the obvious sites and moved on. I've never heard of most of the places that she hadn't checked off. Marker 61, marker 67, Tiburon Wall, Peligrosa Rock…"

Lloyd snapped his fingers. "There you go. Dangerous curves. Peligrosa Rock. Peligrosa means dangerous in Spanish."

Stop being cleverer than me.

I scanned the map with my finger, inappropriately noticing that I needed a manicure and would have to head to the bar/salon at the airport. "Hey. Peligrosa Rock is near where I'm going with Renny today, right near Dolphin Bay. Could that be one of the new reefs she was studying? Can you print out the bathymetric maps from my phone?"

"Bathymetric? You just might be a scientist after all." He printed from my phone and rushed to the printer.

He spread the new documents across the desk. "Full disclosure. Marine biology is one thing that I do not have a degree in. The whole discipline is a little wishy-washy for the most part, in my not-very-humble opinion. Let's see if there's anything these relief maps can tell us." He took a moment, circling the desk, looking at it from every angle. "Her notes are just a series of frustrations, but yes, this unclassified reef is very close to where you are going. It's all up to you, Encyclopedia Brown."

"I warned you about calling me that."

He rolled his eyes. "Isn't that what they call a private joke?"

"No." I looked at the maps, feeling a tiny bit stupid since I didn't exactly know what I was looking at. Remembering our conversation from two days ago, I asked, "What did you mean when you said that you had a vested interest in figuring out who did what and when to who?"

"I had a feeling her murder might be about something she found. We had a hand-shake deal that I'd get to look at the reefs or wrecks to analyze what was growing on them to assess their medical value. Before she contacted the Smithsonian Research Station. That's it." He didn't pick up on social cues. Either that or he didn't care. "So let's break it down. Lust. Anger. Greed."

"The only one lusting over her was Hywel, and I'm worried about him. No matter how much he's acting like a fool, I still didn't see it. I'm worried about his safety. And Bella was talking about how happy Jazz was after six months or so. Why would he want to kill her?"

"It's just a question that hasn't been answered. Don't dismiss it."

Nothing is dismissible with Lloyd. I know he was on his best behavior, but if you pressed him, the shark would be back in the line-up.

"Anger is easy," I offered. "If this photo is going around, and it is, Cam could have completely exploded. I never knew, but his temper seems to be legendary. But who took the picture? That's what we need to know. It just doesn't make sense that it would end up with all of them: Jazz, Cam, and Hywel. And does Daisy have that picture? I mean, in the last week I've seen Cam out of control, and as for Daisy – hell hath no fury and all that."

Lloyd was tapping his lower teeth with his pointer figure,

lost in a world of his own. He ground his cigarette butt into a small black ashtray. "And greed? Well, that's anyone who knew about Santa Amaro. The only person we're sure who knew about it was the least probable choice of lover, your other boss. If she passed a note to him saying, 'Goodbye Santo Amaro,' he knew about a possible location more than anyone. And if she was telling him to stay away from it… If the urban legends are right, ten million dollars is about ten million motives to strike down our dear friend in her prime. You can be sure Cam knew about it."

Bella certainly didn't know anything. The maps meant nothing to her. "So, who knew?"

"Maybe Renny to your disappointment ? It's not clear, but since they've been working together for years, it's probable. So, yes, your little boyfriend might know." He frowned to the world in general as he suffered a human emotion. "But maybe you want to rethink your cruise to nowhere."

"It's not the first time we've gone out on a boat together. And he's not my boyfriend. We sing, eat, don't swim. There's no way he'd think it anything otherwise."

Elbows on the desk, he pointed two fingers at me, tongue poking into his cheek. "Make I make an observation? I'm certainly one not to avoid drama, but if I lose you, who's going to help me come off as an affable fellow?"

"From what you and LaGuardia have said, the reason I got to go to last night's event, the reason Bella talked to me, the reason that all those society Bocans give a little something up to me…is Bocans the word for them? The reason they trust me is because I am no one. Not like that. Not what I meant.

"LG is not welcome in those coteries. There seems to be a virtual wall against telling him anything. Everyone seems to give him half-truths if they are covering for half-truths. What I meant is, I am not a cop. I have the rare opportunity to ask questions and I elicit a real answer without police interference.

"I can see your face. You aren't pleased. He trusts me. I can just go out with Renny, a.k.a. greed, for regular friend stuff. Then I can see Daisy at her club, a.k.a. lust and anger and greed, and see what I find out. It's just a day. It's just an outing. And as Bella said, 'ask Renny.'"

"And if it's a date, watch yourself."

"It's not a date." I blushed. "He'll know something, at the very least about Santo Amaro. Don't worry – I'll let LG know."

"Then stop with the chemical adrenaline." Lloyd wasn't convinced either way, but still said, "You tell LaGuardia, there's no way he's going to let you go."

Leaving LaGuardia in the dark? I didn't feel particularly comfortable about that.

Don't be so hard on yourself.

If it weren't for you, there'd be two unsolved murders on this island.

You know what you are doing.

"I feel like I'm doing something illegal."

Lloyd shrugged. "Illegal is a relative term." He lit another cigarette. "I'm quitting this indulgence tomorrow. Extraordinary times call for…and all that. Here. Take the rest of the day off and prep for your non-date slash investigation. Check in though. A text will do."

Lloyd walked to the other side of the room, opening the door to the office, looking at the broken glass and a group of concerned men standing in the middle of the detritus. Had Crabby Paolo been crying? I felt bad. Not bad enough to give him a hug or anything, but enough to pity him for whatever was about to go on in Lloyd's office. "Paolo? Can you come in here?"

He nodded his head, resembling a second-grader who must go sit on the naughty step and think about what he's done. He followed Lloyd into the office, and I closed the door behind us. I went back to sitting where I was on the couch, but Paolo chose to stand, ready for the firing squad.

"*Lo siento.*" Paolo nervously crossed his arms.

I swear I caught Lloyd smirking. He let Paolo stay there for a pregnant minute, then asked, "How would you like it if a bunch of giant monkeys came and made you get high on some berries or whatnot? You could be creating addicts."

"I'm sorry. I'm sorry." He wiped his nose with his sleeve.

"Go home now and think about why I shouldn't fire you. Then come back tomorrow and tell me."

Paolo slunk out of the room, silently closing the door.

Lloyd escorted me towards the exit, and this time I had to stop.

"I really think he's sorry. I really believe that he thinks the monkeys are his friends." Not the kind of conversation that I thought I'd be having that morning.

Not a morning any of us thought we'd be having.

19

SWIMMING LESSONS, PART 5

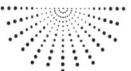

The written reminder on my arm had worked, so I decided to do it again, writing CHARGE SPEAKER on my right arm. My arm looked more like a reminder to char steak, but I'd be able to remember the intent. The driving without music was making me as batty as La Gruta (story for another day). Lucky to find myself with three hours more than I thought I'd have, I drove home to collect myself. I did not want to be rushed while I prepared myself for my non-date-slash-snoop-around.

Everyone liked Renny, but could he be greed, lust, or anger? Could there have been something he knew? That he saw? He probably had spent more time in his life with Jazz than Cam had. Could he have been involved? If Lloyd knew about Santo Amaro, Renny would have to know about it too.

When I got home, I downed a liter of water and lay on my couch with the computer on my lap. I googled Santo Amaro and there wasn't a word about any shipwreck at all. There was very little about the saint himself either, just a few pages on a Catholic scholar's website from 2005 about his periplus and his veneration. Seems like it was possible, if not probable, that Santo Amaro never existed at all. Just like the ship...

While I was busy looking up shipwrecks and getting distracted by what periplus actually meant (it's a document that lists the ports, costal landmarks, and distances between these places for captains to be able to identify on shore... a.k.a. a map), I had a notification *ding*. I had a new friend request on Facebook. I hadn't had one of those in quite some time.

A smile crept across my face when I saw it was from Miguel "Migs" Araya. I forgot that he had an actual full name. "Yes, please," I said aloud.

He sent me a message as soon as I accepted, saying only, "Nice profile pic." It was taken the week that I had decided to move here. I was terrified and excited and proud of myself for making what was probably the first bold decision I'd made in my life. Having drinks with a work friend on a rooftop at sunset on the first hot day of the year, she snapped a pic of me floating around on cloud nine. It had been a really nice day. Six weeks later I was on a one-way flight to Panama.

Stay on point, Lexie.

After messaging back and forth for a few minutes, mostly in stories made up of emojis, I asked what I needed to, typing, "Can I get Bella's phone number?"

There would be time to comb his profile later. I fleetingly wondered if he'd posted any pics from the mess of a wedding he photographed back in April.

I was really nervous to call her, and it turned out to be for no reason. LaGuardia had come to her house right after he and I parted and she told him everything she'd told me and more.

She spoke to me non-stop about planning Jazz's funeral,

and how guilty she felt about everything. "I keep thinking that if I hadn't covered up for her for all this time, maybe this wouldn't have happened. Or if I had told the police the truth as soon as they asked, they would have found whoever did this by now."

"You can't think that way, Bella. It is not your fault." I couldn't imagine how terrible she felt, but I imagined a frenzied version of her usual put together self in my head. Red eyes and frazzled hair.

She went on for a bit before pausing and taking a huge breath on the other end of the line. "I don't even know why you called. Sorry I babbled."

Why was absolutely no one telling anything to the police?

"Does Santo Amaro mean anything to you?"

"That old shipwreck? Jazz has been talking about that for more years than I can remember."

I walked to the door with my phone, stood in the doorframe, looked down the dock at a snorkeling group going by. They all waved at me as they sailed by, and I waved back. "She never talked about maybe finding it?"

"It's just an old story." She sighed. "I consider it an old wife's tale she'd been talking about for way too long. But ask Renny about it. I stopped listening to her about the stupid ship years ago. He dropped off some photos for the service today. He said he's looking forward to seeing you." She must have understood I was still thinking about Jazz's warning, because she added, "Just keep him at an arm's length."

My heart gave a little flutter. Or arrhythmia. Or increased cortisol levels. To think that at one point I called myself a hopeless romantic. I took the opportunity to get his phone number and prepare for our outing.

∼

You'll be pleased to know that I did charge my Bluetooth speaker/car stereo system and had a good chunk of time to loofah off all the writing on my arms. No easy feat. The water was never too hot and had terrible pressure, but that's what one does to save the environment.

Looking through my closet for the perfect outfit that says, 'I don't care,' I remembered Daisy's impressive kick, wondering if I could add it to my arsenal of self defense. Like everything, practice makes perfect. I held one trembling leg in the air while leaning on the frame of my bed. I gave it my best, ending up sprawled across the floor with a definite bruise on the way.

I decided I didn't want to take my car out to Bocas Town to meet Renny and face a third morning of having to get on the death trap bus back down to claim Lady Luck. I also didn't want Renny picking me up at home. It sent the wrong message, and I didn't want to end up doing anything unto-ward. Plus, Lloyd might as well have stamped the word GREED on his forehead.

The Prince of Darkness had even been reticent about me going out on today's excursion. My rational side asked what possible reason Renny could have to come after me. He couldn't have known what I took from Jazz's bathroom. Plus he had told Bella that we'd be out together. I wasn't going to die today. Probably.

I texted him to meet me at the dock near Yarisnori, Larry Breger's restaurant at Bocas del Drago near where I lived. I did happen to try on all six of my shorty wet suits (ok, some of them twice) before I threw the lovely silver and black suit in a bag, which matched the snorkel fins I'd yet to truly utilize.

I walked up Paved Road, my mind all over the place. I'd

been pseudo-crushing (ok, maybe crushing) on Renny for months. Despite the current maybe-he-killed-her thing.

Getting to Yarisnori by foot was a bit of a pain in the posterior. Once at the end of Paved Road, it was just a sandy beach route down the coast. Beautiful, but not when you were in a rush and carrying a bag full of snorkel paraphernalia. There would be equipment I could use on Renny's boat, but my slight concern with bacteria of all kinds kept me using my own.

I'd thrown on a flattering, light blue, gingham dress over my bathing suit. I was currently sweating through it, but isn't that life in paradise? Or is that what Dante was thinking of in the fourth sphere of Paradiso?

I could see Renny talking to a couple of guys by the restaurant, smiling and laughing. The group saw me coming and gave me a nod. I felt a small victory that I was getting occasional nods of recognition.

You're getting there.

This is where you were meant to be.

Though flip-flops made it impossible to look too glamorous, I did my best to gracefully walk the catwalk down to the group of men, wishing there were some trade winds to blow through my hair. Renny looked good in a rock n' roll t-shirt and short, slim-fit board shorts that were all the rage at the moment. He had the great tan of a person not trying to fit a year's worth of sun into six-days-and-seven-nights.

Yup, that's a crush.

And a potentially dangerous one. For all kinds of reasons.

As Lloyd had said, 'baby, baby, baby.'

And he'd also said, "Are you sure you want to do this?"

Snap out of it, tall girl.

"Hey, Lexie," Renny said when I was close enough for him to hear the flip of the flops. The guys turned to say howdy, and Renny came towards me, giving me a kiss on both cheeks. "Thanks for coming out with me. We're going to have a great time." He patted one of the guys on the back. "This is Ned Livingston. He owns the villa where we have our poker games. He loses so much that he's going to have to sign his villa over to one of us soon."

"Not like you're doing much better than me, *chookiana*."

Renny gave him an affectionate shove. "Yes, but the difference between you and I is that I pretty much know I'm going to lose. It's the price I pay for unfortunately wanting to hang out with you guys."

Renny continued with the introductions, "And that's Dino Calvitto, slumlord hotelier." Calvitto wasn't too friendly. He shrugged without acknowledging me and walked off. He was a handsome man of maybe 60 with a head full of grey hair, but a sour disposition which made me happy not to shake his hand hello.

"Eh, he's complicated," Ned commented.

Dino shook his head while turning to Renny and returning to the group. "I have to remember to never get stuck passed out on lounge chairs with you. Snoring all night to wake the dead."

"Firstly, I didn't pass out. I went to bed in a comfortable lounge chair. Secondly… I don't snore."

It's not something he wanted me to know.

"That was you? I assumed the window rattler was Dino the slumlord." Ned turned to me. "There are plenty of bedrooms, but Breger's idiot cousin went in to use the bathroom and drunkenly locked all the doors to house. I could hear it through my window. Worst night's sleep of my life."

Dino looked happy once he could start making fun of someone. "Imagine sleeping outside with him. Waking me up every twenty minutes. You've got to get that nose of yours looked at, sailor."

"Later, you bunch of degenerates." Renny put his hand on my back and started leading me towards his boat, turning back just once. "And Calvitto, remember…it's just money." They had a good laugh and we were on our way. "I don't snore."

Those two missing hours. Renny could be accounted for by snoring louder than a Howler Monkey. Thanking god for sleep apnea as a viable alibi, I'd be allowed to enjoy this trip to its fullest.

He walked me down the dock to his boat, a swank Jenneau Prestige 30 monohull. Living down here was a crash course in boating. It was like LA in a way, where your car is a representation of you; taste, status, personality.

He helped me on the vessel, like all gentlemen do. I put my bag on a table behind the driver's seat and looked around at the boat. There was a cabin and a living space below.

I could get used to this.

"Poker night was one of my favorite parts of the month, but the next day is always one of the worst. Ned has the room service bring up Bloody Mary's and bacon and then we lie around in pain for half the day. Every month I say never again… well, it's easy to forget. It's a little notorious. One of the guy's wives refuses to let him gamble anymore. Don't ask me who - his wife completely forbids him from playing poker anymore. But he loves it. These nights have become so regrettable the next day. So we agreed to say he wasn't there. He told her he was going out all night with that guy, Crabby Paolo, on a slug research expedition. He's in on the cover up. It's getting a little complex"

All night slug research. Doesn't surprise me.
Sunday night cover up? Curious.

"Please?" I bat my eyebrows the best I could, hoping it looked coquettish and not like something was in my eye. "Just tell me who."

"Nope, nope, young lady. A secret is a secret."

"Bocas del Toro seems to be the world capital of secrets."

"Then all I can say is that you've never been to Turks & Caicos." He flashed me that winning smile.

"Is it always the same guys as this week?" More fluttering of the eyebrows.

"Detective LaGuardia is rubbing off on you, isn't he?"

"Harmless game, right?"

"Usually six or seven guys show up, but it's a rotating group of twelve or so." He scoured his mind for the usual gamblers. "I'll be honest. Detective McDonough on more than one occasion. That cop Romeo just once. Dr. Nolan usually – he loses more than anyone and can't particularly hold his liquor but he's fun to watch. Larry Breger. Breger's shady cousin. Geez, who else? Brain dead. Let's just move on to singing, cool?"

I'd try again later.

He grabbed a couple of bottles of water from the cooler and tossed me one. I wiped the condensation on my forehead and arms before taking a sip.

I don't know who I was kidding. As McDonough had once said, "If it looks like a fish and swims like a fish, it's a fish." The terminology was a little skewed but I got it. This boat trip was not a boat trip. It was a date. And I was getting shy.

"I think I brought enough for the next few hours. I've got pulled pork on coconut bread, a papaya salad with sweet peppers, and katuk greens. Champagne to celebrate after your water victory." He winked.

"It's a beautiful day, but I'm not sure I'll be going in. You might want to hold off on the champagne." I pulled my hair back and sat in my regular seat next to the captain. "I'm a little nervous."

"I've seen you. You're always a little nervous but Jazz has been coaxing you in one step at a time. You're so close, Lexie. You're ready to let go."

"I don't think you have any idea how uptight I am." I cringed. That didn't come out right.

He laughed. "Why did your parents never teach you to swim?"

"I think I ran away when we were at pools. And at summer camp I spent a lot of time in the nurse's office. Not exactly a daredevil." Saying it aloud sounded ridiculous.

"You're truly an original. Want to get going?" He cozied up in the driver's seat.

I couldn't forget to dig. "Before we go…I wanted to say… this must be hard for you, being out on the water without Jazz. Not that you were always on the same boat together, but I know how memories can hit you."

"They haven't." He turned and gave me a sad smile. "I'd been seeing much less of her. She'd withdrawn from me a little bit. Really just on Sundays like you.

"I guess I still don't believe it. Like I still think I'm going to see her next Sunday and go out like we always do. I've never lost a friend… unless you count this guy named Marzzy in college who went on a stupid surfing trip to the Sea of Cortez and never came back. They never found his body. It was like a legend, a legend at Cal State Long Beach. Everyone comforted themselves by thinking that he'd floated all the way down to Galapagos or something and was living like a king. You don't really understand mortality when you're nineteen, do you?"

"No, you don't."

"I just wish I had some idea of what happened. It keeps me up at night. "It's hard to believe that at the moment we were acting like idiots playing poker.

Is that an invitation to probe a little deeper?

He didn't want to talk about anything yet. Understandable. I could give him a little time. "Ok, Lexie, ready for me to rock your world?"

I want to say yes, but no.

I must have looked petrified because he clarified, "What music do you want to sing along terribly with me as we go?"

"Oh. The Cure's Head on the Door?"

"Your wish is my command."

It was an easy ride to Dolphin Bay, though we ruined the peace with our terrible voices shouting over the motor. I took in the beauty of the bay as we motored south. With a three-bottlenose dolphin escort for a good bit of the ride, we finally arrived at the reef and dropped anchor. There were a number of other party catamarans in the vicinity, a few outfits I was familiar with. The bay was surrounded by mangroves on three sides with palm trees along the far shore. As promised, the sea was calm and clear.

Renny took his shirt and shoes off and asked me, "Do you want me to put any of your stuff below so it doesn't get wet?"

No matter the state of your body, you have to get used to being seen in various stages of undress when you live in the Caribbean and hang out on boats. Your natural state was in a bathing suit, like various sized versions of Malibu Barbies.

Though he'd seen me in plenty of them, I was suddenly shy when I pulled my dress over my head and tossed it to him. He noticed the awkwardness and smiled in some kind of appreciation of my misplaced modesty.

While he was below, I scrambled to get into the tight wetsuit quickly. Most people didn't wear one to snorkel, but if I was going to actually do this, I was going to count on all the buoyancy I could get. Water wings too, if available.

Renny came up from below and quickly checked me out. "Cute. What do you say we get your hair wet today?" He had his fins and masks in hand ready for action.

"Do you mean in the water?"

"Just one more step is all you need, Lexie." My energy wasn't matching his enthusiasm and he could see that. "You don't have to do this. I'm not going to pressure you to do anything you don't want to."

I slowly looked around the large bay at the dozens of other swimmers submerged and looking at a batfish or what not. I'd been prepping for this forever and could easily identify anything I saw in that new world below. I glanced around with a level of jealousy at the ease that everyone else was enjoying.

"Jazz had said, 'It's such an easy slide.'"

"It is."

"Ok. I'm ready. I think that I'm ready. Maybe. I don't know." I crossed my arms and shifted my weight to my right side.

"Here. You're going to love this." He tossed me a life vest. "Your namesake."

Thank you, Avanti.

It seemed strange to be sitting here with Renny teaching me to snorkel, after my Sundays with Jazz. On the swimming deck, webbed feet dangling in the bay, listening to a speech about the basics of snorkeling that I knew by rote.

He tossed a foam surfboard in the water, with rings of rope hanging off. He took my hand in a reassuring way. "I rigged that up for you. We're doing this one step at a time. Just chill on the ladder like you always do, just up to your shoulders. If you feel like it, you can grab one of the ropes on the board. Then two if you want.

"I'll be there with you until you feel safe. When I can see that you are breathing the right way and enjoying what you are seeing, I'll tap you. That means I think you are ready to let go of the board and give it a shot on your own. You don't have to. But you can. And I'll be right there with you."

Almost in slow motion, I took one step, two steps, three steps down the ladder. The water was so warm, unlike when someone had tried to drown me during a rainstorm in April. I closed my eyes and pushed the fear out of my being the best I could. I reached out for the rope, tightly and securely affixed to the surfboard. And I slid.

Wow, was she right. "It's so beautiful down there," she had said. "See the reefs before they disappear." What a tragedy we were heading towards.

It was like going into the most fantastic dream. Dozens of species of fish. Brain coral. Feather stars. Skinny trumpet fish. Neptune himself would be in awe.

Renny tapped me on my shoulder. Could I? I could. One hand after the other let go. After about three seconds, a violent-looking fish charged toward me. Was it a barracuda? Enough for one day.

I grasped the surfboard, which Renny still held steady. We held on to opposite sides of the foam core, taking off our masks. "So? You did good, Lexie. You did great."

He had water dripping off his body. I was delirious. "Maybe one day in the future, I can live down there."

Delighted, I smiled deeply, ignoring the imprint of the mask around his welcoming face.

"You were spectacular." He pulled himself up and slightly over the board, taking my face in his hands and kissing me, slowly and perfectly.

I kept my eyes closed, savoring the moment. I smiled dreamily. Then I remembered that there were 12 meters of water below me. "I think we should get out of the water."

I reached over, grabbed the ladder, and moved to the swimming deck to take off my fins, like I'd watched everyone do over the months. Renny followed, sitting down next to me and kissing me once again. I took a deep breath with my eyes still on him, and said softly, a little regretfully, truthfully, "I am pretty sure I'm not ready for this yet. I'm sorry."

He propped himself up on his elbows, giving me a dreamy gaze.

"I respect that, Lexie. I promised to be a gentleman." He took my hand, kissed it and got up, walking towards the cabin.

What just happened?

And wasn't it great?

Let's just reel it in and heal a little bit more.

He came back up with a picnic basket, wearing the same t-shirt he'd arrived in. He tossed me a towel. I dried off, leaving my hair to dry in the sun. We put the damp towels down on the deck and lay there for a while, saying nothing, but basking in a bit of a daydream. We ate our lunch, and at the end he grabbed a chilled bottle of champagne and fine plastic champagne glasses out of the cooler. Everyone knows you can't have glass on a boat.

Despite what I said, I didn't want the moment to end, so we stayed on the towels, fingers touching fingers.

"What are you thinking about?" He turned to look at me.

I had to ruin the mood eventually. "Do you mind if I ask you a few questions about Jazz? I've come across some interesting stuff over the last few days and maybe you have an idea… I think you probably knew the true her better than anyone." My heart was beating on double time. I tapped my finger nervously on the side of my plush cream seat in anticipation.

His gaze seemed to be elsewhere, as if he was weighing the pros and cons of confiding in me. He turned to me and caught my eye for a long, intense moment. "Of course. Ask me anything."

I took my phone out to show him the pics I'd snapped of Jazz's envelope.

I passed over the phone and showed him the photo of Jazz and Hywel. "Have you ever seen this before?"

It only took him a second for him to say, "Yup."

"Both Hywel and Cam had a copy of the same picture anonymously delivered to them last week."

"That part I didn't know. She got that photo maybe a month ago?" He looked at the photo, enlarging it to see the lovers' faces. He sighed. "Look, she was happy. This is what I know. I knew about Hywel for several months. They absolutely made no sense as a couple, but something about them really worked. And they laughed.

"I'd say that for the past few years, Cam and Jazz have been together, but not together. When she was with Hywel, though, I could see that he was filling something in her that had been absent for a long time. And you never know how someone really is until they're behind closed doors. To me, Hywel is just a goofy surfer with a third rate hotel."

"Hey, take it easy. I work there. It's not third rate."

"Dangerous games, you know? And she was being blackmailed. That's what the photo was about. She never told me who it was, but they were threatening to expose the affair to her husband if she didn't hand over a big chunk of cash. You've seen us bickering on her catamaran lately. She was so frustrated with me. Snapping. Probably part of the reason she was distancing herself from me. You know, people think

Cam's the one with the cash, but she's got plenty and then some. Do you know about the family's chocolate plantations?"

Greed.

But he's off the hook, right?

"Yes."

"I told her just to hand over the cash and be done with it. Get rid of whoever was shaking her down. Why wouldn't she tell me who? Not that she didn't lose sleep over it. Her stupid delusion was that she was going to stand up to this person, say no to handing over the cash, tell Cam about the pic herself, and most likely leave her husband. You saw him Tuesday night at their house – an uncontrollable temper. The person was only asking for a quarter of a million. A stretch for the rest of us mere mortals, but not for Jazz."

I could eek out ten years of sustenance with that.

Don't say that out loud. Lloyd will have you on a list of suspects before you can say 'drunk monkey.'

I couldn't help looking at him in a bit of a first kiss fuzziness, but I tried to get back to the serious business. "I know that you talked to Detective LaGuardia on Monday, but did you tell him about the blackmail?" We all were running around grasping at straws, and knowledge of blackmail sure could have sent us in the right direction. Sent the police in the right direction.

I'm not part of this investigation, you see.

Who are you kidding, Lexie? Get to it.

"No." He looked at me, pursing his lips, embarrassed. "I'm working up to telling you, ok?"

"Ok." I nodded my head. "She really was a proud woman."

"Too proud for her own good." He didn't wait for an answer and turned the ignition key.

Was I going to lose his candidness if we moved on? On

shaky ground, I stood and moved a little closer to him, talking over the motor. "Before we go, can I ask you about Santo Amaro?"

He turned off the boat and took off his Ray-Ban Wayfarers, rubbing his eyes. "You know about Santo Amaro?"

"A little. Does it exist?" We were getting into Indiana Jones territory now. I'd be lying if I said that it wasn't a little thrilling.

"Yes. I'm pretty sure. I didn't think it did for a long time. Okay, I never believed it was there 100 percent. She said that she'd been fascinated by it since she was a kid. I think that's probably why she went into marine biology.

"Jazz originally told me the story over twenty years ago. She was going to find it and get famous. Over the years, she'd get obsessed with it for a while. Then she'd abandon it for years to get back to her other business. Then she'd get reinvigorated.

"She didn't care about the fame anymore, and even less about money. In fact, she was very well versed on the legal aspects of maritime salvage. She even attended UNESCO's Convention on the Protection of Underwater Cultural Heritage. I can see that I'm boring you with that one. She wanted to find it and lay some claim to it with the Smithsonian Research station. Research, not treasure salvage.

"She never was completely open with anyone about the full details she'd charted, but there were enough people who knew about her story. Bella, Cam, some of the guys you've met on Sundays, Hywel I'll assume. When she was obsessed, she was completely obsessed, so we knew we thought she was close. We were going out more often until… until we weren't. She's picked this up and dropped it so many times over the years that I wondered if she'd just gone off it."

I scrolled through the pics on my phone and passed him over the reef map and the bathymetric maps. "Why would she pass a note to someone saying, '*Cuidado con las curvas peligrosas. Adios, a Santo Amaro*.'?" Beware of dangerous curves. Goodbye..."

"Goodbye, Santo Amaro," he almost whispered. "Who was the note to?"

"Hywel. She had me give it to him on Sunday after our trip."

"It means someone was on to her. And maybe she actually found it. And it means that Hywel might know where it is. It means to stay away."

"He said it was a private joke when I asked him on Sunday."

"Some kind of joke... what does he say now?"

I had to believe Hywel, but my faith was getting shook to the core. I didn't even want to say it out loud. "I don't know. He's kind of... disappeared." Ten million motives.

"You know him. You don't think..."

"I don't." He shook his head. "But... I have to digest all this."

"You looked shocked when I mentioned the boat. I'm guessing you didn't tell LaGuardia about it, but it seems pretty important. Blackmail could mean everything."

"I'm not proud of what I'm going to tell you. Look... things work a little differently down here. I didn't say anything to the police because I was scared. Like I said, I wasn't the only person who knew about Santo Amaro. She used to talk to Cam about it, and I think all he saw was dollar bills, despite what he said. That's why he wanted to believe. She'd stopped talking about it to anyone. His business wasn't doing well, and he wanted that treasure. Their finances had always stayed separate and he knew about leaving her fortune to the Smithsonian. Have you heard about his temper?"

I thought back to Migs shaking in his flip-flops. "Have you heard about his temper? I've heard a little bit about his anger issues, but that maybe it's more bark than bite. Could that be true?" Flashback to him socking his friend in the face. Maybe more bite.

"Yes, but maybe it's more bark than bite."

"He can be pretty terrifying. A year ago Jazz and I were heading out a lot more. He was paranoid. He started joking with me that she and I were treasure hunters, and that if I knew where the Santo Amaro was, me and this 'used crap heap of a boat' would be found at the bottom of Grandma's Garden. I froze. Then he'd pat me on the back and say, 'Joking!' I don't think it was a joke. I never would have thought her death had anything to do with stupid Santo Amaro."

"Do you think Cam could have done it?"

"I can't imagine anyone I know being able to kill someone, but someone has, so they have... I should have said something."

I put my hand on his. "You need to talk to LaGuardia about this."

"I will. I promise I will."

He got to change the subject with the beginning of the sunset. For as long as it lasted, we could be silent. At one point he refilled the champagne glasses. After pouring, he held up his glass to mine. "To Jazz."

For sure. "To Jazz."

"She did good."

Indeed she did.

Surely ruining the moment, I got back to the story.

20

THE END OF THE WORLD

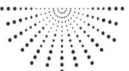

(AIN'T NO PARTY LIKE A DAISY PARTY)

hen we docked in Bocas Town, I'd agreed to a goodnight drink at Tango Vista, and though I may have been playing with fire, it sounded like a perfect end to a perfect day.

We had low alcohol Aperol Spritzes, thankfully not lowering my inhibitions. I insisted on paying for the drinks as a thank you. Rustling through my bag, I found that I'd forgotten something in my swoon: Daisy's Tickets to the End of the World. If that wasn't foreboding, I don't know what was.

Did I trust him enough to ask him along?

Did I trust yours truly enough to ask him along?

"Semi-strange question." I raised my eyebrows (or I tried, since everyone else seemed so good at it) and bit the side of my lip. "I told you how Crazy Daisy is still a suspect. She's been flitting all over the islands, one step ahead of LaGuardia. I had the displeasure of running into her on the top of the hill between Old Bank and Wizard Beach. Does a place called Cuckoo Cloud really exist?" It was totally possible she lured me in another direction.

"I haven't heard of it."

I'm losing my mind.

"Well, my next stop tonight is The End of the World. She gave me two free tickets to her club night tonight. Care to come with me and poke around?"

He looked pleased, even though he might be about to confront a murderer. "You sure?"

It was 8 p.m. when we finished our drinks and walked the short path to the quick ferry to Carenaro Island. My level of adrenaline was crazy high. Knowing that I might be walking into fatal danger with walking next to a guy who I'd just shared a spectacular kiss with, had my mind spinning at double time. "This is a day that I will never forget."

"You and me, Lexie. You and me." He took my hand and we walked the rest of the like that. We were just about to get on the ferry when he stopped me. "I have no intention of going against your wishes, but can we just pretend for a night? That we're... something. I know that sounds strange, but I'll get you in your carriage to get home before midnight with your virtue intact." He tenderly tucked my hair behind my ear.

Just one night.

His hand still holding mine, I drew him close and kissed him slowly and intimately, still feeling my lips tingle as we parted. "Ok, for tonight."

Before we docked on Carenero, we could hear the music pumping from any number of clubs. The cacophony was killing me, putting my nerves on high alert. It was such a small island compared to Isla Colon, barely a mile tip to tip. It was clubs and hostels and third-rate surf camps known for their beginner's waves. Home to the Pickled Parrot, which should tell you something.

Her club was the biggest and most notorious on the island, probably the only place in the whole province with a neon sign. Some of the letters had burned out, giving the impression that the joint was called, 'End Of he old."

It was a huge building that looked like it should be condemned. It resembled a sniper's tower, but the real party was further out on the dock with swings, cozy dark corners, and fire eater,.

Had LaGuardia found her before I did? This was my last chance to be a fly on the wall. He'd find her here eventually.

"Well, we're here," I said, hoping I'd brought my antibacterial wipes.

He slyly smiled. "Who says I don't take you to the best places?"

The line was short and filled with very fit Generation Z's handing over relatively big bucks for drinks. The guys at the door were large, bald, and not particularly friendly when I handed over the passes. One said to the other, "Daisy doesn't give these out very often. VIP section to the left and up to the stairs next to the DJs. I'll show you – it's easy to get lost in this place. And that's intentional."

"Is she here?" I looked around through the chaos as best I could.

"Nope. Haven't seen her. At all."

Hmmmmm.

We followed him through a sea of half-naked, drunk, twenty-somethings. How could ten years younger make such a difference? Granted, I was never much of a bikini, get-sloshed wild girl, but even so.

When we reached the VIP section, it wasn't the life of the

party. A few bored older men with young women in skimpy clothes sat around, not talking but slowly dancing in their seats to the latest club music. However, it gave us a great view, looking down on the rest of the party, party, party. Some dancing, some falling, some selfies, and some people doing flips off abandoned lifeguard stands and into the dark water.

The bouncer started walking away, then turned around. "House rules." He pulled out one of Daisy's fake tattoos. "Turn around and show me your booty."

What kind of insanity was this? I grew slightly angry. "I'm a VIP, remember? I'll take it on my arm, please."

He looked annoyed, but acquiesced, slapping the tattoo on my upper arm, then walking away. "Have fun," he muttered.

I examined the vampiric angel on my right arm, not enjoying it. But what are you going to do?

Renny checked it out. "Not what I'd pick for you, but it actually doesn't look bad."

We walked over to the bar, where the two bartenders were dancing in synchronicity. I spoke loudly over the bar, "Two Bitches on Wheels, please." I handed over my drink coupons. Renny looked surprised at my order. "It was recommended. Good luck to both of us."

We toasted with our plastic cups. Renny shrugged. "Well, here's to whatever this is?" He coughed on it. "Whatever it is... it's terrible."

Daisy was nowhere in sight. I started asking anyone who looked like they might work there. With their terrible poker faces, they looked like they had a clue but weren't going to share it. I went back up to the bar, asking one of the bartenders.

He looked very annoyed. "Like I said, *no lo se*."

I didn't break his gaze when he shot me a mean stare. "Listen, I've got a message to give to her…from Hywel. Do you think she's going to be happy if she doesn't get word of that?"

He's going to think I'm lying.

Because I am lying.

And not very good at it.

He scanned the room, looking at the few Very Important People and the club staff coming to and fro. This guy couldn't crack a smile if he wanted to. "Maybe she'll show up at 11 or so. I don't know. Haven't seen her."

"Do you think I've got hours to wait around to hope that I see her?" I didn't like standing up to this guy. I could imagine him sucker punching me just like Cam did his friend from Boca Raton the other night.

"Whoever you are, you owe me. And you didn't hear it from me." He pointed behind the bar. "Go past the kegs, take a right, then she's got an office two doors down on the right."

"And who are you to Daisy?"

"No one of consequence." Half way through his sentence he abandoned me to serve a couple at the other end of the bar. It was starting to get more crowded. It made sense – the club was for a late night crowd, not the early bird special which is Lexie Marino.

Renny had been leaning against the wall, something that I didn't think I'd ever want to touch. He'd abandoned his drink and had his hands in the pockets of his shorts.

I wanted to kiss him so badly that it physically hurt. But I didn't. There'd be time for that another day. Maybe. Maybe is dangerous business. Maybe can be torture.

Another kiss might never come.

Just enjoy tonight.

"She's got an office behind the bar. Ready?" I went through the door that no-one-of-consequence had offered up and into a shambles of a back room mess. No rhyme or reason, with boxes and booze all over the place. Completely a fire hazard. Two bare bulbs hung from the ceiling, slightly swaying along with the bass line of the music. I turned on the flashlight feature on my phone, making the room seem even more dirty and creepy. Please no banana spiders.

"I am not sure he knew his right from his left." I frowned, seeing four doors on the left and none on the right. "I guess we just try them all?"

The first was locked, and I immediately gave up trying after I pulled my hand back covered in some sticky substance. The second was locked as well, and I began to think that the bartender had sent me here to get me out of his bar. Or to set me up by locking me in this scene from a horror movie.

As the old saying goes, third time's a charm. Or is it bad things come in threes? Or good things? No matter, the door-knob turned and we were in.

"*Que mierda!?*" Daisy shouted from under the blue light-bulbs illuminating the small funky office.

"Oh my god," I exclaimed. Sometimes you can't un-see a thing. All I will say is that Little Miss Blondes-have-more-fun was *in flagrante delicto* with a man who was most definitely not Hywel. My phone flashlight paralyzing the deer in headlights, and I did what came naturally. I took a picture.

Slamming the door behind me, I put my hand to my heart. "That was not what I expected to see."

Renny started laughing, but caught himself. "I'm sorry. It was just...hilariously disturbing."

From the other side of the door, I could hear Daisy

screaming in Spanish, and objects unknown crashing around the room. My fight or flight gene kicked in, and that gene was definitely telling me to run, but I froze and waited. I had come here to confront her, so against every bone in my body I stood firm, waiting for the door to open and to face the fury I'd unleashed. I put my phone in my bag, trying to forget that this woman was a tiny kung-fu master who could hypothetically crush my windpipe with the flick of her too long fingernail.

The door flew open, and Daisy bounded out looking frazzled and angry.. She was in bare feet and a little yellow dress with a pattern of delicate purple flowers. I had no idea that short hair could get so rumpled. "What are you doing back here? Who sent you back here?"

A handsome and buff man with no hair and a goatee emerged, and she pushed him away in the direction of the bar. "Get going now. I don't want to see you. Ever."

He was confused but scurried away. She looked me up and down, taking in both me and the situation. She put her hand on her hips and pointed at the man who was currently making his way back into The End of the World. "That's not what it looks like. So why don't you delete that picture? You really don't want to make an enemy of me." She snapped her fingers in my face three times.

Even with Renny by my side I felt we were no match for Daisy, but she finally really had something to lose. "It doesn't matter if I delete it or not. It's already synched up with the cloud." That hypothetically would be true if I could regularly get service. "Detective LaGuardia will most obviously pick it up and show it around trying to find you. You know he's out looking for you."

"Yeah, good luck with that one." Daisy was whatever the island version of street-smart was. She was intelligent, a grifter, and a huge trouble maker. She was calculating how to get out of this mess. She motioned towards Renny. "I know that guy's face. What is he? Your boyfriend? Good lips."

My face flushed, which betrayed something inside me. "He worked with Jazz."

"Does he talk or is he just your sweet delicious?"

"Yes. He speaks two languages just like you."

Not proving my point Renny crossed his arms, staring her down.

"About this sitch… you deffo did not see what you…" She put on that big beautiful saccharine sweet smile of hers.

"It doesn't matter what I think I saw, but I'd be interested to see what Hywel's opinion on the photo would be." The truth was that a mourning Hywel would probably be pleased at seeing the pic, feeling he was finally free. I felt kind of gross pretending that he would be bothered at all.

If it was physically possible to blow steam out of your ears before you were about to blow your lid, Daisy's stare and expression said it all. "What is this? A shakedown?"

I shook my head and shrugged. "I wouldn't know how to shake someone down if I tried. I want you to be honest about you and Jazz and the conversation you had on Saturday night."

She knew she was stuck between a rock and a hard place. She and Hywel were broken up – she could do what she wanted when he wasn't around, but he was the definite aim of her arrow. Yesterday she had told me about her ten commandments, and she had said, 'Boils down to this…thou shall stay away from my man.'

"So are you saying that if we talk now, and I pony up this info, that Hywel doesn't know about this picture?" She puffed out her cheeks, making her look like the very young woman she was. Just a very dangerous girl with a broken heart.

"As long as you tell me the truth."

"Fine, but not here. This room looks like a crime scene. Come on." She quickly walked through the seedily lit hallway back towards the club. She stopped before she got to the door back to the bar. She put her hand on her heart, took three deep breaths, and literally shook her vulnerability off. She ran her hands through her very blond hair and turned to me. "May I borrow some lipstick?"

Of all the strange things that had happened over the past few days, that was somehow the most surreal. In hopes of a smooth conversation I dug into my purse and passed her a shade of plum that was much subtler than her normal color. "Do I look okay?"

The best way to deal with crazy is to just go along with it. "Just smashing."

She put on her boss façade and walked confidently into the bar, after peeking out to see if it was safe to come out of her bunker. She turned to the bartender-of-no-consequence. "Can you bring three Bitches on Wheels to suite B?"

The club was like a maze, up some stairs, down some other stairs, and finally to a small room with slightly too-old rattan furniture. It was like being in in a box in the balcony at a Broadway theatre (what can I say? You can take the girl out of Broadway, but you can't take the Broadway out of the girl).

"Sometimes people need privacy. It is the End of the World after all." She leaned over the rail to take in her Bacchanalia.

Renny finally showed his vocal cords, his annoyance singing through. "Daisy. The quicker you talk to us, the quicker we're out of here. This is your chance to come clean, and I don't imagine that you're going to get any decent offer from the police."

"Two conditions: you don't tell Hywel about what you think you saw and you delete that photo off your phone and then you invite me over to your house and delete it off the cloud and your computer. I see zilch reason I should trust you. That was all kinds of shady."

The door opened and the waitress put down the drinks. "Here's your three Bitches."

Sigh.

"I've got another photo for you though." I searched for what had perplexed us all from the start. I passed her the phone, and she looked at the picture. She kept her anger in check, which shocked me. She was familiar with the photo.

I snatched the phone back, in case she decided to drop it in one of the cringe worthy drinks. "What were you and Jazz really arguing about on Saturday night? I'd put money you didn't find out about their love affair through the little-bird-told-me situation you told me about. You didn't react at all when I showed you that photo."

Renny took a sip of his toxic drink, with a grimace again. "Geez is that grim." He shook his head quickly, wanting to get the taste out of his mouth and his memory. "What's more important to you? Losing Hywel forever or telling us what you know."

She was not used to having her head on the chopping block. "You're right. Despite what you just *think* you saw, getting Hywel back is all I want. I'm not a nut job. Maybe I was lurking a few times or so when he was giving Jazz surfing lessons. I wanted to chuck up when I saw the way he was looking at her. Because I knew she was just toying with him." She slammed half of her Bitch on Wheels, forgetting how horrible it was and cringing the same way Renny had.

"You told me it was rancid," I said, reminding her of our nice but bizarre conversation at the surreal Cloud Cuckoo. "What do you have to do with that photo?"

She banged her fist on the table. "Why is this my life?! Fine. Fine. I paid one of my bouncers fistfuls of cash to start following her. It was all mostly by boats, so I had to fork over more cash to get someone to take him out. I wanted 100 percent proof. And on that first Sunday after I paid the *pendejo*, he comes back with a stack full of photos of them on a boat headed south. And the following Sunday he found that little hideaway near Paunch where they were doing whatever to each other. Mugging me off. When I knew everything, when I knew about her little bait and switch going to her sister's house before she'd sneak out like a little sneaker, I knew what I had to do.

"The next Sunday I waited for her at like 5 a.m. at the marina where she keeps her boats. I snuck down to her favorite boat I know she uses those mornings. When she was alone and out far enough on the water that no one could see from shore, I came up on deck, I scared the kitty cat crackers out of her. I showed her the photos, it's obvious what I did next. I let her know that if she didn't want me to go to her fat bastard of a husband with the pics, she'd better break it off with Hywel. I gave her a month to pie him off."

"And she didn't reach your deadline." Renny brushed some odd crumbs off the seat he was sitting on. A man after my own heart.

I was being as patient as I could. She'd done something horrid, but how horrid? Was it a coincidence that they had a stand-off on Saturday and Jazz was murdered in the wee hours of Monday morning? "Tell us about Saturday night."

"It wasn't anything heinous really. Or so I thought. At the beginning of last week I had the picture delivered to both

Hywel and Cam. It was going to blow up in her face like it or not. It would ruin her marriage, and when I first went to her it seemed that she absolutely didn't want that to happen. And I've heard that Cam can make some pretty terrifying threats. I stay far away from him, not like that's hard. He's not my kind of people. And sending it to Hywel? I know you've seen how he literally runs away from any conflict."

That I had.

Though hard as stone, Daisy started to cry. I couldn't hug her, but I could hold her hand. We needed this story to be over. "So Saturday night, Jazz shows up at the club. My turf. It's not supposed to go that way. We smack a tattoo on her right mediocre buttock and have it out in this room. She told me that she'd come to understand recently that she was ready to leave Cam. She'd subconsciously been waiting to leave him for a very long time. She was done with me and Hywel was done with me. She'd been confronted with the photo by Cam, but Hywel hadn't mentioned it to her." Her crying eyes turned mean again. "Still not sorry she's gone. Rest not in peace."

Renny sat, mouth agape. "You're a horrible woman."

Daisy wasn't offended. She smiled. "Don't I know it…"

"I'm going to ask you one last question; the same one I asked you the other day, but I want you to answer honestly. Where were you between 2 and 6 a.m. on Monday morning?"

"What! You think I killed her? I may be a Bitch on Wheels, but I'm not a murderer. And I can tell you exactly where I was! Whaaaaaaaay down south on Popa Island from Sunday at sundown until we woke up somewhere on a beach Monday afternoon. You're a little too prudish to hear this, but there's a crazy spiritual dude who's known as the Incan Pharmacist of the Eclipse Rave. You can see how rare an event it is since you have to wait for an eclipse. We dilute red frog poison to ingest for enlightenment. I'm sure you'd love it…" She gave me a look of pure sarcasm. She took out her phone and queued up the video highlights. "There's a private video. You need a code to watch it. Here. You can see the time stamp. And I can put you in touch with a dozen people who were there."

"I don't recall there being an eclipse on Sunday night." Renny took her phone.

"Hey, I don't make the rules." She stuck her tongue out. This gal was an enigma.

He turned away from the phone, shaking his head in disbelief. "Lexie, you aren't going to want to see this. Trust me."

I stared her down. For once I felt my height was an asset. "No, but LaGuardia is going to see it."

And probably Lloyd wouldn't mind.

I have to think about the company I keep.

She tried to look defiant, but couldn't.

I continued, "Write down the web address and the pass-code, but I would go and show it to the detective yourself if I were you. You're in enough trouble as it is. Blackmail is a crime you know." I thought it best to not mention that she could be found guilty of contributing to Jazz's murder. But I had turned the tables. "And if you don't show up by ten, that photo of what I definitely saw happening is going straight to Hywel."

If he's okay…if he's not in trouble…or dead…or responsible for what happened. My heart sunk when I realized that Hywel was now the only suspect without an alibi for those early hours of Monday morning.

She shrugged and got up, ready to leave the room. Her

last words to me were, "You're more badass than I assumed. Big ups to you, tall girl."

I turned around, almost forgetting a crucial question. "What does Santo Amaro mean to you?"

"Nothing. Why? What is he? The patron saint of cheaters?" She uttered a sound of disgust.

"Nothing of consequence," I said, repeating the bartender's phrase.

With that we walked away.

LEAVING The End of the World brought on an enormous sigh of relief. The club was now packed with stumbling drunk folk. Well, I guess there's something for everyone.

There was a beautiful crescent moon in the clear sky full of twinkling stars. Nervously, I did something that was completely uncharacteristic of me: I reached out and took Renny's hand in mine. "Thank you for a great non-date. Considering the circumstances."

We walked towards the docks with waiting water taxis. Without stopping or looking at me he said, "There's a little time until your carriage turns into a pumpkin. Care for a night cap?"

I simply nodded and we walked back over to Tango Vista. It wasn't too crowded and we were able to get a nice table on the water. We ordered two glasses of pinot grigio, but they were hardly touched between our conversation and short, sweet kisses.

Not the time or place.

I took his hand and looked at his watch, which proclaimed the inevitable time of 11:30. "Walk me to the water taxi?"

The range of emotions I'd felt that night was more intense than I'd ever experienced in my life. There was nothing to do except say goodnight. Before I stepped into the water taxi, I nervously said, "One goodnight kiss." It was sweet and sad and wonderful.

And then Cinderella was on her way home.

DAY FIVE

21

BEYOND HERE THERE BE DRAGONS

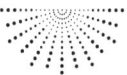

To be honest, I don't know if I slept at all. Did I dream I was awake, trying to put it all together? Was I tossing and turning, too ramped up to close my eyes, scared of who might be showing up at my door? No sharks, no Cam, no Renny to save the day.

As usual, I woke up a little clammy in last night's tank top and put my hair in a top bun. As if the gods were eager to push me into another very long day, I was up at daybreak.

Two large cups of Dunkin Donuts coffee and a cold shower (cry, cry, cry) would be the next move of the day. I sighed when looking at the 23 coconuts I had sitting in the corner of the kitchen. Maybe I could barter with my favorite smoothie guy in hope of a couple freebies.

And like the rest of the world, before even brewing my coffee, I looked at my phone. Email full of junk, so I headed for Facebook, showing a few messages and a couple of notifications.

Ugh. An all caps email from my dramatic mother asking why oh why I had forsaken her by not posting promised daily pictures on my feed. In this case, preoccupied didn't begin to explain it. Her use of the word forsaken was probably a bit of an exaggeration, but that was Mrs. Colleen Marino.

I scrolled through the recent pictures on my phone that I hadn't posted. Biometric maps and photographs of fatal lovers wouldn't entirely be appropriate for the general public. I desperately wanted to delete the offending photo of Daisy in her club, but knew I had to keep it for just a little bit. I scrolled back further, posting a couple of surfing pics from last week. I captioned it, "Another perfect week in paradise."

A few minutes later, another notification popped up, and I clicked on it right away, gobsmacked.

'Hywel Lange has reacted to your photo.' What the flying ferret!

I clicked back to the post on my feed as soon as was humanly possible, and his like was gone as if it was never there at all.

I was livid. I was glad he was alive but furious that he didn't let me know this fact. He wasn't being kept captive either, as I doubted some nefarious killer would give him access to Facebook. I got it. He had fled – not because he was guilty, but out of fear.

LaGuardia had seen him on Tuesday afternoon, less than 48-hours earlier. How far could my surfer have gotten? There was a province-wide warning to look out for him. His picture was plastered all over the airports and the ferry ports. His name wasn't on any flight itinerary, but besides that there just weren't enough cops to keep an eye on every marina, dock, and beach in the area.

He wasn't at Wizard Beach, and not at Bluff Beach. Where would that scared man run to? Daisy had said something about a love nest near Paunch beach. Hywel had also mentioned somewhere he cooked for Jazz.

Where oh where?

Too much information from the past four days was running through my head, but he had not mentioned Paunch Beach to me.

Playa Escondida. On Tuesday Hywel had told me about the pad that his friend Jake owned and abandoned, a.k.a. barbeque love nest. It was between Paunch and Bluff, and a small beach ten minutes from each. Daisy could have easily mistaken one for the other.

I grabbed the first t-shirt and cutoff jeans I could get my hands on. Sneakers in case I had to run, which was a distinct possibility.

I jumped into Lady Luck, remembering my fully charged bluetooth speaker. I grabbed the first t-shirt in my dresser, which said: 'Sloth Running Team: We'll Get There When We Get There.' There was an illustration of an adorable three-toed Bradypus sloth, smiling and hanging from a tree.

Hywel wouldn't be going out for his early morning surf unless he was a complete moron, but he had accidentally liked my photo, so I couldn't rule it out. Like I'd said to LaGuardia, he ran from trouble, didn't search it out. Jazz was leaving Cam to be with him. That's no motive. But $10 million in sunken treasure is quite the incentive, especially if your girlfriend plans to give it to the Smithsonian instead of sharing it with you.

Daisy was running around the rainforest with the Incan Eclipse Master. Cam had been on an overnight expedition only returning around noon. And Renny had been at an all-night drunken poker game. Snoring. That's a shame.

Two out of three: lust and greed. Please, no.

Music? I put on the Work-Out playlist (that I've used

twice in my lifetime – don't judge!) to encourage enhanced driving speed and was on my way, ending up driving just as fast as would be safe. I had no death wish.

Playa Escondida was not a large beach. As far as I remembered, it was only populated by a couple of surf lodges, one luxury (by I don't know whose standards) boutique hotel, and a handful of homes close to the beach, nestled in the rainforest.

I pulled over in front of the short path to the semi-luxe boutique hotel, *Casa Amor.* How could a fancy hotel be called the House of Love? Oh well. The islands were full of misnomers, which was just another thing I loved about it.

I took my shoes off and stuck them in my bag. Then I mussed up my hair, trying to look as surfery as possible. Sunglasses added to the slightly hungover surf-bum façade of someone who just might be a friend of Jake.

Aiming for luxury, the hotel had a well-dressed gentleman sitting behind a desk. He looked me up and down. "Can I help you?"

How bad at role-play was I? "Yeah, dude. Do you know a bro named Jake who lives right around here? I was supposed to crash at his pad, but I so do not remember where he lives. What a ding-a-ling, right?"

He was a young guy, kind of a beach version of a hipster. He scratched his goatee. "Yeah, I know Jake. But how do you know Jake?"

Good question. "Yeah, I shared a house with Hywel in La Jolla in Cali, and came to surf here for a couple of weeks. You know, the guy who owns Grito Mono up the road? Anyway, total bummer, the dude only has a tiny one-bedroom cottage, so Jake's been super rad about letting me crash. Totally cool. But I had a wicked long night and couldn't find this place. I had no idea where to sleep besides this beach. I'd like a bed and a shower. I was bitten by chitras. I've got a key, but I just don't know for where." I held up my own house key.

I doubted that my surfer talk was current at all, and I had no bug bites, but it was the best I could do.

The hipster concierge deemed my story to be the truth. "Walk about two minutes north. If you look to the left, there's a wooden planked pathway going up the hill. There are four cabins, I think. Jake's the second to the right. Tell him that Manny says hello."

"Totes," I said, giving him a wink as I walked out the door.

After reaching the path, I put my sneakers on and quietly made my way to the cabins. Second on the left; a cozy little bungalow which was bigger than Hywel's with a huge deck. I could see why Hywel would have liked to cook for Jazz there. That was a somber thought.

He wasn't very good at playing hide and seek. I peered through the window and spied him, shirtless, sitting in front of the TV with a PlayStation 4.

This isn't a murderer. This is a sixteen-year-old who never grew up.

I knocked on the window, making Hywel jump off the couch and drop his controller. The surprise on his face was epic. He didn't move at all, just stared at me.

"Come on, Hywel! I'm looking right at you. I want to help you. Let me in." I banged on the window again. We were looking at each other eye to eye, and he had no surfboard to jump on to run away. And I had sneakers on.

He let me in, closing the door quickly and locking it immediately. Sitting back down on the couch, he looked up at me like a school kid sent to the principal's office. "Hey, Lexie."

"Don't 'Hey, Lexie' me. Do you know how much trouble

you're in?" The place was clean and comfortable. Lush enough for Jazz. Plush furniture, framed 1950's movie posters on the wall, and elegant doors with paneled glass leading out to a massive deck with a luxury grill, where Hywel must have cooked his legendary meals for Jazz. Was he a great cook, or was Jazz, full of love, just eating his mediocre offerings of adoration? This place, just like Hywel's, was a huge contradiction to what I had thought it would be.

When did surfers become such great interior decorators?

"Do you want a coffee?" He got up and trudged to the kitchen.

"Are you not aware that I'm trying to have an serious conversation with you?" I followed him, where he started fiddling with a coffee maker.

"I know. I just need a coffee. I haven't really slept for days." He sat down on a stool in the island kitchen. "How did you find me, anyway? Does anyone know you're here?"

On the off chance that he was the murderer, I didn't think it was wise to tell him that I was there solo, of my own volition. "Yes, Jazz's friend, Renny. And I will have a coffee. I didn't sleep last night either."

I sat next to him, settling in for what I hoped would not be another case of him messing me around. "I'll give you a hint, Hywel. If you are ever on the run again, don't press Like on my Facebook page."

"Could you, like, triangulate where I was or something?"

"No. You told me about this place a couple of days ago. I listen, you know. Just tell me the truth. If you do, I can help you. As it is, when the police track you down, you're suspect number one."

His eyes were brimming with tears. "I was in love with Jazz. She inspired me to be better. To excel. She saw something in me that I never did. Do you think that I don't know how bad it looks that sleeping alone was my alibi and that I lied to the police left and right about our relationship? And sharks? I know how idiotic it was for me to hide out here...you don't need to tell me. I was an idiot that thought that if I ran away for a little while they'd figure out who killed Jazz and I could come back. I was so depressed about it, I just wanted to be alone and cry. But you found me.

"What did you do Sunday night into Monday morning?"

"I swear, Lexie, I told the truth on that one. She generally showed up here around 8 p.m. I'd bought steaks, wine and mangoes, and everything she loved. She was late. I waited. We never texted or emailed because of...you know, Cam. I got stupid and drank the two bottles of wine, fell asleep, and woke up. Alone. Super sad. Super sad. Went out for my break of dawn surf, and there she was... I couldn't leave her out by those palms. Like, I didn't know what to do. I don't know how to live without her." He turned back to the coffee machine, rather than allow me to see him cry.

I felt horrible. "Did you know that Daisy was blackmailing her? That she was going to go to Cam?"

"No."

"Or that Cam got the same picture that you got last week? And that Daisy is the one who had it taken."

"Daisy? That evil little... I was going to show Jazz the photo when she came over Sunday, but... I had no idea where the picture came from. I was just waiting. But... Daisy? She killed Jazz?"

"No, maybe, I don't think so. She was at an all-night rave on a different island. But I think you are going to know something that will help the police put this to bed."

He poured two cups of coffee, then pounded his fists on the counter. He took a deep breath to compose himself, not turning to me when he said, "We're out of milk and sugar. You'll have to take it black."

He brought the hot drinks to the table, giving me a teaspoon for absolutely no reason. "So, what now?"

I looked at his bare feet. If he ran now, he wouldn't get too far. "I need to take you to see LaGuardia. Not at the police station. I'm meeting him this morning at Lloyd's company, ANANKE. It will be comfortable for you there. There won't be any other cops."

Just a high-security building that you couldn't get out of if Lloyd didn't want you to.

He simply pouted, drinking his black coffee.

"Hywel, do you know how many cops have been running around trying to track you down, instead of concentrating on the real murderer?"

"I never thought about it like that."

I spent the next ten minutes convincing him that he was going to a safe place. I did most of the talking. Hywel just nodded from time to time. "So, are you ready to go?"

He nodded for quite a long time before saying, "Yes. I'll follow you in my car."

"Oh no, you won't. I'm driving." I texted LaGuardia to let him know that I was bringing Hywel to him at ANANKE, hoping that service was good enough that it went through. "We're bringing this to an end today."

Hywel had beaten me in the competition for the most ridiculous t-shirt of the day. His was a picture of a surfing cat with the words, 'Schrödinger's Cat Is Alive And Well And Living In Hanalei Bay.' Maybe he was. The shirt looked like it was the only clean thing Hywel had left to wear.

I opened the door to Lady Luck, and watched him slowly get into the car. I'd never wished I had handcuffs in my possession before, but if anyone I knew was going to do a runner, it would be Hywel. He seemed to have no fore-thought, wearing only flip-flops and forgetting his sunglasses.

Still, every time I slowed down or stopped, I'd keep an eye on him and watch if his hand was getting closer to the door. He stared straight ahead down the Paved Road, his mind elsewhere, listening to my overly empowering gym mix.

We pulled into the driveway behind the two SUV's I'd been expecting: LaGuardia's official one and Lloyd's Land Cruiser. Almost forty years younger than mine, it was probably the nicest car on the island.

ANANKE was a place that I'd be afraid to go into if I didn't work there. It was The Dark Place owned by the Prince of Darkness. Hywel reluctantly got out of the car. "This is the place that's supposed to be comforting? It looks a little on the diabolical side."

Today it seemed particularly foreboding. It had hardly rained in almost a month, and this was an island whose middle name could be 'Humidity.' Rain was overdue. It was hurricane season in the Caribbean, but with Panama being just nine degrees latitude, it was too far south to suffer hurricanes. It was one of the reasons Americans loved to retire there. Still, thunderstorms would come soon.

"Ready, friend?" I asked Hywel.

He weakly smiled. "What's the worst thing that could happen?"

Don't ask me that.

My hand didn't work on the hand recognition security, repeatedly displaying a red light instead of the welcoming green. Why did Lloyd have to make everything hard?

Ringing the silent doorbell, we waited until Lloyd opened the door. He grinned when he saw Hywel. "Well, who do we have here? Good to see you, Hywel." When I'd left the islands in April, I was told that Lloyd was considering investing in Grito Mono. I wonder if he ever had. They'd hit it off, so it wasn't outside the realm of possibility.

"Is the security down? I couldn't get in?"

He smirked. "No. I've disabled it. I've let most of the guys know we're closed for a bit, but not Paolo. I want to scare him a little bit. Teach him a bit of a lesson."

Hywel was curious. "Is Paolo ok? What happened?"

Lloyd's face changed from curious to mad (mad-angry or mad-as-in-madman I wasn't sure.). "He was getting the Capuchin monkeys drunk. Unacceptable."

"Don't ask." I pushed by Lloyd, leading Hywel into the building. "Don't ask at all."

I walked the distance to Lloyd's office with the two gentlemen following me. It was back at its temperate constant of 71 degrees. His usual spotless desk was covered in scattered papers. He'd finally found a problem that he couldn't solve from behind his desk.

LaGuardia was pacing when we got in the office, unshaven and looking very angry. When he saw Hywel walk into the room, slouched and defeated, LaGuardia's anger blew. "Hywel, you sit down. You're in a lot of trouble, surfer boy." He directed Hywel towards one of the club chairs by Lloyd's desk.

Lloyd also sat down, took the pack of cigarettes out of the top drawer, then thankfully put them right back. Maybe a three-day relapse while dealing with a murder and drunken monkeys was enough.

I was about to sit down when LaGuardia turned his frustration towards me. "And you? Lexie 'Avanti' Marino? Do you have a death wish? All I got from you yesterday is a text asking me to meet you here to go over some new information with you and Lloyd. I get here, and you've let this complete *el demente* send you into the arms of danger." He gave Lloyd a look that would have terrified me. "You fraternized with two suspects yesterday, putting yourself in a really dangerous position. And here you are, showing up with the most likely killer of them all?"

Both Lloyd and LaGuardia started to talk, but I interrupted both of them. "Look, LG, you told me on Tuesday, when I was going to Cam's house, to keep my ears open because I had access to people who would never be truthful with you. I don't get this island. No one talks to the police. It's like everyone has a closet of secrets they are trying to hide. But I have plenty to tell you."

"When you were going to Cam's house, we knew where you were. It was an event filled with dozens of innocent people. And you let me know about it! Now I find that you've gone out for an afternoon boat ride with a possible suspect, then proceeded to go to the place of work of Crazy Daisy. Because of the suggestion of Lloyd Wilson? I can't protect you if I don't know where you are!"

"Lloyd did not suggest I go out on the boat. He warned me away to be totally honest." I felt it would somehow be disrespectful or dismissive if I sat down, so I stayed standing. "I'm ok. And I only figured out where Hywel was this morning. And I wasn't worried about finding him because I know he's innocent."

"I don't even fully understand why we are here at your offices, Lloyd. How do you play into this?" LaGuardia had been over Lloyd since April.

Lloyd started, in his slow, rational, slightly condescending way, "Jazz was my friend and I have a vested…"

"Vested?" LaGuardia was annoyed, and was Lloyd trying to put himself in the suspect pool?

Lloyd was just as annoyed with the detective. "It's a medical research thing. You wouldn't understand."

Before this conversation went off in who knows what direction, I butt in. "This is just the wrong way to do this."

La Guardia stopped me in my tracks. "Hywel should have been answering these questions at the station days ago. Lloyd should be hiding away in his sub-bunker doing whatever insane people do in the dark. And you, Lexie, should be talking to me before you put yourself into perilous situations. You can't let some braniac who you work for part-time convince you to act as his toy robot if he's got a hunch about something."

Lloyd lit up a cigarette after all. "Hold on, Mr. Half-an-excuse-for-a-cop here. There is a decided and calculated reason…"

"Enough! Stop talking, both of you. Like I said, it was my choice." I was tired and frightened, and maybe a little bit over being treated like a child. "It's not the two of you playing chess. I chose to play a part in this because I cared about Jazz, and more so, I didn't want a good friend to be arrested for something he didn't do.

"If there's anything that this entire island chain knows about me, it's that I don't take risks. So all my choices of yesterday and today were measured. My choices. I'm not Lloyd's Encyclopedia Brown puppet. I'm not a helpless child. And it all paid off. I have mountains of information to tell you, LG.

"It's 100 percent true that what I did yesterday was a little reckless, especially for me, and not thought-through in any ultra-analysis. But here it is, the next morning, and I'm sitting with the two smartest men I know, much closer to helping you figure out who did this."

I knew what each of them was thinking. Lloyd thought

that Detective LaGuardia was still an idiot, and LG was sure that Mr. Lloyd Wilson was walking around with a few nuts loose, but they stayed quiet. For one of them to start talking civilly was to lose face, so I asked Lloyd to go and get some coffee for Hywel. On any other day, a request for him to retrieve anything from the kitchen would be met with one of his bone-chilling stares that meant, 'Don't you know who I am?' But... today wasn't most days.

As the next hour passed, I felt terrible for Hywel, even though LaGuardia was treating him with kid gloves. I had a good feeling that my surfing boss would keep true to his promise of coming 100 percent clean, but I stayed in the room to make sure he did.

When Lloyd came back to the room with coffee (and very lovely French macarons), he sat silently to the side, listening, letting LaGuardia lead from behind the boss's desk. If the investigation could have only started with truthful conversations like this...

Hywel blew his nose on his t-shirt and said, "I know when it comes down to it, I have zero alibi. I was sleeping in a house by myself and surfing a hundred feet from where I found Jazz's body. I didn't know. How could I have known? I hope you keep looking for the truth. I know I'm the jerk, but she deserves more."

"You still have to come down to the station, Hywel," LaGuardia kindly said, "We need to do this by the book."

Hywel shook his head, letting his blond bangs fall in his face. You can only paddle away on a surfboard so many times until you have to stop. "This is real, isn't it?"

LaGuardia asked Lloyd, "Is there anywhere secure I can put him while the three of us talk? Then we won't have to worry about him doing a runner again..."

Lloyd motioned towards the door. "I'll put him in Lexie's

office. But of course, you couldn't get out of this place if you wanted to when all is activated. Security and all." He escorted Hywel out the door, and I could vaguely hear him ask the surfer if he could buy his t-shirt.

LaGuardia seemed to like sitting behind Lloyd's desk and stayed put. "Ok, I need to solve a murder, and I've got Lloyd, this *vampirico loco,* trying to tell me that I'd be an idiot to rule him out as a suspect. Why does this man plague me?" They'd been at each other's throats soon after they'd met. Understandably, as Lloyd had been arrested for murder.

Lloyd returned to the room, plopping down on the sofa. "That boy has some serious problems."

La Guardia turned his attention to me. "Now let it spill, Lexie. I need to know exactly what you were doing yesterday. You could have put yourself in some serious danger."

It was better to let that last comment go. It was hard to remember who knew what, so I started at A and ended as close to Z as I could get. I left out kissing Renny, but what would there be to say anyway? If I was ever going to want to bare my soul about my romantic entanglements, I was going to have to make a BFF that was a woman.

Jules? Bella? A thought for another day.

They both stared at me wide-eyed, all the way from Renny's candid talk about Jazz to our strange journey through the End of the World. The only time either of them interrupted me was when Lloyd said, "Did you just say Incan Pharmacist of the Eclipse Rave? Fascinating."

Why yes, Lloyd, I did.

"I didn't know there was an eclipse on Sunday night."

"I don't think that there was to be honest."

"So where do you go from here?" I asked LaGuardia.

Lloyd tried to put himself back in the driver's seat. "So you've got scared surfing loverboy in the other room who couldn't hurt a fly, but has no alibi. Then three suspects with alibis... four suspects if you count me, which I would, but I to have an alibi."

"Sometimes I think you are brilliant, and sometimes I think that you just talk to hear your voice filling space," LaGuardia spoke the words I'd wanted to say for months.

I counted it out for them. "Daisy was video time-stamped at the all-night Eclipse Rave, and Renny was having an all-night poker blow out at Red Frog Beach with the fellows I'd met before we got on his boat yesterday. Renny snores. Not like I know, but according to these guys, that accounts for your two hours in question."

"I'm still going to have to check in more about this poker business, but we've got confirmation from Ned Livingston that Dino Calvitto was stuck next to Renny. A few others have been elusive as well. There's a few of the players that we haven't been able to track down yet. And I'll want to confirm the snoring, god help us, with Dino Calvitto." LaGuardia turned around to look out on Lloyd's terrace, where three Capuchin monkeys were knocking on the glass door.

"Cute, when they aren't drunk." Lloyd waved at them. "What's the husband's alibi?"

LaGuardia rubbed his temples. "He was out on a two-day fishing charter with Larry Breger, from Yarisnori..."

Two and two made a possible four in my mind. "Hold on. Just hold on. I think I have a plausible theory. Supposedly Cam and Larry were out together on the boat. But Renny said Breger's sometimes plays with them. And here's where it gets kind of interesting. Renny also told me the guys were covering for *someone* whose wife forbids him to go to these poker parties. If the wife asks, he wasn't at the game. And on the other hand, Paolo was covering for Larry's fake alibi by saying they were out on an all night slug hunt together. The wife really hates gambling. Like Divorce hate. Breger is Cam's alibi, but could he have actually been at the game and not with? It's plausible that he got off the boat somewhere, isn't it?"

The two of them processed my treasure trove of information. I think I had even confused myself. I mumbled, "Trust me, I know?"

Was my treasure trove full of gold or trinkets?

LaGuardia shook his head and sighed in disappointment. "We talked to Larry Breger on Monday, Lexie. Said they made it almost as far as Colon. But it's possible and we have to go down every avenue there. Breger's a standup guy though. Why would he cover for Cam?"

"Probability dictates that nothing is certain." If there was one thing you could count on Lloyd being, it was being Lloyd.

My adrenaline informed me that this was the right track. "Renny didn't share who was secretly at the poker game. I don't think he thought that one could have anything to do with the other. But if it turns out this could be about Jazz's murder... he's not going to care about lying to someone's wife about a game.."

Lloyd was on it. "And I'll let my Crabby herpetologist know that if he wants his job then he'll give me the skinny on this slug hunt. The man is strange. And not in a good way.."

As a nice switch, the guys were both looking at me for my analysis. "It's possible that the poker contingency didn't have any reason to not believe Breger. If Cam is believed to be cleared, would his alibi ever surface?"

I excused myself to call Renny, while Lloyd got Paolo on the horn. I didn't want to go in my office and see poor Hywel, so I headed to the kitchen to use one of ANANKE's landlines. The unknown lay before me. Had I cracked the case? And how was I going to react to hearing Renny's voice?"

After enough rings for me to assume my call was going to voicemail, Renny answered in a slightly sexy gravelly voice that only comes from waking up before one wants to. "Hello?"

I paused for a pregnant moment. Should I say anything about last night? Should I deal in niceties? No time for that now. "It's me, Renny. Lexie. Sorry to wake you. You might have the key to solving who killed Jazz."

THE TRUTH now lay before us. Larry Breger was part of the all night poker party, rushing out after coffee with the guys to run to Yarisnori. He was a good guy who everyone liked. Why would he lie about Cam? He had to have left the boat for at least a night. And Crabby Paolo let on to Lloyd that the restaurateur was not with them on the inland slug-fest. He was just an innocent guy ready to be a poker player's cover story. I had a strong feeling I'd never want to meet his associates he was with on that particular quest.

I could see clearly. Cam's the man with a one-two punch. He greedily wanted Santo Amaro and angrily wanted his wife, Jazz, dead when he saw she didn't want him.

LaGuardia looked at his phone, surprised at the perfect service he was getting in the bunker. "Let me call McDonough. We'll go out to Cam's, and I'll have Romeo go find Larry Breger to get the read story. I hope he..."

"No." I was so surprised when I uttered it that I didn't even think it came from me.

"Excuse me."

Flashing back to the events of April, there was one thing

that I understood with absolute certainty. "No. Rich people get away with things. Rich people have ways to disappear. You'll travel down to Tierra Oscura, and Cam will say he was on his boat all night. Even if you toss him in the clink for 72-hours and can't confirm anything... Larry Breger is going to get caught up frazzled with the truth. Why would he cover for him? And while all this is going on Cam's on a luxury catamaran to Columbia."

"So what do you suggest we do?" Everyone waited with baited breath.

My heart was beating double time. "I'm going to tell him I know the location of Santo Amaro."

22

THE LEGEND OF SANTO AMARO

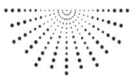

*A*ccording to legend, Santo Amaro was a well-heeled, fifteenth-century nobleman from Persia on a quest to find earthly paradise. When no man could guide him, god appeared to him and said that he must build a boat and follow the path of the sun across the Atlantic Ocean.

His many year journey brought him upon unbearably beautiful semi-immortals, as well as the most dastardly of beasts, and apparitions of ghostly women who instructed him to pour all of his wine in the sea. By a nunnery high upon a mountaintop, he waited for instructions on how to approach his final destination.

Almost to paradise, he came upon a dazzling castle built of gold and rubies, with a gatekeeper who would not allow any mortal to enter. After begging for months, Santo Amaro was allowed to peek through the keyhole. He saw the Tree of Life from which Adam ate, young musicians playing unknown instruments, and birds whose songs were so beautiful one could remain entranced by them for a thousand years.

When he finally looked away from the keyhole, three hundred years had passed. He returned to the coast where he landed to find all his friends gone and a city named after him.

There is no moral to this story.

There was a ship named after this long-forgotten Saint. It was said to contain treasure when it sunk. It was never found.

Were either real?

Before LaGuardia had escorted Hywel out of ANANKE and into his car, I'd stopped to ask him one question. "Did she ever find Santo Amaro?"

Suspense had us all at the end of our seats. The question left Hywel deflated. "No."

IT WAS four in the afternoon when I met Cam at the restaurant. He was dressed like most middle-aged men in the tropics, in a white polo shirt and khaki shorts.

The friendly doohickey-king I'd grown kind of fond of had shed his benevolent costume, and I could clearly see the wolf in sheep's clothing. Though he still looked like the big goof I'd known him as now all warts were on show.

Late afternoon at a sparsely populated restaurant in the middle of a luxe resort sounded safe and anonymous enough to me. Lloyd had slipped into the restaurant. He was sitting at a table far away reading *The Lives of Saints* at the bar, surreptitiously keeping an eye on me. A few solos and couples dotted the chill room, drinking signature Blue Lagoon cocktail, ignorant of the seedy side of the islands. Romeo sat with who I assumed was a female cop. LaGuardia's face was too familiar on the island to sit in the restaurant, so he stayed back in the kitchen.

Despite his new role as grieving widower, Cam checked me out in my winning outfit. Lloyd had made me watch a six-minute video on how to do smokey eye-make-up.

Trying to summon confidence, not fear or anxiety, I attempted a stoic expression when I sat down at Cam's table. I feared his poker face was infinitely better than mine. He had his normal drink of scotch with two ice cubes. He skipped hello to simply say, "I don't know what you drink."

"Coca-Cola is good." I mentally shook my head. Femme fetales do not drink coke. I should have ordered a champagne cocktail and pretend to sip it.

Awkward didn't begin to describe how I felt. When my drink came I smiled."I just wanted to apologize for Tuesday night. I should have known better than to lock Jazz's office. Or to go in her bathroom at all. I wasn't thinking."

"I appreciate the apology, but I owe you one as well. I overreacted. I don't know how to act. What to say. What to do. Where to go." He stirred the ice cubes with his big finger.

"The worst thing that could happen to you, did. You lost the woman you loved. There is no right or wrong in how you act right now." I drank my coke through the straw. Not great.

"Well, thanks. It's nice to know you thought about it. As you saw, I wasn't on my best behavior. I can blame some of it on this." He motioned towards the scotch.

That's where our small talk ended. I caught Romeo's eye, who gave me a nod indicating he was still with me. I've never had less to talk about with anyone. So I jumped. "You probably figured out that apologizing to you isn't the primary reason I asked you to meet me here."

He looked around, perplexed. "Um."

Operation Femme Fetale commencing. "There's something that you and I have in common that you probably don't know about. It's safe to say that you and I need each other."

He misunderstood my intent, and why wouldn't he have? He let his eyes drop to check out my cleavage, then met my eyes again, attempting something of a lascivious glance.

Yuck.

I'd take Crabby Paolo in a New York minute.

I took a sip of my coke as if it were Dom Perignon. "You do understand what I'm talking about."

He downed his scotch in one sip. "I think I do."

Here we go. "Santo Amaro."

It was not what he expected. He looked shocked and said nothing.

"And I think we both did similar things to go for it. I need assurances before we go forward from here."

Was he buying it?

"Santo Amaro?" He looked at me with hate. He wasn't going to admit anything, but he wasn't going to let me get away with anything either. "You're a bit of a gold-digging piece of work. Just another in a line of idiots chasing sunken treasure. I should talk to the police. Sounds like you should be on the list of suspects."

His tone terrified me, but I held my stare, almost shaking as I met his challenge. "You may have fooled everyone else, but I know what you did. And if that's not a literal gold digging piece of work, I don't know what is. Desperate times call for desperate measures, *n'est ce pas?*"

Wrong language, Lexie.

"What are you talking about, little girl?" If he wasn't going to punch me with his fist, he was giving it a go verbally. "I liked you, Lexie. You were a good lost girl taking a chance moving here. But look at you! You're a snake."

"I liked you too, Cam. That's why I'm here. And I understand why you had to do what you did." I glanced around the room. Lloyd was drinking a Negroni while keeping an eye. Romeo was fully at attention as well.

"And what do you think I did?"

Take a deep breath and say it.

"You killed Jazz. I don't blame you. But I want you to say it."

"You are an insane... something. Jazz was my wife. I loved her. She's not even in the grave and you're pulling this crap. " He spoke with every word spaced out, trying his best not to make more of a scene than he already had. "I'm walking away, little girl."

"I'll see you again." I called after him as he walked away.

He turned for just a moment. "No, Lexie. No, you won't." He walked away in the angry huff I'd grown to know so well.

I'd lost my chance.

Lloyd walked over and sat at my table, Negroni still in hand. Unable to display emotions or sympathy, he patted me on the back. "That was intense."

LaGuardia appeared out of the kitchen. He went over to Romeo and my knight-ess in shining armor, speaking to them quickly in Spanish. They got up and exited the restaurant in a hurry. Cam was out of earshot but still visible walking down the beach towards the jungle shuttle. LG sat down and took my hands in his. "Hey Lexie, are you okay?"

"I am. Disappointed in myself. I blew our chance."

"You didn't. It was so bold of you to sit there and try to get a confession out of him. And we now have his fishy alibi to go on. Romeo and Theresa are going to tail him for the rest of the day, so we know exactly where he is. Then I'm going to go talk to him again. As you know, I don't need a reason to detain him for 72 hours. And I think I have plenty of reason."

"Blue Lagoon, please," I said aloud, but to no one in particular. Lloyd was off to the bar in a second. "I don't think I'm made for this kind of work. If something like this happens again, please recommend I take a one-week trip to an all-inclusive resort in Cancun."

Lloyd returned with my Blue Lagoon, having got the gist of my conversation with LG. It was that smelling fish expression again. He tapped the side of his glass, looking pained. "I don't particularly like visitors, but I've got a five-bedroom house. I've only slept in four of them, so it might be prudent that you stay the night. As you might have surmised, it's a high-security home."

"I don't like to agree with this *pendejo* but I'd guess you'd feel safer if you stayed with Lloyd for a night or two." LaGuardia looked at his watch. It was getting later in the afternoon. "I don't think you don't need to worry about anything, but I want you to feel safe. It's been quite a few days for you."

Lloyd never stopped thinking. "Maybe you'd like to stay in the guest house. Still secure. You might want your privacy." If nothing else, he was consistent.

I smacked myself in the head with my open hand. "As is my M.O. for the week, I've left my car at ANANKE. If this is cool, could you take me home in the boat, LG? I'll pack quickly and Lloyd? Maybe you could drive up from Bocas Town and pick me up? That's the last annoyance you'll get from me. This will maybe take an hour?"

Not changing his expression, Lloyd sincerely said, "You're not an annoyance."

DECKED out in sweaty gingham taffeta and a pair of sneakers,

I was a bit of a sight as we all took the jungle shuttle back to Red Frog Beach marina. I held the Louboutins like a safety vest.

Lloyd got on the ferry to Bocas Town while I went with LaGuardia in the police boat, which always gave me a bit of a thrill. Not today, though. I just wanted out of Red Frog Beach. The dolphins swimming alongside us had lost their charm to me as I stared past them into the far mangroves. I'd tried my best and failed.

LaGuardia was getting regular updates from Romeo about Cam's movements. All was as it should be. When we pulled up at my cabin, he helped me out of the boat and onto the rickety dock. "He's still at the Aqua Point Marina. Yelling at some of his staff. So don't worry."

I made us some Earl Grey tea, which was still a novelty to LG. He sat at the kitchen table, making police phone calls while I packed.

How long was I going to be at Lloyd's? I was strangely relieved for a moment when I realized that his compound would definitely have air conditioning. My oversized luggage seemed to be the obvious choice in my plan to bring everything I owned, including the last of my strawberry frosted Pop-Tarts.

I screamed when I opened the suitcase and two giant stick spiders calmly crawled out to say hello. Venomous? Yes, but harmless to humans. Ugly as the devil, but not on my list of a thousand things to be scared of. Added to travelling case: two bottles of toxic insect repellent.

LaGuardia appeared at my bedroom door immediately. "What? What's going on?"

I weakly smiled. "Nothing. Just some stick spiders in my luggage."

"Jesus Christ, you can't do that after what we've been through today."

"You'd have screamed too." Five pair of flip flops, two wet-suits I probably wouldn't use, six dresses and as many cut-off jeans & t-shirt combos as would fit.

"So, McDonough is on the way to talk to Breger at the restaurant, Cam's still at Aqua Point, and Hywel is in a cell downtown. I don't know what else to do with him right now." He caught sight of one of the stick spiders and crushed it with his shoe. It's man against insect in the tropics.

Contact lenses, eco-friendly bamboo toothbrush, which just worked terribly, and a picture of my mom. American Advil. The two lipsticks I had that hadn't melted in the sun. "I can't wait to get out of here. I love this place, but not tonight."

I texted Lloyd: 'How's it coming?'

With his mysteriously perfect cellular service, he wrote back immediately: 'Not far. 30 minutes?'

I was packed and ready and dropped my bag by the door. Biding my time I walked out to the dock, where LaGuardia was pacing. "You don't have to stay with me. I'll be fine. I'd rather you were out there hauling that lug to jail."

"I can stay."

"I wish you'd go. Lloyd's like around the corner."

"You sure? I know you are safe, but I want you to feel safe. I just worry. You're like the little sister I never had."

"Your little sister who I believe is older than you."

I swatted away a small army of chitras as I watched LaGuardia leave. I waved goodbye, and went back to the house to sit at my desk and search online for cost-effective security solutions. I rummaged for the last of Hywel's sugar babies in the bottom of my purse, and then opened Jazz's red envelope again to look at her papers. The desperation in her scrawled post-it notes was evident.

It meant nothing, but I wondered if Hywel kept her last note to him.

Beware. Dangerous curves.

Too much time had elapsed. Dusk was falling. I didn't like it and texted Lloyd to see what was going on. I hoped he hadn't made some ridiculous decision to do some psychological experiment on me by making me wait for him.

His response was unfortunate: "Sloth crossing. Police shut down road temporarily. National emergency it seems." I'd been stuck in sloth related traffic incidents twice. One took ten minutes, the other felt like hours. Why was I so worried? Cam would be detained soon. Maybe already? I texted LaGuardia my update on the unfortunate sloth incident.

While waiting for the message to go through, a wave of texts that I hadn't received from the last half hour barraged my phone. One from my mother, a cocktail-beach-wink emoji message with a question mark from Migs, and three in a row from LaGuardia. His cops on the case had lost Cam somehow, and he was on his way back. And was I with Lloyd? And finally:

"?????????????"

I grabbed a black backpack from my bedroom and snatched the necessities out of my giant piece of luggage, taking just what I'd need to get out of my house. Glasses, a clean pair of underwear, and when it comes down to it, isn't that all you need anyway?

In fifteen minutes I could make it to the Paved Road, and hopefully, Lloyd would already have turned down my driveway.

Almost to the door, I heard the familiar sound of

LaGuardia's boat pulling up at my dock, and I flung the door open to welcome the safety.

It wasn't LaGuardia. It was Cam in his luxury speedboat. Alone.

Cam hadn't seen me yet, his attention still on tying his boat to the dock. I quietly closed the door, noting that my lock was almost as poor of an excuse as the one at Hywel's board shack.

I turned to reach for my safety blanket, the baseball bat that was always propped up in the corner. The memory of letting those little boys play ball with it outside on Sunday hit me like a slap in the face.

Maybe he just wants to talk.

Maybe he just wants to take you up on your offer.

Maybe.

I sent messages to my two delayed friends (yes, I said friends plural) and turned on the audio recorder on my phone, sliding it under the sofa. I noticed I should have been dusting behind there more often.

Should the very worst happen, Cam would have taken my life, but a recording would remain of whatever he'd said to me. If I kept it on my person, then he'd undoubtedly smash the phone as well.

I positioned myself on the arm of a chair, with two heavy bronze candleholders within arm's grasp.

Don't telegraph and you just might make it out of here alive.

Cam had the decency to knock first, so I opened the door. It seemed like the safest choice. What to say? Pretend not to be scared. "I knew you'd be back."

"Well, congratulations. That and a dollar won't get you to Bocas Town." He pushed his way into the house like he owned it.

His expression was familiar. I'd seen it when he'd found

me in Jazz's office, and when he'd socked his Florida friend in the face. When he'd got off his boat the day after Jazz was found, with two men to hold him back, his expression was the same. I wondered if this was the last thing Jazz saw before she was gone. "Santo Amaro. What do you know about that stupid old legend and why are you coming to me?"

"Ten million dollars worth of riches. I know the location. You've got the maritime tools. You'll take half, or both of us will get zilch." I was sweating through the taffeta. Dress ruined. But the sneakers were still good.

"You've known Jazz for 32 seconds. Why would you know the location...if it even exists?"

"Because I stole all of Jazz's notes when I was at your house. You can't think that I locked that door by accident. You can't think that you were the only one who knew about it. I'd assume that $5 million is enough to save your company. From what I've gathered, you knew she was leaving no money to you in any inheritance. She was on to you." Who was this woman I was conjuring?

"You usually come off like a pathetic lost thing. That's not you at all."

Pathetic?

I refused to change my tune. "Listen, Cam. If you don't get that $5 million, your precious business is going under. You'll have to go back to the Greater Houston area and hope to make your way up to doohickey-king once again."

"Show me what you have."

"First, you say it. Say it, and all I have is yours. It's the only way I have your word." I'm sure he could hear the fear in my voice. "There's no one to hear us. It's not like I haven't done similar. If we're on the same page, we do this, we part richer and we never see each other again."

He was viewing me angrily as a fly in his ointment. He slowly looked around the room, judging my dingy home. He rubbed his mitty hands together. "Similar?"

"You tell me and we'll go from there."

"I'm not stupid, little girl. What's this similar business?"

Crikey. What was my similar business? Let me go for the Oscar and then be done with performance for the rest of my life. "Do you really think that I moved down from New York City to work at a third-rate surf camp?" (It wasn't a third-rate surf camp…) "I heard all about this when I was here in April. I knew about Hywel and Jazz then. I was in it for the long game. You might know that he hasn't been seen since Tuesday night."

"I've underestimated you."

"That was the plan."

"Ok, extortionist. I killed Jazz. I killed her, and I'd do it again."

I felt my eyes widen and heart rate increase but that to keep it under wraps. That had come way too easy.

"Jazz came back home after that Sunday trip she takes with you all – she was surprised to see me. She thought I was gone for another night like everyone else did. I let her go on and on about her big plans with Bella for the sake of watching her lie and asked her to cancel so we could go on a late afternoon boat trip to talk reasonably about what was going on between us…" He laughed.

"I already knew about her and that boy. I had for months. I knew exactly where she'd be going that night. If she was going to leave me, and completely cut me off from the money she'd grown so protective of, then it was time for her to say goodbye to this world. Simple as that."

"It was that easy for you?"

He took a step forward, dwarfing me. "No, it wasn't easy. It just needed to happen."

"How did you do it?"

"No, how did you do it? Miss Quid Pro Quo?"

Automatic default. "Red frog venom. A classic." Not a classic.

"Crushed her windpipe. Quick. Maybe painless. I don't know." There was no remorse in his voice or expression.

"And you left her at Hywel's lodge?" It was the most peaceful way I could express what happened.

"As far as I was concerned, he could have her."

He was pure evil. I glanced at my trusty candlestick friend, ready for action. There was not one word I could imagine uttering.

"So, Lexie, show me. Partner." He sat on the couch.

This part of the play hadn't been written. If at *Playa Bajja Plage* as soon as he said that he killed Jazz, he'd have been arrested. There were no police lying in wait now. All cards on the table.

Jazz's red leather envelope was still on my kitchen table. I didn't want him to know where Santo Amaro was, or if it was. I could pretend it was all lies and then get pummeled at best. What if those maps revealed that the shipwreck had been found? Cam surely would know what he was looking at. But it would buy me some time.

"I'll get it right now, partner." Saying the words made me sick. And I sounded like John Wayne. I walked to the other room and, hands shaking out of control, I straightened the papers and shoved them back into their elegant keeper.

Back in the living room, he greedily grabbed it out of my hands, tearing the papers out of the envelope, carelessly throwing one page after the next on the floor. He glared at me, "What are you playing at? This is all scribble! This is what you're giving me?" He was about to blow, red seeping up through his dark tan, but he was giving me another chance. "What do you think is going to happen now, little girl?"

I had no idea. I eyed the distance between me and the door. All I needed was five seconds of distance between us, as my self-defense teacher had taught me. My right hand grabbed a candlestick and swung it at him, missing his head but hitting him firmly in the neck.

He screamed and stumbled towards the door instead of away from it. He pried the weapon from my hands, but he still had a moment of staggering pain. It was enough for me to get as far as the bathroom and lock myself inside. Certainly, by now, the sloth had crossed the road, or LG was on the way, and someone would be coming to save me.

Right?

The lock wasn't secure, but if he had trouble with that he could easily punch the window in from the outside. "The police are coming, Cam! You've got time to get away; otherwise, they are going to be here real soon."

He pounded on the door, his voice gravelly when he replied, "I'll take my chances. I don't think anyone's coming to get you any time soon." My bathroom. The most terrible place in the house. No matter how much I cleaned, I wouldn't go in there without flip-flops on, even in the tiny shower. It was small, and tiled, with a tiny sink and extra small shower. A shower curtain with palm trees.

There was nothing in the bathroom that resembled a weapon in the least. Even my bamboo toothbrush was packed up in my luggage, waiting for Lloyd to get it and me.

At least I was currently wearing sneakers.

There was no sound from the other side of the door. Was he going to wait me out? Or was he going the outside route to come in through the window in case the police arrived?

I hopped up on top of my wooden clothes hamper to get a better look out of the window. It was much higher up than I'd thought. There was no way he'd be able to attack me through it, but conversely, it was no means of egress for yours truly. His one way in was my one way out.

He banged on the door repeatedly, all the while barking at me. "How about instead of giving you five million dollars I give you no million dollars? How about I crush your windpipe too?"

I wrapped my hand in a towel and smashed through the high window. He wouldn't know that it wasn't a standard height window that I hadn't escaped through. Would he?

He didn't seem to care. "Little Pig, Little Pig, Let me in…"

Not by the hair of my chinny chin chin.

Not that I had hair on my chin,

Cam was throwing himself against the door, probably shoulder first. It was only a matter of time before the chintzy lock gave and he came barreling through.

Looking at things from a slightly different point of view, that is, two feet higher than usual atop of my laundry, I saw a possibility.

It doesn't take a hulk of a man to crush a windpipe.

I conjured that terror of a tiny dynamite that had made everyone's lives a living hell. Daisy came to me, with a power stronger than she could hope to harness. She'd terrified me with her crazy kick, but it was going to save me.

I stabled myself against the solar shower, as I could clearly hear the doohickey king finally busting through. The door creaked open like a haunted house, his hand coming into the room before his giant head appeared. I raised one leg like the karate kid and waited.

I was not strong enough or trained enough, but I was scared enough. When my foot hit the side of his head, it left him stunned for about thirty seconds. He clutched his head and screamed every name in the book at me.

I'd lost my balance and fallen into the tiny solar shower, bringing the curtain down with it. Not by my doing, part of the rod holding up the curtain collapsed on both of us. I ended up on top of him, but the rail ended up smacking him on the head, doing double duty on his bruise. The terrible curtain, translucent but printed with a map of Europe, fell on top of me, and my arms flailed, trying to get out of this vinyl hell.

As I struggled to get out from beneath the curtain, I capsized the hamper, which I seemed to take Cam down a notch as well. It was like a game of Mousetrap. I finally understood the game that never actually worked. It was just a big old mess. But he seemed down for the count. It would buy me my five minutes.

While he was still curled up in a fetal position, I eased my way by him, running to the front door and throwing it open. I stood against the frame, candlestick in one hand.

How would I detain him? He was barely knocked out, just groaning on the floor. Both LaGuardia and Lloyd were on the way, but how far away were they?

Safety was always my first line of defense. And I had a giant basket of industrial strength insect repellent.

Isn't that what he was anyway?

I had no rope. No locks. No way to restrain anyone.

On a last glance to the kitchen I spied my two-dozen coconuts.

So repellent and coconuts it was. And just like a chitra or a rhinoceros beetle or hard-shelled hornet (the worst), I sprayed. I aimed, and I went overboard. He screamed, but it was temporary.

From the corner of my kitchen I grabbed a coconut and held it close like a safety blanket. I'd clearly miss hitting him hard but every second counted. Who knows? I might not have been able to kick like a kung fu master, but my aim was true.

I just might make it after all.

He wasn't going anywhere. Coconut in one hand, repellent in the other, I was already out the door.

Lust. Anger. Greed. Everything that is evil boils down to those three words.

Fairly poetically, the sun had finally set. All lights on the property were turned on as I walked down the dock, nocturnal insects flocking to them like a cliché.

Do you know how cool it is that police boats have sirens? The sounds and lights beckoned me to safety as I sat by the bay.

For at least a moment, I was invincible.

23

EPILOGUE: AVANTI, UNBOUND

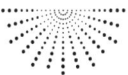

I'd spent about a week in the air-conditioned bliss of Lloyd's guest bunker after the madness ceased. A wall of windows allowed me to curl up on the couch, catching up on my reading. Outside, a torrential rainstorm spent a week's vacation in Bocas del Toro. The house was as sparse and grey as ANANKE, but comfortable with an extraordinary bed where I slept like the dead.

Positives were that I didn't end up in the hospital. And that I helped catch a killer.

I didn't much want to see anyone for a while, but allowed a few visitors. LaGuardia and his wife Gabby came a few times, bringing wine and dinner, and letting me know how quickly the island was settling back to status quo.

What can you do but go on with life? The night I arrived, LaGuardia came back to my temporary digs and stayed until I felt safe.

They'd talked to Larry Breger about being with Cam during those fatal hours. Larry had covered for Cam on many occasions, this being on of them. There was a mistress he'd often covered for. Breger had come clean. The case had already been closed, but this was the cherry on top.

I sat and pondered that for quite some time.

Finally I made my request clear, over a snack of chips and salsa and low-calorie margaritas. "I don't want anyone to know about my involvement. I don't want the attention. And I want to become just a person here, not anyone else."

"Whatever you want, Lexie. You saved the day again. Your wish is my command." He scrambled for the last crumbs of tortilla chips. I was lucky for his friendship, despite how he hoarded food. He was number one on my phone's favorites list.

Goal for the end of the year: fill up those missing favorites.

OF COURSE, the question of the hour: how did it end with Cam? He remained incapacitated like the wasp he was until Romeo bounded up my hill to officially apprehend the villain.

LaGuardia ran to my side. "Are you okay? I shouldn't have left you."

"How could anyone have known? There were a thousand variables and probability states that nothing is certain."

Oh no. Lloyd was rubbing off on me.

"Not that this will ever happen again, but I'll never leave your side in any dangerous situation."

"You just jinxed it. Kidding."

Tensions were heightened as Romeo finally escorted a very damaged looking Cam to the police boat. I avoided his stare for the most part. But I had to take a last glance. He didn't look nearly as huge anymore. I'd conquered the monster.

He got the last word. Turning to me, evil in his eyes, he said. "Watch your back, little girl. You never know what might be coming for you."

~

THE FOLLOWING MONDAY, I received a text from Migs. I was surprised he was still in town. He asked if I wanted to join him at the ex-pat gathering at *Playa Bajja Plage*.

Of course I didn't. How insensitive can someone be?

Truthfully it wasn't insensitive at all. The best thing to do is get back to normal. The best thing to do was live.

We met in Bocas Town to take the ferry to Red Frog Beach together. He was looking good in a plain white t-shirt and salmon colored skinny pants, which were all the rage at the moment.

"Lexie Marino, looking like a million bucks like always. Happy to have you on my arm, or whatever else you want to be on." He smirked at his offering.

I blushed and looked at the ground. When I was done being a high school freshman I looked up and pushed him. "You wish."

He linked his arm with mine. "Doesn't mean I won't stop trying."

Safer to stick to Migs, my non-attainable (despite what he said) crush-at-a-distance; the handsome photographer.

The closer we got to the restaurant, the more I felt like I was going to have a panic attack. It wasn't because of fear of my conversation with Cam, or facing the familiar faces who may or may not know what I did. It was the thought of seeing Renny. Excited? Frightened? I had no idea.

Like my last event with Migs, I clung to him like a safety

blanket, almost cowering behind him. "I'm a little frazzled. Stay next to me."

"A little frazzled? You're all over the place." We went to the far right side of the bar; a Blue Lagoon for me, a beer and whisky chaser for my escort. I scanned the room for familiar faces.

The regular Sunday morning snorkeling crew was gathered in their usual corner. Dr. Nolan was talking animatedly with a duo of women I wasn't familiar with.

Surprisingly, at a high top table across the room, Lloyd was talking to another woman with the same bored look he'd had when we'd last come together. I had to give it to him – he was attempting to be normal, maybe courting a social circle for the first time in his life. Was it possible for him to grow?

And like always, my eyes caught Renny's across a crowded room and I immediately looked away. You can never go back to being friends, can you?

Migs wasn't one to miss a clue. "Not you and him? Tell me it's not true. Why choose ground beef when you could have T-bone?"

I pushed him again. "You've got to stop it. You're on overdrive tonight. And I am exhausted. Can you just turn it off tonight, because I need a friend."

"Whatever the lady wishes. But that was some electricity if I've ever seen it. I'm happy to be buddy-buddy tonight. Last thing I'll say is that if you don't want me to worship you, you might want to come out in jeans and a t-shirt and not this sexy thing. Yes, yes, I'm done. So, what do you prefer? Two-toed sloths or three?"

"Definitely two. They never hold up traffic."

"Fair enough."

After ten minutes of completely inane conversation,

being completely distracted the entire time, I asked, "I'm feeling a little crazy here. Would you be up for heading back to Bocas Town for drinks?"

"Whatever the lady wishes. I'm leaving Wednesday morning, so I want, in a friend way, to spend some quality time with you before I buzz off? Ya dig?"

"I dig."

I caught no one's eye as we left, walking quickly towards the jungle shuttle. Ten feet away from the restaurant, one of the snorkel crew yelled after me. "Hey, Avanti!"

I turned and smiled.

"Will we see you this Sunday?"

That's the question of the decade, isn't it?

Isn't it?

A new normal.

"No. Maybe. Sure. Yes. I'll see you at Aqua Point."

Maybe Renny and I could be friends after all.

I HEMMED and hawed about Sunday's snorkeling adventure all week. I hadn't left Lloyd's yet, and I'll admit that it was really growing on me, the brutalist iron curtain Prague luxury hotel that it was. I was tempted to go back to work at ANANKE. I wanted talk to Lloyd, to weigh the pros and cons of going out on the boat with Renny Lloyd's words of yesteryear echoed in my mind. "This BFF thing? It's not working for me."

Another goal for the end of the year: Make a new BFF. Non-serial killer category.

In the end, I took that one step forward and showed up at Aqua Point for a Sunday morning excursion. Who knows what the future held? For anything.

I welled up as I walked toward the ship. A giant banner on the back of the boat temporarily renamed the vessel: SS JAZZ LOVE.

Back to Grandma's Garden, the group was in the water one after the other, lickety split. And as was my routine, I sat with my mask above my head on the ladder by the swimming deck, watching the fun everyone was having. I felt very solo. Very me.

Did I dare?

Rung after rung down the ladder, I submerged myself, past my knees, past my waist, right up to my shoulders. No one was paying attention, and that was okay. I put my mask on and slid right in.

Like I said, it was beautiful down there. And if last time it was five seconds, I think I managed for ten. It looked like a batfish was out to attack me, and I was out as quick as you could say *Playa Bajja Plage.*

When everyone eventually came back, I welcomed them as Jazz would have, and they replied with the magnificent things they'd seen on the reef. One day I'd see.

I got to towel off my hair for once. Good times…

We got off the boat like a group of old friends, everyone commending me for the fine remedial job I did. I felt like one of the gang for the first time.

I walked over to the water taxi rank, and just before I stepped into one of them, a voice chimed out behind me.

"Can I talk to you for just a minute?"

I turned to see Renny running down the marina after me.

I'm an adult. I couldn't not stay and talk. "Of course."

We walked towards his boat and sat. He looked like he wanted to grab my hands but didn't. "I wanted to say that I really enjoyed our time together a few weeks ago. And it's got nothing to do with the action-adventure part of the night. It was everything else."

Heart flutters. Or Stable Angina. Or Takotsubo Syndrome.

What could I say? "It was nice."

He was having a hard time getting out what he wanted to say. "Listen. I understand why you don't want to get involved yet. I just wanted you to know that I haven't felt like this about somebody for a long time."

I was stumped at what to say, so repeated, "It was nice."

I don't think it was the response he was looking for. "All I want to say. All I wanted to say. Is that I'll wait for you."

Isn't that what every woman wants to hear?

Do you really have to say goodbye, Lexie?

How about ,'See you later?'

There were a million reasons that I should walk away, and just as many on the list to stay. "I can't do it right now, Renny. I want to find myself here before I start anything. It's not that I don't feel something for you...what I'm saying is that I do. I do. But don't wait."

He looked hurt. Then surprised. Then maybe okay. "Maybe I'll wait anyway." Without a goodbye he turned and slowly walked down the dock, while I still sat on the back of his boat. "I know you are worth it."

Lexie, the point of you being down here is to be okay.

Avanti or not.

You are allowed.

He might be worth it too.

"Hey, Renny!" I didn't move from my sitting direction, but I smiled genuinely.

When he turned back hope not sadness was in his expression.

I nodded at him. "Just wanted to say I'll see you next Sunday."

THE NEW NORMAL. As ever, that evening was an outdoor dinner at McDonough's pad, with folks really beginning to be my friends. Who knows? With a few more weeks of Gabby's lessons I could be chatting in *Espanol* like the best of them. No drama. Laid back. The new best time of my week.

Wearing cut-off jeans and a terrible t-shirt that said, 'Why is abbreviation such a long word?' I did not have the answer to that.

I was surprised to find McDonough's house was just up the coast of the bay from me. It was certainly nicer than mine. I had no wish to go back to my cabin yet, but it was nice to sit out on a lounger wearing my favorite sunglasses. I was over the moon to find out that they were serving marlin fillet and lobster tails. The sun was nice after the vampire bunker at Lloyd's, but I shouldn't complain. I liked it there.

I sat next to LaGuardia, who was also basking in the sun. After not talking for a while, he said, "I know we haven't talked about this, per your request, but I want to update you. Cam's in jail in Panama City awaiting trial. Between the recording on your phone, and the admission of Larry Breger that he was not with Cam on the second night of their supposed trip, a conviction is in the bag. You won't be hearing from him for a very long time, and most likely never."

"It's a comfort."

"You don't have to worry, is what I'm saying.' He grabbed an ice-cold beer, drops of water rolling down the bottle. "The crazy thing is that he really believed that Cam was innocent. Breger got off the boat, got back on the boat on Monday, and lied. We talked to the mistress on Isla Solarte, but… How could Breger not have seen it?"

"I get it LG. Devotion can be blind. He believed in Cam, and I believed in Hywel. And Hywel's alibi looked just as hopeless. I just had the luck of having Detective Alajandro LaGuardia as my friend."

"Thanks for that."

"And what about Daisy?"

"300 hours of community service. Role to be determined. She actually speaks very highly of you. But The End of the World goes on."

"Doesn't it always?"

"Last thought before I go gorge on lobster tails... like I said last April, you're good at this. Investigation... we should figure out a way for you to get you doing this... officially."

Ugh. "Thanks, but no thanks. I'd rather sell flip-flops and magnets in Old Bank."

"Fair enough, Lexie. Fair enough."

Day became night. My new normal.

LIKE A MURDER INVESTIGATION, it's imperative to wrap up all loose ends.

What happened to Hywel?

Most intriguing, what about Santo Amaro?

Both remain mysteries.

Hywel was hiding out somewhere, as he does. Business went on. De Souza and Jules took over the day to day, and I returned to do what I did. Nothing thrilling, but I liked my routine.

Where was he?

He'd said that the shipwreck was never found.

Was it?

Jazz's obsession may have lay somewhere in the reefs of

Bocas del Toro. Ten million dollars in anyone's grasp. In an archipelago of islands that most of the world didn't know existed, it could stay on the ocean floor for eternity.

For the sake of some kind of justice for Jazz, I hoped it did.

THE END

ACKNOWLEDGMENTS

Where do I begin?

My first thanks goes to Ned Livingston, who read along week by week as I wrote the first draft of The Wipeout Affair, helping me work through making this a tight mystery and assuring that I finished what I started.

For helping me add depth of character and story, I'd be nothing without my first round developmental readers; Michael McDonough, Lawrence Paone, Peter Breger, Joe Roland, and A J Epstein.

For pushing me even further, I send heaps of adoration to my beta-readers and fellow writers; Roland Scahill, Annabelle Hunter and Liz Tully.

Huge thanks to my editor, Meredith Rodriguez, and my 11th hour secret weapon, David Calvitto.

Gratitude and adoration for Tim Marrs for creating another stunning cover, and Scott Fowler for laying everything out so gorgeously.

To my husband John Reynolds, forever thanks for your love and support. I am a very lucky lady.

ABOUT THE AUTHOR

Rachel Neuburger Reynolds is a playwright and mystery novelist. She is currently working on the Red Frog Beach Mystery Series and the Evelyn Bay Mystery series. Her plays have been produced in London, New York, and Edinburgh. Previous to being a writer, she was a theatre producer for many years. A former New Yorker, she now lives between London and the south coast of England, with her husband, John, and a greyhound named Comet Jones, Esq. who has a thousand more Instagram followers than she does.

To hear more about her adventures and be the first to know about the 3rd book in the series, Beach Cover-Up, check her out at: RachelNeuburger.com

facebook.com/rachelneuburgercreative

twitter.com/rainyday11

instagram.com/rainydaywrites

Want to know how the party started? Check out Drowning Lessons, Book 1 in the Red Frog Beach Mystery Series.

A destination wedding to die for...

Welcome to Bocas del Toro. Five days of glorious sun and lush rainforest await the forty guests celebrating Bridezilla Olivia's dream wedding—but will a murder sink the catered affair?

Before anyone's got time to work on a tan, an snorkelling accident eliminates a member of the wedding party. Maid of honor Lexie is thrust into investigating, to solve the case before her bestie's trip down the aisle gets tropically derailed.

Can this unlikely sleuth stay afloat as she's hit by wave after wave of wildly entertaining characters, including an alpha bride, surfing detectives, and a high school flame long forgotten?

Purchase now on Amazon!

Printed in Poland
by Amazon Fulfillment
Poland Sp. z o.o., Wrocław

51371733R00179